# SELENA'S MEN

## *Ravens of War 1*

## Elle Boon

MENAGE AMOUR

Siren Publishing, Inc.
www.SirenPublishing.com

**A SIREN PUBLISHING BOOK**
IMPRINT: Ménage Amour

SELENA'S MEN


ISBN: 978-1-62741-829-4

First Printing: August 2014

Cover design by Harris Channing


Printed in the U.S.A.

**PUBLISHER**
Siren Publishing, Inc.
www.SirenPublishing.com

# DEDICATION

First and foremost, I'd like to thank my husband and my children. Without their love and support I wouldn't have been able to accomplish my goals. Love you all.

To the wonderful Debbie Ramos, I'd like to say thank you for her endless hours of reading all my versions of this story. You have helped me more than I can say. To Valerie Tibbs and Margie Hager for believing in me and always being there to boost my spirits. Truly grateful for you ladies.

Many thanks to Siren for believing in me and giving me a chance. You guys rock! From the editors, to the authors, and of course most importantly to the readers, thank you all very much.

And, as always, to my friends the "bitches," thank you ladies for your encouragement.

# SELENA'S MEN

***Ravens of War 1***

**ELLE BOON**



## Chapter One

*Max King stared at the ethereal creature before him. In all his years never had he seen a more alluring vision. He'd never had such an overwhelming urge to drop to his knees and beg. Until now.*

*The tiny female wore a gown so sheer her luscious body was visible through the fabric. When the wind blew her long, silvery-blonde hair, a peek of her pert, rounded ass was visible. He wanted to see if the perfect round globes would fit in the palms of his hands, wanted to see if the front was as gorgeous as the back. His hands literally tingled with the urge to touch.*

*A soul-deep pull, unlike anything Max had ever known, drew him to the woman like an invisible thread, and his feet were moving him closer to her.*

*So completely enthralled by what he was sure was his Fated, Max didn't realize he wasn't alone with her until he heard a masculine groan to his right. He didn't want to take his eyes off of the mystery woman out of fear she'd disappear, but years of training won out. His twin Malcolm had a look of awe as he too moved toward the vision.*

*The feeling of being incomplete was always with Max, except when he and Malcolm shared a woman. In the moment of the dual joining, Max felt his soul reaching out to Malcolm's and the woman they shared, as if searching for the connection that would make them whole, only it was fleeting at best.*

*That same part of his being seemed to be stretching out to the woman on the hill.*

*She turned, giving him his first glimpse of her body, except her face was shadowed, hidden by her long hair. His breath stilled in his chest. The gown was as transparent in the front as the back. He didn't know where to look first.*

*Somehow he found himself standing before her on a hill that overlooked what appeared to be Mount Olympus. He hadn't seen his home in thousands of years, and at any other time he would have rejoiced to be there again. But the woman in front of him held him spellbound.*

*He shook his head, wondered if he was somehow being tricked, if this was how he was being led to his death. If that was the case, Max thought he'd happily die.*

*His brother didn't have the same misgivings as him, obviously, as he took one of the hands she had lifted toward them. Max decided if he was to die, he'd at least know what it felt like to touch the skin that looked like silk. Electrical currents shot into his hand where they touched, flowing up his arm like a wave of energy at first contact.*

*A feeling unlike any he'd ever known, a sense of oneness radiated where they were all three connected, palm to palm. She was their center. Their Fated. They'd found her.*

*Her breasts were perfectly formed for his hands, not too big, not too small. Her nipples were hard little points begging to be sucked, touched. Gods he wanted to do everything with this woman. To this woman.*

*With his left hand still engulfing her much smaller one, he lifted his right hand to brush the back against her breast. The soft inhale delighted him. His twin mimicked his action.*

*He didn't think her nipple could get any harder, but as he rubbed his knuckles back and forth the little point became stiffer.*

*Max tried to focus on her face, wanted to memorize everything about the woman whom he planned to spend eternity with.*

*Mist swirled up, separating her from him and Malcolm. He didn't want to lose the connection. Her hand was the greatest anchor in his world, a world he was sure he didn't belong in.*

*"Don't go." The anguished words came from deep within his soul as her fingers slipped from his. No matter how hard he squeezed he couldn't hold onto her.*

*The beautiful hills and valleys of Olympus were swallowed up by an oppressing darkness. Malcolm echoed his cry as they both dropped to their knees.*

* * * *

Max rolled out of bed, his latest dream even more real than the last one, leaving him hard and aching for a woman he'd never met. Hell, he wasn't even sure she existed. It had been thousands of years since Zeus had sent them to Earth to find their Fated and most of his fellow Ravens had given up, or assumed there was no such thing.

A quick shower had him feeling marginally better. He rubbed a spot on his chest where the loss of the woman was still like a living pain. He needed to adopt more of his twin's philosophy and start loving and leaving, but that just wasn't his way.

*"Max, you up?"*

*"Hey, Mal. What are you doing up so early?"* Max ran his hand through his hair.

It was easier to mind-speak with his twin rather than picking up a phone and calling.

*"I don't know how to say this, so I'm just going to say it. I've been having dreams."*

Malcolm's words were not what Max expected to hear. Sure, when they were younger, Malcolm would share images with Max. But never a dream.

*"Malcolm, I swear to all that's holy I will fucking kill you if you have been pulling me into one of your messed-up shit of dreams."*

*"Are you saying you've been dreaming about you and me and a woman, Max?"*

With as much detail as he could remember, Max described the dream from last night as best as he could, and then he described his other dreams where the mystery woman was always there.

*"Mal, I have dreamt about a dream girl with silver hair for weeks now. Only, until last night I hadn't been able to touch her."*

*"Shit!"* Max heard the confusion in his brother's one-word exclamation. He honestly had no idea what the dreams meant or who the woman was.

A disturbing notion that she was someone from Malcolm's past, maybe an old lover, made Max want to punch his twin.

*"Dude, you need to stop gritting your teeth."* Malcolm was openly laughing at him. Max realized he was broadcasting his every thought without a filter, something they'd all learned to do early in life. "*I've bedded a lot of women, but I swear I don't recognize her,"* Malcolm reassured him.

*"If you dream of her again let me know and I'll do the same. This can't be a coincidence."*

Max wasn't sure if he wanted to dream of her again or not. Since the first time he'd dreamt of his silver angel he'd been unable to think of any other woman, let alone date one. His dick was only able to get hard when he was dreaming or thinking of his dream girl. Zeus, or Fates, had to be punishing him.

* * * *

Malcolm stared at the ceiling fan spinning above him. After he stopped communicating with Max he knew sleep wasn't something he'd be getting back to.

The sound of the waves hitting the rocks outside drew him to the patio. He pictured the woman from his, and obviously Max's, dreams, standing there in nothing but her skin. He never brought women to his home. It made them get ideas of happily ever after. Malcolm didn't do happily ever after. Being as long-lived as he and the other Ravens were, they outlived most of the population. But he could see *her* in his home.

"I'm getting maudlin." Malcolm gripped the door frame and shook his head. He had a flight plan for later in the afternoon, but saw no reason not to move it up.

With a nod of his head he turned back inside to make some calls. Maybe if he left the country he'd stop having dreams of a petite woman and sharing her with his brother Max.

Just thinking about never seeing his angel again felt like he'd been stabbed in the heart, even if it was only when he slept. Yeah, time to get the hell out of Dodge.

* * * *

Selena Ramos was officially freaked the eff out. Her first intuition was to call up her best friend Tamara and tell her about the dreams she'd been having. If anyone would know what was going on it would be Tam. And if Tamara didn't know then her mama would.

When she'd had the first dream of her mystery men, she imagined it was because of the books she read. What woman wouldn't love to be the sole focus of two gorgeous, uber-rich men who only wanted to please their woman? But that was only make-believe, and Selena didn't believe in fairy tales.

The unmistakable sound of Buckcherry's "Crazy Bitch" blared from her phone on the nightstand. Tamara's personal ringtone always brought a smile to Selena's face.

"Hola, chica. What's bothering you?" Tamara asked in her slight accent.

"Why do you think something is bothering me?" *Evasion is a good tactic when you deal with a Seer. Not.*

"Oh, baby girl, are you now gonna try and lie to Mama T? Don't make me come over there and kick your little white ass."

"Bring it on. I'll beat you with one hand tied behind my back." Selena rolled out of bed and headed to the kitchen to get some coffee. By her best guess, Tamara would be walking in the front door within the next five minutes.

"So, you into the BDSM thing now, are you? I didn't have you pegged for that kind of kink," Tamara drawled.

Selena trudged down the stairs on silent feet, making her way to the kitchen without turning any lights on, only the barest light from outside illuminating the way. Another quirk she didn't share with many people was the fact she could see almost perfectly even in the dark.

She came to an abrupt halt at the sight that met her eyes. "Dammit, Tamara. Why did you call if you were already here?" Selena groused.

Seated on top of the island was none other than her best friend Tamara in a pair of fleece pajama bottoms with skulls and a black tank top. A pair of fuzzy slippers lay on the floor where Tamara kicked them off before she hopped up and made herself at home.

Tamara held a mug of Selena's favorite coffee out to her. As ploys went it worked. Anyone who knew Selena knew that she was a bear before her first cup or two of coffee.

She took a sip of the nirvana. Blissful cream- and sugar-laced coffee met her taste buds. Exactly how she liked her morning drink. Her eyes closed as she savored her first taste.

Being the smart woman that she was, Tamara waited until the cup was empty before she began what Selena called the Spanish inquisition, Tamara Mejia-style.

"So spill, or so help me I'm calling my mama. You do not want me to get her up this early." Tamara flashed her pearly-white smile.

Selena thought Tamara was one of the most beautiful women in the world. With her mixed Spanish and Cajun ancestry she stood at close to five foot nine without shoes, with black-as-night hair and chocolate-brown eyes. If Selena swung that way she'd totally have a girl crush on her.

But no, she seemed to have a thing for two hot men in her dreams.

"I've been dreaming about…men."

Tamara held her coffee cup between her two hands, looking at Selena like she was crazy. God, did she want her to spell it out? "Me and two men. Like, as in together. The three of us." Selena stuttered like a fool, holding up three fingers.

She spun around and popped another cup into the Keurig coffeemaker.

"I don't see the problem here. I mean it's a little out there for you. But it's not, like, totally uncommon." Tamara held her mug out for a refill.

Selena stared at her best friend, sure that her mouth was hanging open at Tamara's words. "Have you ever done that?"

Tamara cocked her head to the side. "Not me personally, but I'm not against it."

"Okay…" Selena had no idea what to say to that. She thought she knew everything about Tamara. They'd been best friends for over ten years.

"I see the wheels spinning in that dirty little mind." Tamara laughed. "Tell me about your dreams, and stop trying to evade my questions."

Selena explained as best she could. It was like she could recall how large they were. How they smelled. Even how their skin felt in the palms of her hands, but when she tried to bring up what they looked like she was kicked out of her own dreams.

"So when you are with them in this dream world, does it look familiar?"

Selena thought for a moment and realized she had not truly focused on her surroundings so much as the men. "I was on a hill but nothing looked familiar. Fuck…" Selena screamed. As she tried to focus on remembering other parts of the dreams a sharp, stabbing pain brought her to her knees.

"What the hell, Lena?" Tamara kneeled beside her.

"I don't know. It's like someone took an icepick to my brain." Selena rubbed her temple.

"This is not good, baby girl. Not good at all. I think we need to call my mama."

"No! Absolutely not. She'll call my parents, or make me come and stay with her, or worse, send one of your brothers here. No way. We are opening our last club if we can find the right place. And I think I've found the perfect spot."

The pain began to subside to a dull throb. Selena took a deep breath, focused on the ache, and sent a healing light to the area that still seemed red. A wash of relief flooded her senses.

"Promise if you need me you will call me no matter the time, Lena."

"I pinky promise." Selena held her right hand in a fist with pinky extended toward Tamara. They locked pinky fingers, kissed their fists, and sealed the deal. They'd been doing the same thing since they were teens, even though Tamara was three years older than Selena.

They discussed the new location of the club Selena wanted to open. Their clubs were a mix of honky-tonk and hip hop. She hired big bad-ass bouncers, but her bartenders and waitresses were all primarily gorgeous women.

"Kansas City, huh?" Tamara hitched herself back up onto the counter.

"Yep. They've revitalized their downtown district. I think Redneck Paradise would be a huge hit in the Midwest. It's also a big sports area with the local NFL and MLB, not to mention close to several colleges."

"Well you've obviously done your research. Have you found any property for sale yet?"

"Actually, I was given the name of a guy who brokers for the property developer there." Selena clapped her hands. Just thinking of the new club gave her goose bumps. "I'm going to give him a call as soon as it's a decent hour." Selena looked pointedly at the clock.

Tamara uncrossed her legs and jumped down from her perch. "You had me worried. I may not be able to see into your dreams, but I felt your fears." She wagged a finger at Selena. "Next time you pick up that phone and you call me. Don't make me have to go all commando and break in again."

Selena rolled her eyes. "You have a key."

"Whatever. You know what I mean." Tamara put her mug in the sink. "I'm heading back home to see if I can get a couple more hours of sleep. Some of us need more than a few to look gorgeous."

"Oh puh-lease." Selena followed Tamara to the front of the house. Her best friend opened the front door, only to stop.

"I know you can take care of yourself physically, Lena. But you need to guard your heart." Tamara looked over her shoulder.

"That's not a problem, Tam. Now go home and get some sleep. I'm going to drink some more coffee and then give Malcolm King a call."

# Chapter Two

The buzzing of his phone in his pocket stopped Malcolm in his tracks. He puzzled at the unknown number.

Shrugging, he answered. "This is Malcolm. How can I be of service to you?"

"Hi, my name is Selena Ramos. I was given your name as someone who could help me acquire property."

Usually the double entendre didn't go unnoticed, but the female caller not only seemed unfazed, but her voice was doing crazy things to his mind and body. His dick decided it was time to stand up and say hello, while his brain simply stopped listening to the words and basked in the tone of her voice.

"Did I lose you? Hello?"

He jerked as if coming out of a daze. "Sorry, sorry. Yes. I can help you. Where exactly are you looking for…I'm sorry, can you start from the beginning again? Service was a bit spotty." He used the lamest excuse in the book, glad he at least had a reason to not only have her reiterate what she was looking for but also to hear her speak some more.

The husky southern drawl was the sexiest thing he'd ever heard. He truly made an effort to listen to what she needed. When she mentioned the city she wanted, a light bulb went off in his head. His brother may not believe in coincidences, but Malcolm believed in fate. And he believed Kansas City and Selena Ramos was Fate's way of bringing her to him.

"Do you think you can find something for me?"

Her words pulled him out of his reverie. "Yeah, I do believe I have just the place. Can you e-mail me the specs you need?"

He gave her his e-mail address and promised to get back to her. What she didn't know was he would move heaven and earth to make sure there was property for her club, even kick his own brother out of one of his properties. The last notion made him chuckle.

"Why are you laughing?" He could hear the smile in her voice.

His unruly cock loved the husky note as it twitched in his trousers. At this rate he was on track to come in his pants with no other stimulation. "I was just thinking of my brother."

"Oh. Are you guys close?"

"You could say that." He chuckled. "We're twins."

"That's so cool. I always wanted a sister or brother."

The wistfulness was obvious in her words. He wanted to flash to her side and comfort her, erection be damned. A first for him. Usually he wanted to pleasure them, several times, then find his own happy ending, then quit them faster than they could offer to cook him a midnight snack. Or breakfast.

"You don't have any siblings?"

"Nope. It's just me and my best friend Tamara, but she shares her family with me. She's like my big sister and her brothers more than make up for my lack of." Again, she husked out a laugh.

He had to adjust his dick and feared he'd have to change his pants before his meeting with his clients. The visible wet spot confirmed his assumption. "That's great. I have ten other pseudo-brothers I'd give my life for."

The Ravens of War were created by the God Zeus thousands of years ago. He and his brothers had fought tirelessly to defeat Cronus and his army of demons. Finally, when they, along with the help from the other gods and goddesses, were able to banish him to Hell, the Ravens were no longer needed.

Just thinking of the gods who had sent them to Earth *for their own good* made Malcolm want to rip their heads off and shit down their throats. Sure they had been given immortality, along with many of their abilities from being created by gods. But it still didn't seem fair that they were willing to give up their lives, had fought tirelessly for the worthless beings who sat on gold thrones eating grapes like it was their due. He snorted.

"That's how I feel about Tamara. I'm not so sure about her brothers. Just kidding. I love them too."

At her words he felt the green-eyed monster of jealousy rip through him.

"Of course if they didn't have their significant others to temper their meddling ways, I think Tamara or I would have probably killed them at least once in the last ten years."

Instantly he began to relax. He recognized the camaraderie of love between non-blood relatives. He and the Ravens, although not related by blood, were brothers of the heart and soul.

"I understand completely. One of my closest friends is in constant danger of being zapped to the nether regions of hell anytime he's in the same room with my brother Max. You'd think he makes it his life's duty to piss my big brother off." Malcolm lay back on the bed.

"So how long do you think it'll take you to find me some property to look at?"

*Shit!* He forgot why he'd been talking to her in the first place. For some insane reason Malcolm was more at ease speaking with a total stranger than he was with almost anyone other than his fellow Ravens.

"After you send me the specs I'll make you my top priority. I can guarantee I'll have something for you within the week. How does that sound?"

She clapped her hands, which he could hear through the phone. "I can't wait. Can you e-mail pics of the locations, too?"

"I'll bombard you with everything I've got." *And there goes the double entendre again.*

"Great. I just sent you what I need. I really look forward to hearing from you."

Malcolm didn't want to let her go. That train of thought was enough to make him end the call. "Listen, I gotta go. I'll get back with you when I get you some properties to check out."

"I can't wait to see what you'll come up with."

He was angry at himself for wanting a woman he'd never met. First in his dreams, and now some anonymous woman on the phone. He never mixed business with pleasure, but here he was wanting a woman whose voice made him hard and nearly ready to come in his pants. "I'm sorry. I just didn't realize how late it was. I have a meeting in less than thirty minutes and have yet to change out of my traveling clothes." *There I go again, soothing the woman when what I need to do is go out and get laid.*

"Then I'll let you get off here. Hope your meeting goes as planned. And thank you again for agreeing to work with me."

Her southern drawl really was the sexiest thing he'd ever heard. He, who'd heard every language spoken, could speak every language including those that no longer existed. At this rate he was going to have to rub one out before meeting his client for their meeting.

"It was my pleasure, Miss Ramos. I look forward to doing business with you." Maybe if he kept it business by calling her by her last name he could keep his body in check.

"Oh, no. Please call me Selena, or Lena. Unless of course you prefer me to call you Mr. King?"

Gods, but he couldn't keep it business with her. He didn't care what she looked like. There was something about her that drew him. "No, please call me Mal, or Malcolm."

After assuring Selena he'd call, he hung up. He opened his e-mail and immediately forwarded the specs to his brother with a terse order to make it happen.

* * * *

Selena pushed the disconnect button on the headset. Malcolm King could be the voiceover for audio porn, she was sure.

It was an easy thing to send what she needed in size for the next Redneck Paradise. The name of her clubs always brought a sense of pride to Selena.

Born and raised in Texas, she was a country girl at heart. Even though she came from money, she still considered herself a redneck. Her best friend Tamara loved to tease her because she never went without either her cowgirl boots or her flip flops.

At Redneck Paradise the uniform was either a pair of jean shorts or a jean skirt and a tank top or shirt with the logo of the club emblazoned across the front. And of course a pair of cowgirl boots, with or without a cowgirl hat.

She kicked her chair back and propped her bare feet up on her desk. How would the Midwest react to her type of bar? Silly question. Who didn't like to see gorgeous girls in cute outfits? Add equally gorgeous guys strategically placed throughout who were not only easy on the eyes, but kicked the unruly patrons out when needed, and you've got a recipe for success.

"What's put that look on your face?"

"Sweet baby Jesus," Selena wheezed, nearly falling out of her chair. "Can't you knock like normal people?"

A raise of one perfectly arched eyebrow was her only answer. Tamara Mejia strolled into Selena's home office in a white pencil skirt with a slit that almost made it indecent, paired with a striped, black-and-white top that molded to her upper body and left part of her midriff showing.

"I'm waiting." Tamara sat in the chair across from Selena's desk.

"I just got off the phone with the broker I was telling you about. He thinks he knows some property for sale in Kansas City that'll work for us."

"Uh huh. That's not the look I was referring to. The dreamy expression I walked in on was one that I'd describe as a woman who was on the verge of orgasmic bliss."

Selena was sure her face resembled a tomato. "Does not."

"Does too."

She grabbed the cute little stuffed dragon sitting next to her keyboard and tossed it at Tamara's head. "Bitch." Selena laughed.

Tamara easily caught the stuffed toy.

"All right, so that's out of the way. So you gonna answer my question?"

"Fine, but don't laugh." Selena waited while Tamara pretended to cross her heart. "I was talking to the broker and I don't know how to describe it, but his voice…it just…" She sighed.

"Made your panties wet?" Tamara dodged the stuffed wolf Selena lobbed at her head.

"I hate you, you hussy."

"You love me, you just hate that I know you. So." Tamara paused.

Selena knew her friend wouldn't stop until she told her what she wanted to hear. "Fine, you're right. There, I said it." She was saved from further embarrassment by the ding of an incoming e-mail.

A giddy feeling took up residence in the pit of her stomach at the unknown sender. With the unmistakable King in the title she assumed it had to be from Malcolm, so she quickly clicked it open. Attached to the e-mail were several specs and even pictures of the space he felt would work for her.

"Oh my gawd, Tam. He did it. Look," Selena squealed.

Tamara uncrossed her long legs to come around the desk. They both looked over the pictures, enlarging them as they clicked on each individual one.

"Dang, girl. That boy sure does work quick."

Selena kept her face averted, not wanting to see if Tamara was doing that Seer thing she did. Although to be fair, Selena knew the other girl would never do anything to hurt her. Just the opposite, in fact.

"What do you think?" Selena asked, instead of addressing Tamara's statement.

"What does your gut tell you, Lena?"

With a hand on her stomach, Selena scooted her chair away from her desk. Tamara hopped her butt up on the desk and crossed her feet at the ankles, looking prepared to wait.

"Perfect. My gut tells me it's perfect." Selena bit down on her bottom lip, waiting to see if Tamara thought she was crazy.

"Then let's do it. You're right. Of course I already knew that before I came here."

"You what?" Selena jumped up from her chair.

"Now now, don't let that temper of yours get out of control," Tamara soothed.

The hair on Selena's arms were standing on end. A twinkling light in the brown eyes of her best friend calmed her like nothing else.

"You are such a…"

"If you call me more bad names I'm gonna call my mama. You know she'll wash your mouth out with soap."

As a diffuser of situations, threatening to tell one's mother was definitely a good one. Selena wrapped her arms around Tamara's shoulders. "Love you."

"All right, now enough of the mushy stuff. Did he give a timeframe as to when we can get started? These things don't happen overnight, ya know."

Even after all these years it amused Selena to see her best friend get all funny when it came to emotions. She made a shooing motion with her hands to get Tam to move out of the way since her butt was still parked on her desk.

A few keystrokes later and the first steps were done in her plans for the next club to add to her portfolio.

* * * *

Looking out at the setting sun with his arms crossed over his chest, Max thought about the poor lost goddess. The last time he'd seen Zeus—his mentor, the man who he'd looked up to, thought the world of—was just over twenty-four years ago. The Ravens were tasked with one last thing, and they had failed miserably.

He shook his head. The prospect of getting up every day without a purpose had always fueled his need to succeed, which he and the Ravens had done without fail, until now. Their time to find the lost child was dwindling with only a year, give or take a few weeks. Even though they'd narrowed down the power source to the United States, all the Ravens had separated, searching for her. Every day he let his senses flare, hoping if she were near his inner light would recognize her. Each night, utter despair threatened to choke him when he failed, with only the hope that his fellow Ravens had better luck fueling him.

If he could have found someone to share his life with, he'd have been content. A female that was made just for him and his brother. *Damn.* Ever since the dreams of the phantom woman, all Max thought of was the three of them coming together as one.

They didn't even know if the dream woman was real or a figment of their imagination. Not to mention if they did find her now, their time with her would be short-lived if Zeus was to be believed. And why wouldn't he be? He could still hear the words as if Zeus had just spoken them. "*If my daughter is not returned to me within twenty-five Earth years she will come into her god powers. An untrained goddess receiving all her powers at once will be disastrous for this world you call Earth. Find her for me.*"

Max scrubbed his hands down his face. Knowing that even Zeus had been blocked by the dethroned god Cronus, and wasn't able to locate the child either, didn't make him feel any better.

He got up from his chair to look out over the Power and Light District. From the top floor of his building he had an uninterrupted view of the entire area, plus a perfect view of the sky. The sun was setting, its fiery descent bringing to mind what the Earth would look like when it exploded.

A smile curved his mouth as he heard his assistant, Kim, talking. When the intercom buzzed, his lips pulled into a full-blown grin.

"Max, your brother just called and said he's sending the contracts for the property back to you. He wants you to get them back to him ASAP."

The way Kim enunciated each letter in a brisk staccato voice made him chuckle.

"Didn't he want to talk to me?"

"Nope. He said to have you call him when you're done. Hold on. The fax is just finishing."

"Bring it in when it's finished."

"Yes, Sir." Sarcasm dripped from her words. He could imagine she'd given him a tiny salute to emphasize the statement.

With a thought, he turned the intercom off and focused back on the skyline. It took only moments before a brief knock signaled his ever-efficient assistant's presence.

"Here you go. Do you need anything else?"

"Shouldn't you be gone by now?" Max looked at the clock on the wall. "I thought it was your bingo night."

"I'm on my way now, unless you need me to fax these back?"

"I'll take care of it. Go win some money."

"Ha. I think I'm more of a donor than a winner. Your brother wanted me to make sure you know this client was super *special.*" The comical way she said the last word combined with the waggle of her eyebrows was one of the reasons he employed her. The fact she was in her late fifties and considered herself his pseudo-mother was another.

Halfway out the door, she stopped, saying over her shoulder, "You know your brother. She must be really…"

He knew what she implied. While he was the brother who put down roots for thirty or forty years, his brother liked to play it fast and easy.

Once he heard the outer office door shut he opened his senses. Usually by this hour all of the staff had already left for the day, but it was too ingrained in him not to check for himself.

The documents his brother had forwarded him lay on top of his desk, with the name Selena Ramos on top. It took him only seconds to scan the papers. Even though there were many bars already filling up the downtown Kansas City area, the urge to give this woman every available space assaulted him.

Within moments he signed in the appropriate spots and had the papers sent back to his brother. But a sense of urgency plagued him. A need to make contact with the new owner of the property below his own offices, the space he had no plans to sell, until his brother called him. *Fucking Fates.*

The contact information Selena Ramos had put on the contract was permanently imbedded in his memory. He tapped his fingers on the desk. To call or not to call? Why was he questioning himself?

Before he could change his mind he punched the numbers into his cell. The phone rang several times, making him think he was going to get voice mail.

"Hi, this is Selena."

"Miss Ramos?"

"Y–Yes. Who's this?"

"This is Max King. I just wanted to let you know I just faxed the contracts back to my brother, Malcolm King, and wanted to personally say thank you for your business. I do believe you are now the proud owner of a prime piece of real estate in Kansas City, Missouri."

"That's great."

There was an unmistakable sadness clouding her voice. "Is everything all right?"

"I'm sorry…yes, everything is fine."

Max ignored one of his golden rules and tried to focus on her memories. It was harder to tap into the thoughts of people he'd never met, but not something he wasn't capable of.

The image of a double funeral with many attendees and a sense of heartache flashed into his mind. She'd obviously lost both her parents in a tragic accident. From what he could see of the season surrounding the proceedings it wasn't recent, which to humans didn't ease the heartache.

"Let me know if you need anything else. My office is always open to preferred customers, and you, Miss Ramos, have moved into that category."

"That's really sweet of you. Thank you."

Before he broke another rule and flashed to her side, he pulled out of her memories.

"You have my number. If you need anything, anything at all, please call me or my brother at any time." Why he felt it imperative to make sure she knew to call him, he had no clue. *Shit!* He needed to find a woman and get laid. "Talk to you soon."

"Selena. Call me Selena."

"Until next time, Selena mine." Max hung up before she could respond.

The clubs below were beginning to fill up. He could have his pick of women, so why did he get hard for a dream girl and his heart ache for a woman who he'd never met?

As he did every day and night he sent a tendril of energy out to search for the lost goddess. And just like every day and night for the past twenty-four years, he came up blank. Nothing. Surely if she were dead Zeus would've paid him or one of the other Ravens a visit and let them know?

A disturbing notion pushed its way into his brain. Had the child been found and all this time he and his brothers had been looking for nothing? Worrying for nothing? Tossed away like they were nothing?

He misted to the lower level of his building, outside one of the busier bars filled with the rowdier crowds. The thousand-dollar suit became a pair of low-slung jeans and fitted t-shirt. Although he towered over ninety-eight percent or more of the crowd, he tried to blend in.

Several heads turned in his direction. Most of the young men froze in place, while the women seemed to come alive. It was always the same, and now he was beginning to sound like his brother Mal.

At least he knew the bartender, liked him, and respected him even though the man seemed a bit scared. "Hey Alan, can I get a Makers on the rocks?"

Alan smiled, more at ease. "Sure, coming right up. We got a great band tonight. You staying for the show?"

"Maybe." He took the short, squat glass, downing the whiskey in one gulp. "Can I get another?"

"Rough day?" Alan asked, taking the glass and refilling.

"Nah, just long." He smiled, hoping to look less harsh.

It obviously worked. The smaller man rested his elbows on the bar and nodded toward the stage, at ease for the first time since Max had met him over a year ago.

A woman with grace and agility, and what men would call sex on legs, moved up to a microphone located center stage. Her voice was a deep, raspy sound that made you think of doing dirty, naked things with her. But she did nothing for Max.

Not wanting to seem rude, he stayed for another twenty minutes listening to the woman sing, watching her graceful movements as she walked across the stage in a black corset and baggy, black pants. Gothic gorgeous is what he'd call her. The men and women alike lined the front of the stage, many of whom were clearly aroused by her. Not Max. *Shit!*

Alan kept his glass full, stopping to chat every now and then. Max made an effort to appear less threatening to those around him.

Without being obvious, he blurred the perceptions of Alan and the other patrons as he made his leave. The tip he left would make up for any discomfort he might've felt.

## Chapter Three

*She stood facing them with her hands at her sides in tight little fists. The usually calm air that Olympus sported was suddenly engulfed with winds that buffeted their bodies. Max refused to allow her to slip away from him, them, again.*

*He closed the distance between them, fusing his mouth over what he decided was the most perfect pair of lips he'd ever tasted. His brother moved in to nuzzle her neck, wisps of her long silvery hair tickling his nose. He broke away to inhale her unique scent that reminded him of honey and strawberries.*

*Warmth, unlike anything he'd ever known, radiated from the alluring creature. His brother claimed the mouth that he'd just feasted on. He stepped around the kissing pair, molded his front to her back. A feminine gasp made him smile.*

*Her ass was high and round, fitting into his hands perfectly. It was by far the sweetest ass he'd ever seen or felt.*

*Over her shoulder he watched Malcolm bend to engulf one of the erect buds of her nipples through the transparent gown. Her hips swiveled against Max's groin. He groaned at the strength she displayed when she reached up and pulled his head down to hers. Her body stretched between their much larger ones had his overprotective instinct to keep her safe burning in Max's gut. He sent a burst of energy outside his body, searching through the mist and fog surrounding them for danger. A sense of peace settled over him when he encountered nothing but the three of them.*

*He traced her swollen lips with his tongue, dipped inside for more of the sweet taste of strawberry honey. The soft moans were music to his ears.*

*Malcolm stood up and pulled on the ties that held the gown together, letting it float to the ground.*

*With a growl, Max turned her in his embrace. His hands roamed down her back and framed her ass before tracing the crack all the way to the heart of her and back.*

*Fuck, she was so wet. He brought his fingers up to his mouth.*

*Though he didn't think he was worthy, he needed this woman with every fiber of his being. His twin and he were so completely in tune with each other that words weren't needed. He released their lady long enough to wave his hand through the air. A bed large enough for three appeared alongside them. Their clothes disappeared without conscious thought.*

*Her eyes, which he could see were an amazing shade of silver, widened. She licked those delectable lips that drove Max to distraction, then with cat-like grace turned and crawled onto the bed.*

*The bed dipped as Malcolm climbed on one side while Max went to the other.*

*Mist and fog began to roll in, nearly suffocating Max with the thickness. He reached for his woman.*

Max bolted upright in bed. The dream seemed so real he could smell the scent of strawberries, could still taste the lingering hint of honey on his tongue.

*"Malcolm. You up?"*

*"I am now. Please tell me you didn't just dream about our dream girl again?"*

*Son of a bitch.* Max swung his legs off the side of the bed. With his head in his hands, he closed his eyes.

*"Dude, I was this close to…Yeah, as far as wet dreams go. That was a good one. But fuck, I'm hard as steel and no woman will do."* Max could picture his twin's scowl. The love 'em and leave 'em

wasn't working out too well right now. At any other time it would've amused Max, except when he was in the same position.

*"I know. I tried, and like a dumbass I thought I'd get drunk. Get laid. And all would be well. And what do I have to show for my efforts other than a minor headache?"* Max looked at his still-hard dick and grimaced. He couldn't even get semi-hard watching half-naked women, but give him an imaginary one and just like that he was ready.

*"I'm thinking you've got the same problem as me, bro. So my question is what are we going to do?"*

That was the problem. Max, the leader of the Ravens, had no clue. For thousands of years he'd led his band of soldiers, first on Mount Olympus, then through countless battles here on Earth. Until they'd finally decided to split up and find their own way.

Of course, beings created by the gods who were immortal but not gods, but not humans, didn't really belong anywhere except together. If Max hadn't had his twin he didn't know what he would've done. All the Ravens paired up in one way or another, although if they ever needed each other they were only a thought away.

But with this he didn't feel comfortable calling out to any of his brothers other than Mal, who shared the dreams with him. If only they knew who the woman was.

*"Max?"*

*"Yeah, I was just thinking."*

*"Don't do that too hard,"* Malcolm joked.

*"I honestly have no clue. I'm...We're flying blind here, Mal. I've called out to Zeus and the other gods. Hell, I've even called out to the goddesses who birthed us."*

He echoed his brother's snort. To call the goddess who agreed to carry them for nine months a mother was a joke. No. They weren't what anyone would call normal by human standards or even god standards. The Ravens were full grown adults within their first year, but they still had hearts that beat. They still had feelings.

To be thrown into training with soldiers who were hundreds, if not thousands, of years old seemed normal to them at the time. But looking back with the knowledge they had now? Max shook his head. They had been disposable then, just as they were disposable now.

*"Let me guess. O Great One didn't answer any of your calls. But I bet you still expended energy today looking for his lost little brat right?"*

*"Mal, if he's right, and the goddess isn't found, Earth has a ticking time bomb that is less than a year away. Who's to say we will survive if she explodes?"*

A tired sigh stretched out. "*Would it be so bad to finally meet the All Creator?"*

Max didn't have an answer to that. No. He had an answer, but to voice it out loud felt like he was betraying someone. "*I don't know, Mal, I just..."* He trailed off. His twin knew without words what Max felt.

*"I'm going to be out of the country on an extended trip, if you need me you know how to reach me, bro."*

*"Of course. I think I'll take a little trip and do a little radio silence myself. If you need me..."*

*"Yeah, yeah."*

*"Take care, Malcolm."*

*"You too, Max."*

* * * *

"No, no, no..." Selena groaned. "Why can't I have normal wet dreams where I get to the happy ending like normal people?" she asked the ceiling.

The cloying mist that wrapped around her reminded her of the dreams she'd had when she was a child. Her parents had spent thousands of dollars on therapists who all said it was a manifestation of her biggest fears. Hello, who wouldn't be scared of being dumped in a garbage can and left for dead as a baby?

But that was not why she was scared of…fog or mist, or whatever the hell was in her dreams. She wanted to get it on with one or both of her dream men, dang it.

The loss of her parents when she was twenty-one was devastating, but wasn't such a stabbing pain to the heart whenever she thought of them. When they'd been in their mid-fifties, taking on an infant must've been a difficult task, but they'd been the best parents a child could ask for. At seventy-eight and seventy-nine they were still too young to die, but they had lived a long and happy life and she was grateful for all the time they had had together.

They'd taught her to never take anything for granted. Her mother was always saying, "*Lena, mia bambina, you must not dwell on the past for it is gone and can't be changed, nor look to the future for it is yet to be decided. But do you know why they call right now the present? Because it is a gift and should be treated as such.*"

She would then nod her head and go back to baking, or whatever thing she happened to be doing at the time.

With that last memory in mind and a smile on her face, Selena got out of bed with a lighter heart. Her parents would always be with her in spirit, but they'd want her to live life to the fullest.

Now she had to talk Tamara into stopping by Malcolm's office in California while she was out there doing whatever the heck she was out there doing. Sometimes the Mejias could be downright spooky with their voodoo, seer abilities. Selena snorted at that.

"Who am I to call others weird?" she asked the empty room.

While she waited for Tamara to answer her cell phone she made her way to the kitchen. After filling her coffee cup she took it out onto the back patio to enjoy the early morning quietness.

When Tam didn't answer she left her a brief explanation with Malcolm's office address and his contact information. A flash of her best friend showing up in one of her patent miniskirts that showcased her long legs topped off with a too-tight and too-short crop top had Selena seeing red.

Jealousy wasn't an emotion Selena associated with herself. Her first and only love Tim had been the older, more experienced guy. They'd met at Tamara's brother's house party, and he'd seemed so sweet and kind. At seventeen she'd been a bit naïve and too trustful. Her parents should've known better than to let her date a college guy for her first boyfriend. She shook her head. Looking back, if it hadn't been Tim it would've been someone else. At least he knew what he was doing when they did the deed.

She snickered. Here she was, twenty-three, and still called having sex "doing the deed." After she finally gave it up to Tim, he thought they should do it every day. Or in his own words, he'd find someone else who would. *He was a healthy twenty-one year old guy*. The last bit made her sober. It seemed she was always losing those close to her. Within months of their relationship Tim was taken from her too. Of course she had no illusions that she and Tim were meant for happily ever after. Had he not been in the wrong place at the wrong time and been killed, their relationship still would've had an end date.

The ringing of her phone broke into her reverie. "Hey Tam, did you get my message?"

"No, I was just calling to see how my baby girl was doing."

"Don't you listen to your voice mail?" Selena rolled her eyes even though she knew Tamara couldn't see her.

"Are you rolling your eyes at me?"

"Why do you ask that?"

"Because you got *that* tone. When you get *that* tone it means you're rolling your eyes. And don't answer my question with a question."

"You answered my question with a question and then you just made an asinine statement."

"Girl, I will smack you for…So you want me to go by this hunkalicious guy's office and pick up the paperwork, right?"

"So you were just messing with me? Why does that not surprise me." She laughed. "You are such a brat. You know that right?"

"Takes one to know one. Anyhoo, I'm on my way there now. I've already called and made an appointment all professional-like and everything."

*And, there goes that green-eyed monster again.* Jealous over a man she's never even laid eyes on? Maybe it was time she stopped being a born-again virgin and took one of the cowboys who frequented Redneck Paradise home for a night of hot, sweaty sex. Her stomach cramped thinking of some anonymous hookup.

"You're the best, Tam. Let me know after you seal the deal." *Shit on a stick.* She wanted to call those words back and tell Tamara to keep her panties on and her hands to herself.

"Will do, girlfriend. Talk to you soon."

* * * *

Malcolm stepped off his private plane, pleased to be back in the United States. "Damn, spending other people's money is fun."

The pilot laughed and shook his hand while the flight attendant, a pretty brunette, offered her cheek for a kiss. The look in her eyes said she'd offer more, but he never slept with employees. Anymore.

The sound of his phone ringing saved him from any further conversation. With a jaunty wave he continued to his car, a '66 Chevy Camaro SS. "Yo, Max. What's up, brother?"

"I just got a call from a contractor that wants to come and begin working on the new club. When do I get to meet the new owner?"

Malcolm threw his bag in the backseat before vaulting over the side to land in the driver's seat. "Shit, man, I haven't even met her yet. I do have a voice mail from her partner wanting to meet tomorrow."

Just thinking of Selena Ramos's smoky voice made his dick stand up at attention. Not a comfortable position to be in when one was wearing a pair of tight jeans in a low-slung, antique muscle car. His brother's knowing chuckle brought his focus back to their conversation.

"You mean to tell me you took on a client you've never personally vetted?" Incredulity laced his voice, and something else that Malcolm was sure he wasn't going to like.

Yep, Max was definitely laughing at him.

"There's something." Malcolm cleared his throat. "I don't know how to explain it, but…when I first heard her voice, it was like every hair on my body stood up and took notice, along with other parts of my anatomy."

He could picture Max's eyebrows rising to his hairline at the admission. If roles were reversed he'd be doing the same thing.

"That's how I felt when I first spoke to her," Max said, with a bite in his tone Malcolm didn't hear very often.

"Seriously? What do you think it means?"

"That we are getting old," Max sighed.

"Why do you sound so edgy? Do you need to get laid? I thought you'd been seeing that bitch Steph…" He cleared his throat. "I mean the delightful Stephanie."

"Fuck off, Mal. Her name was Tiffany, and you know it. To answer your question though, I gave her walking papers a while back." Max sounded more amused than angry.

Malcolm listened as Max gave him the condensed version of events with his now ex. He couldn't help but laugh at the image of the banshee of a woman. He'd hated Tiffany on the spot, and couldn't understand the woman's appeal in the first place. But, "to each his own" was his motto.

He and Max were more than identical twins. They were two halves of a whole. With Max being the more serious, Malcolm made it his mission to lighten him up.

He'd flash images to Max at the most inopportune times. Like when Max had been in counsel with over a dozen of their elders, Malcolm would share with his twin what he was doing at the time, which just happened to be the daughter of one of the elders. His brother would have to stand or sit during the meeting, all while Malcolm shared the experience.

Of course Max always retaliated with a bitch slap upside Malcolm's head, but the chuckle he received far outweighed the blow. He'd suffer a thousand hits to the head to make his brother smile. Max carried too much weight on his shoulders, always had, and probably always would.

Malcolm whistled through his teeth. "I told you before, Max. You never hear anything good when you eavesdrop." He grunted at the unseen blow that knocked his head forward, still laughing at the curses he heard on the other end of the phone.

"If you weren't thousands of miles away, I'd kick your ass." Max growled.

"You could try, bro."

"Listen, I gotta go. Let me know the details of when I get to meet Ms. Selena Ramos. The woman who gives Romeo a woody over the phone."

Malcolm sent the image of flipping Max the bird before he agreed and hung up. He adjusted the mirrors in his car before starting the engine. The loud rumble of the big block engine was one of the things he loved best about muscle cars.

By the time he hit the highway that led to the winding road to his home he decided to call Selena's office. A quick glance at the modified dash showed him it was just past five. He figured Selena had already left for the day. He shifted down to second gear as the winding road climbed up the hill, making the outside noise minimal. He waited for voice mail to pick up, and had planned what he was going to say, only to have his breath freeze in his throat at the husky sound of the woman's voice on the other end.

"This is Selena."

From the impatient way she sounded he assumed that wasn't the first time she'd said those words. He opened his mouth, but nothing came out.

"Good evening, Ms. Ramos. This is Malcolm King," he finally croaked out.

"Please call me Selena, or Lena."

The sadness he heard in her voice had an overwhelming urge rush over him to flash to her side and hold her, or fuck her, or just hold her. He wasn't sure which would win out, not with the pole trying to bust out of his jeans. His heart constricted at the hitch in her voice. That was another first for him.

"I got your assistant's voice mail and just wanted to let you know I'm available to meet anytime tomorrow. Or I could fly down to meet up with you tomorrow or the day after and save both of you a trip."

The concept of finally being in the same room with the woman who made his dick twitch and his heart ache simultaneously scared the crap out of him. "Give me a day or so, and I can fly down to Texas with the papers."

"That's very kind of you, but Tamara, the one who left the voice mail, she's my partner, and just so happens to be in LA this week. She can just stop by your office if that's okay? I'm going to be tied up for the next few weeks and I'd rather get this deal taken care of."

Malcolm heard the lingering pain in her husky tone and wanted nothing more than to hold her. The loss of loved ones was hard. He'd lost many people he'd called friends over the years.

"I'm beginning to think you're avoiding me. Do you know what that can do to a man's ego?"

She laughed. The sound sent a thrill through his body straight to his balls. *What the hell?* With a grimace he adjusted his legs, hoping to alleviate the tightness in his groin. He tried to remember the last time he'd ever gotten hard from just the sound of a woman's voice or laugh, and came up blank.

"I don't think there's a woman alive that has ever avoided you, Malcolm King."

"Shit," Malcolm cursed, barely making the curve without hitting the guardrail. The way she said his name almost had him coming in his jeans. Another first for him.

She giggled as he cursed some more.

"Are you laughing at me, woman? You are completely crushing my ego now." He'd stand on his head and make faces if it kept the sadness from her voice.

"Do you need me to stroke your ego?"

His purely selfless thoughts flew out the open top of his car at her innocent question. The image of her hand stroking him to completion nearly undid him. He chanced a look down at his denim to see the obvious bulge.

What if her words weren't as innocent as he thought? He laughed and broke one of his brother's cardinal rules. He tried to tune into her thoughts, slamming into a mental brick wall. His head flew back against the headrest. "What the fuck?" A painful throb pulsed at his temple.

"Excuse me? Are you okay?"

"Uh…No, I was just thinking about something," Malcolm muttered.

Selena cleared her throat. "Listen, I need to go. Thank you for calling to let me know you'll be available. I'll call Tamara. What time works best? Or would you rather liaise with her yourself?"

He tried again to look into Selena's mind, easing into the forefront. A vast blackness seemed to surround him, which was better than a brick wall, but was clearly some sort of mental shield. He slipped out, not wanting to alert her to his presence in her mind.

"Let Tamara know I'll be around all weekend. I can meet anytime at my office." He never invited women to his sanctuary up in the hills.

An overwhelming need to have Selena there rocked him. He wanted to welcome her into his home and be welcomed into more than her mind. He shook himself before he said something that would likely scare Selena.

# Chapter Four

Malcolm missed the husky tone of Selena's voice as they disconnected. He came to a stop at the twelve-foot gates that surrounded his land and entered the code into the state-of-the-art security system.

An immediate sense of peace settled over him when he opened his senses to scan the area. A lone wolf howled, Smokey, his pet that had adopted him as his owner when Malcolm had bought the property.

He wondered what Selena would think of Smokey. An overwhelming urge to have her in his home, his bed, anywhere he could have her nearly undid him. And he still had no clue what she looked like. Sure he could assume she was small and petite with dark hair, dark eyes and dark skin, with the name Selena Ramos. But with every internet search he did, there was always something blocking a shot of her. A puzzle that was fast becoming an obsession of his that even being a country away didn't make go away. He loved women of all shapes and sizes, from blondes, to brunettes, to redheads, short or tall or anywhere in between. He was first physically attracted to a woman and then came…for him, nothing really came next of his so-called relationships. He treated women well. He wined and dined them. Made love to them until they were both beyond sated. And then they parted ways until the next time they met up. No promises of happily ever after. He wasn't thinking of forever with the mystery woman. He just needed to get her out of his system. That was all.

Thoughts of being with the same woman until she turned old and gray, and then died, made his dick, which had been at full staff since he first heard Selena's voice, finally go soft.

A push of a button by his sun visor had one of his garage bay doors opening. He eased his Chevy inside, before another press of the button shut the door. With a jerk of his hand he opened the door and stepped out of the vehicle.

The sound of nails clicking on the cement floors was his only warning as a large silver-and-gray wolf slammed his paws against his chest.

"Hey, boy, did you miss me?"

Smokey gave a growl. He stood on his hind legs with his face only inches from Malcolm's. Standing close to six feet tall, the large animal would intimidate most men, but Malcolm stood at six feet five inches himself.

Malcolm scratched Smokey's head. "Down, boy," Malcolm said, trying to step back. The intelligence shining in the animal's eyes staring back at him still had the power to amaze Malcolm.

He made to lift the large paws off his chest when Smokey raised his right leg up and smacked Malcolm in the side of the head.

Stumbling back, Malcolm growled at the animal that seemed to be scolding him, reprimanding him like his twin Max would've done. With another rub behind Smokey's ears, he grabbed both legs and pushed them off his chest.

He padded into his home, trailed by Smokey, who looked to have a grin on his face. He bared his teeth in a snarl that made the wolf's tail wag back and forth.

Giving up, he headed for the master suite. The room was built large enough for three in mind.

Zeus had told them they'd know when they found their Fated. They all assumed that meant one for each of them somewhere. But Malcolm always felt like he was half of a whole and Max was the other half. The woman who would be his Fated would be his brother's Fated too. It was a bone-deep feeling deep in his gut that was the way it would be for them. Maybe not for all the Ravens, but for him and Max he was sure that was how it was meant to be.

The bed he'd had custom made equaled the size of a double King. The closets were also large enough for three. Everything in the room was built with the thought of him and his brother sharing with their wife. All the things pointed at a triad in his mind and heart.

An image of a naked woman sandwiched between him and Max rolling around on the bed made his breath freeze in his throat.

He stripped his clothes and dropped them to the floor on the way to the bathroom, another room he had designed with the thought of three in mind. "Shit."

His dick was so hard with thoughts of a faceless woman he began to worry for his own sanity.

With a thought, he had all the showerheads turned on and heated to his preferred temperature. He stepped under the spray, braced his feet apart, and placed both hands on the tile in front of him. The tension in his shoulders eased as the jets pounded him from all directions.

He imagined Selena kneeling in front of him. He tried to think of what she'd look like. With a name like Selena Ramos he pictured her as a petite Hispanic woman with brown eyes, but the image kept blurring to a tiny woman with long, curling, blonde hair.

Something niggled at his brain, but with his dick still hard as a pike, he couldn't focus.

With a wave of his hand, he turned the water to cold. Mentally he started reviewing things he needed to do, but his mind kept hearing Selena's voice and her husky laugh.

With a curse, he grabbed his cock and rubbed his thumb over the head, spreading the pre-cum around. He stroked up his shaft and back down slowly before he cupped his balls in his palm.

He conjured up an image of a dark-haired, dark-eyed woman with dark skin. The vision morphed into a tiny blonde woman on her knees instead. He focused on the new sight, and imagined her hand rubbing and stroking him.

Heat exploded from the base of his spine to the tip of his cock. Without any warning, his balls drew up, spurting cum all over the tiles. Malcolm watched in fascination as it swirled down the drain.

"Son of a bitch," he panted. The image that made him come like an untried youth wasn't the faceless Selena Ramos, but the angel from his dreams. He was ten kinds of fucked up.

He grabbed the soap from the ledge and washed in record time. Stepping out, he picked up a towel and rubbed himself dry. Padding naked into his bedroom, he threw open his closet door and chose a loose pair of white linen slacks, a short-sleeved, blue silk shirt, and a pair of sandals.

He looked in the mirror and grimaced at the flush on his face. His little one-man orgasm was better than anything he could remember.

* * * *

Selena hung up and breathed a sigh of relief. She fanned herself and peered at the screen to see a smirk on Tamara Mejia's face through the computer. "What are you looking at?"

"Oh, I don't know. Maybe you sitting there with a goofy look on your face." Tamara giggled.

"That man's voice." She sighed. "I mean, dayam, I'm going to have to change my panties," Selena joked.

"I'm not wearing any so I guess I'm okay. Hang on, hun. My mama's calling."

The thought of Tamara meeting Malcolm in one of her patent miniskirts sans underwear had Selena rethinking sending the other woman to meet Malcolm.

Tamara was everything Selena was not. At five feet nine with long, black hair and snapping brown eyes, Tamara was most men's wet dream come to life. At five feet four Selena was average height, with blonde hair that had streaks of white, and gray eyes. She was just normal.

She couldn't compete when it came to Tamara.

The hair on her arms stood on end, and tingles of electricity arched across her nerve endings. With supreme effort, she steered her angry thoughts away from things better left alone.

Laughing, Tamara cleared her throat. "So what's the plan?"

* * * *

After they logged off, Selena pushed back from her desk with a sigh. She stared at the moon in all its glory and wondered if Malcolm preferred the view of the setting sun, or the moon like she did.

Her parents said they'd named her Selena because when they found her, it looked as if a moonbeam had shone down, highlighting her presence. She smiled at the memory.

*"Mommy, how come I don't look like you and papa?"*

*"Well sweetheart, that's because we adopted you," Selena's mother, Theresa, whispered.*

*"What does that mean?" Selena asked. Her mother looked over at her father, and shrugged her shoulders. At three years old, Selena spoke fluently in Spanish and English, and talked more like an adult than a normal child.*

*Her father knelt in front of her and clasped her hands. His voice shook as he spoke. "One night, when your mother and I went on an evening stroll, we were so sad because we didn't have any bambinas. Then we saw this beam of light leading us to this little bundle. And there we found you. Your mother and I were so surprised to see this baby with blonde, curly hair, and eyes like liquid silver. It was a miracle. We just picked you up and carried you home." Jose wiped his eyes and motioned for his wife to continue.*

*"You're a gift from God, and we thank him every day."*

Selena had known she wasn't like normal children very early. Her first memory of being a baby was more like a fairy tale. When she'd told her parents, they hadn't believed her and told her not to tell anyone else.

Giant men and beautiful women surrounded her. Everything seemed to shimmer in gold and silver hues, with lots of feelings of love and happiness. Her next memory encompassed an angry man, and the golden light was replaced by a cloying darkness.

* * * *

The air crackled as her body temperature rose. She inhaled in an attempt to control her breathing. Her eyes closed, while she focused inward on the here and now.

With an abrupt turn she walked out of her home office, stopping to turn on the sound system. Drowning Pool's "Let the Bodies Hit the Floor" pumped outside at ear-splitting decibels.

She rolled her shoulders, unsnapped her jeans, and lifted her top off before stepping onto the back deck in her sports bra and boy shorts.

Her pulse thundered. The chorus was on the third repeat and she was more than ready.

She didn't want to destroy any of her beautiful surroundings, and from past experiences, she knew if she didn't wrest control of herself she'd do just that.

In the middle of her backyard she took a deep breath, lifted her arms up, and brought them back in front of her body. She bowed to an imaginary opponent and began the intricate steps to Tai Chi, which quickly flowed into the fluid steps of Krav Maga.

By the time her playlist flowed into Metallica, sweat covered her scantily clad body. Her steps slowed and her body felt more like her own.

No longer did the air crackle.

Her hybrid wolf-dog Katja barked, sounding more like a mournful howl.

Selena glanced at the sky, shocked to see the moon had shifted toward the horizon.

She dropped to her knees into the damp grass and bowed her head. A wet snout nudged her arm. "It's okay, girl. I feel much better, but I stink." Selena wrapped her arm around Katja's head. They stayed that way a few minutes. Looking down at her sweat-covered body, Selena grimaced.

In unison they both stood. The large pool called to Selena. Not bothering to shower first, she dived into the cool water while Katja sat at the end.

Only able to swim one lap before her muscles began to protest, she turned to her back to float and wait for the moon to finish its set in the sky. Katja barked, alerting Selena to the time yet again.

An eternity could have passed, she was so relaxed.

Finally she pulled herself out and went to the rock wall attached to the deck with the custom outdoor shower. The water flowed over her head and cleaned the chlorine from her body.

She was too exhausted to do more than wrap a towel around herself, wring her hair out, and dry off before heading inside.

With a look toward the stairs leading to the master bedroom, which was too far in her opinion, she set the alarm. With another glance at the stairs and the inviting, overstuffed couches, Selena shrugged her shoulders.

With a weary sigh, she fell onto one of her couches and pulled a quilt over her legs. Sleep claimed her immediately.

* * * *

She groaned, and ignored the infernal ringing of her cellphone. "Thank the gods the damn thing stopped," she mumbled, and turned over, pulling a pillow over her head.

And bam, just like that, the ringing started again. "Fuck me. What do you want?" she snarled into the phone.

"Well I would be happy to do just that, but I don't think even my impressive manhood could reach you from here."

Selena's face heated at the sound of Malcolm King's voice. She tried to scramble up from the pile of pillows that swallowed her up, making the task almost impossible. "Malcolm?"

"Fantastic, you already recognize my voice. Now, I just need to learn to leap tall buildings, and I could take care of you."

Her pulse raced. "What are you talking about?"

After flinging several pillows off the couch and untangling her legs from the blanket and the still-damp towel, she managed to stand up.

"Did I wake you?" he asked instead of answering her question.

"Why are you calling me so early?" Two can do the "ask a question instead of answer" game, she thought.

"What do you mean, 'so early'? It's afternoon here on the West coast and you're two hours ahead of me."

She nearly tripped over Katja as she stumbled to the patio doors. The sun had clearly been up for hours. "Shit, shit, shit. I can't believe I slept so late, damn it."

"Were you up all night partying?"

Selena wondered at the anger that laced his words. They mimicked the anger she felt when she thought of Tamara meeting Malcolm.

From the lateness of the hour she knew he'd probably already met with her partner. Probably already fell head-over-ass in lust with the gorgeous half-Spanish, half-Cajun woman.

She snapped the curtain closed, shutting out the blinding sun and the green-eyed monster. "Did you need something, Malcolm?"

"Do you know you answer a question with a question?"

Selena's heart skipped a beat at his deep, rumbled laugh. "Hello, Pot, said the Kettle. But to answer your question, no, I was up working and time got away from me. I think I crashed around five this morning."

"I wanted to call and let you know I'll be meeting with your partner in about an hour and just wanted to make sure you didn't have anything you wanted to add before I give all the documents over. Since you are the majority shareholder I just wanted to double check."

"Tam has every bit as much power as I do." The relief washed over her like a tidal wave.

"That's fantastic. I hope we can get together and I can thank you personally for your business. Your partner was almost hesitant to meet with me. It could give a man a complex if he had self-esteem issues."

"Ha. I'm sure it didn't faze you one bit, Mr. King." She laughed.

"You wound me."

Again she heard laughter in his voice, and shivers raced down her spine. She trudged up the stairs and stripped out of her clothes. With the phone tucked between her ear and shoulder she turned on the faucet to her large tub, and added scented bubble bath before grabbing a large bath towel.

"I don't think there is a woman alive who has the power to hurt you."

Silence stretched so long and thick the tub had filled completely.

"That is where you would be wrong."

She wondered at the sadness that had crept into his voice. "I'm sorry…"

"Listen, I really was hoping I could meet you and thank you in person for the use of my company. I'll tell you the truth and that is"—he paused—"you were my easiest client."

She stepped over the ledge into the garden tub full of bubbles and exhaled a loud sigh, happy to hear the eagerness in his words.

"I'd love to meet you too, but I truly can't right now. But when the club opens I'll give you a VIP invite and expect you to be there on opening night along with your brother."

She picked up a sponge, and squirted her favorite body wash on it before lathering it up, running it over first one leg then the other. The swish of the soapy water sounded loud to her, but the soft cloth as it ran over her body made her forget she was on the phone.

His next words jolted her back to reality.

"Um, yes I…What are you doing right now?"

"Oh. I'm just…Look, I need to go. Thank you for all your hard work. When I have the dates set I'll make sure you get an invitation for yourself and a guest." With a face that had to be bright red, Selena was more than happy he couldn't see her.

"You do know it always takes longer for renovations than what you are quoted, right?"

"Not in my experience. I already have the floor plans, plus the same contractor I've worked with several times. He's never let me down or gone over budget."

He grunted. "That's a miracle in itself. Are you sure we couldn't meet before that?" He sounded so eager, but she couldn't fit a social life in her calendar right now.

"I really can't, but I'm grateful for your quick work." Regret was thick on her tongue.

"It wasn't all that hard. One quick inquiry to my brother, who was ready to get rid of some property, and there you go. Easy."

"I remember. You're twins, right?" Oh, she'd always had a fantasy of her being the focus of two identical men. At least that had been her dream fantasy for a while now.

"Yes."

He trailed off and when he said no more, she squirmed in the water. How could his voice alone excite her more than the physical touch of any other man? "I better let you go. I'll send you an invite for you and your brother. You can each bring a guest if you like."

She hoped he brought a date. If he didn't, she was liable to jump him right in the middle of her club. She closed her eyes, thinking about what he looked like. Her eyes sprang open when she realized she'd never actually seen him.

The image of two identical, tall, dark men standing side by side sprang to mind. It was so real her nipples ached for their attentions.

"That would be great. Oh, and Selena…" He paused until she thought he wasn't going to say anything. "Make sure you wash all the good parts in between."

His words flowed over her like liquid honey, making her pussy clench. Sitting with her mouth open and the phone gripped in her hand, she realized he'd already hung up. "Damn the man." She laughed and did just as he instructed.

Trailing her hand down her stomach, unerringly zeroing in on her pleasure spot, Selena rubbed and pressed, bringing herself to a quick and explosive orgasm that left her wanting more.

# Chapter Five

Malcolm hung up the phone and adjusted his cock. He knew the vixen was in the tub while talking to him. When she'd first answered the phone, her already husky voice sounded even sexier and when she'd muttered, "Fuck me," his cock had hardened immediately. Ready to drill.

Her assistant Tamara was due in less than a half hour and the last thing he wanted was a VHO, or a visible hard-on.

"Malcolm, there is a woman here to see you."

"Who is it, Sharon?" Malcolm asked his secretary.

"Her name is Tamara. She said you were expecting her."

"Send her in and see if she would like a drink."

"Don't tell me how to do my job, Mal," she groused.

"I would never do that, please forgive me. Go ahead and give yourself a raise, would ya?" He'd been trying for years to get her to do just that, and it had become a standing joke between them.

"Shut up. I'm sending her in. And Mal." She waited a beat. "Be nice, please."

"I'm always nice." He was still laughing when Tamara entered his office, ushered in by Sharon. He knew she wouldn't be able to see him properly until her eyes adjusted. With his back to the bank of windows and the sun streaming in, the newcomer would be temporarily blinded. A trick his brother had taught him.

He walked around his desk and reached his hand out to shake hers when she gasped.

He was shocked at her reaction to him. "Are you okay?"

"No…I mean yes, I'm fine. Sorry." She gripped his palm in a surprisingly strong hand. "It's nice to finally meet you."

The nervousness was clear to see by the way her pupils dilated. He admired the way she masked her emotions and got right down to business. Malcolm led her to the chair in front of his desk, before he strolled behind and sat back down. "Would you like me to go over the details?" She was tall for most women. He wondered if Selena was as tall.

"No, I'll just read them real quick." She bent her head and scanned each page, nodding her head and murmuring to herself. She raised her head and held her hand out for a pen. She signed her name and passed the papers back to him, carefully avoiding any contact with his outstretched hand.

He double-checked the documents. "Looks like everything's in order. My brother said the contractors have already begun the remodeling."

She pushed back, and he stared as she gave a dismissive wave.

"Yep, they work quickly. Thank you, Mr. King. Selena will be very happy." She tried to smile, but to Malcolm it looked more like a grimace.

"Are you feeling okay? I mean you look kinda ill." He instantly regretted his choice of words when her back snapped straight and she looked him in the eye for the first time since entering.

"I will see myself out. Thank you for your time."

He stood as she nearly ran out the door with the papers clutched to her chest. Sharon looked up, but with a puzzled look and a quirk of her lips, she said nothing.

"Shut up," Malcolm mumbled.

She raised her hands, palms out, and quickly turned them, giving him a two-finger salute.

"Will you marry me, please?" Malcolm asked and got down on one knee by her feet. He gazed at her through the screen of his lashes, causing her to laugh. He leaned back on his haunches and dropped his shoulders in mock defeat. She slapped him upside his head and gave him a shove.

"Get up, you loon. What did you do to her?" Sharon asked.

"I've no clue." He stood in one fluid motion and pecked her on the cheek. "Do you think they're more than partners in business?" He wagged his eyebrows.

Sharon grunted. "Just because that woman didn't fall at your feet doesn't mean she's a lesbian."

"Women do not fall at my feet." He saw the way Sharon's eyes bugged open and amended his statement. "Hey, that wasn't my fault, but that's not why I asked. You never fall at my feet. Hell, I was just at yours, asking you to marry me."

"Pfft. I'm old enough to be your mother." Sharon turned her back to a smiling Malcolm and answered the phone. Summarily dismissed, he walked back into his office. Old enough to be his mother? Yeah right. Sharon may be on the upside of fifty, but he was on the upside of a millennia.

* * * *

Malcolm sighed, adjusting his pants again. Selena Ramos made his dick hard with just the sound of her voice. But picturing her in a bath naked, he shifted again, trying to get his massive erection somewhat comfortable. He'd call his brother and see if the contractors were on the up and up, since the last of the paperwork was done. He also wondered if Max ever got hard just hearing a woman's voice, and decided he was so not gonna ask him.

"What's up, buttercup?" Max asked.

Malcolm pulled the phone away and double-checked if he dialed the right number. "Why the fuck are you in such a good mood?"

"Because it is a sunny day and the local baseball team just won."

His brother had moved to Kansas City several years ago, which wouldn't be bad, except the local sports teams were not the best. "Ye gods, tell me you are not becoming a Royals fan."

"What is wrong with my home team?"

"First off, they are not your home team. Second, they have the youngest team in the sport and third…" Malcolm ticked off each point and waited a beat before he continued. "Third, they fucking suck."

"You better shut it, brother, or I'll make you eat those words."

"Up yours." Malcolm laughed. It was a long-standing joke between them. Max always put down roots, or as much as they could when they had to move every twenty years or so. People got suspicious when you didn't age a day in that many years. Malcolm was just the opposite. He didn't get attached to anything, except his brother, fellow Ravens, his wolf, and his vehicles.

"So if you aren't calling to hear my sunny voice, then why are you calling me, and why are you in such a grumpy mood?"

Malcolm told him about meeting Tamara, and her reactions to him. He could feel his eyes cross as Max started laughing, and from the sound of it, he wasn't going to quit anytime soon. He focused his mind and sent a mental head-butt to his big brother. Hearing a groan, he smiled until Max punched him in the stomach. Even thousands of miles away, that really hurt, Malcolm thought with a grunt, listening to his brother laugh. Again.

"Okay. Whew, I needed that laugh. Thank you."

"I'm so glad you're amused. Not," Malcolm said, but grinned.

"I think I need to meet this woman who ran from you. On second thought, maybe not, she might just hate the way you look. She'd probably run from me too."

"Nah, I think she may have eaten some bad fish or something. Anyway, I spoke with Selena"—just the sound of her name rolling off his tongue made Malcolm horny—"and she said her contractor will have the renovations complete within months." He heard his brother snort. "I know. I already told her to be prepared for delays and such, but whatever. She said we would get an invite to the open house and we could each bring a guest." Was that a growl he heard in his own voice? *What the fuck?*

"Are you going to bring anyone?" Max asked.

Malcolm shook his head. "No. How about you?"

"We'll see. You never know what could happen in the next few months." Max, like all the other men in their group, had been looking for the one woman who would complete them. Even though they'd been searching the world for the last twenty-four years looking for the lost daughter, they still had their hopes of finding their elusive Fated. Whatever that means, he thought with a sardonic smile.

"I don't plan to bring anyone, just in case my dick reacts to the sight, as much as the sound, of Selena."

The brothers talked for a few more minutes before they hung up. Malcolm turned in his chair to stare out at the sun, thinking Mount Olympus was somewhere up there. Having been sent to Earth so long ago, they all knew they'd never get to go back. Although they were created by the gods with many of their traits, they were not gods, and they didn't belong there anymore. Oh sure, they were good enough to fight for them and protect them, even give their lives for them, but the gods and the goddesses had all treated them as lower-class beings.

With a shake of his head he dropped his arms and jumped up, striding out of his office with one purpose. He stopped at Sharon's desk and dropped a kiss on her forehead. She thought she was old enough to be his mother, while he silently wished she could've been. Not that the goddess who so generously birthed him was a bad person. None of the women who carried the twelve Ravens of War were. They just weren't needed to be a mother when their charges were all grown men within a year of their birth.

"Go home, woman." Malcolm growled before softening his tone. "I'll close up and then I'm off."

She looked at him like he'd grown two heads. Maybe I have, Malcolm mused.

Sharon had worked for him for over five years. In that time, he'd tried to get her to go home early. She never agreed, but this occasion she would since her daughter had called and explained it was Sharon's birthday and they planned to throw her a party.

He'd gotten the invite, but there was no way on god's green Earth he'd be going to a family party at some chain restaurant with all of Sharon's family. "Don't argue with me either." He gave her his most stern look, the one anyone who spent time with him knew meant business.

With a huff she nodded and he exhaled a breath he hadn't realized he'd held. He pulled her chair back and she stood on her tiptoes, giving him a motherly peck. "I'll go, only because I planned to leave early. It's my birthday, you know?"

"Yes, I'm aware of that," Malcolm said, deadpan.

"Fine, then I'll be off."

He opened the door and escorted her to the elevator. With their office suite on the twelfth floor, he always walked her to the parking garage if he was in town. This time he had a little bounce to his step, like a little boy who had gotten all As on his report card. He scowled at the absurd thought.

They rode the elevator in silence until it reached the basement garage.

"Malcolm, you don't have to walk me to my car. I'm perfectly safe," Sharon scolded.

He knew she was. He'd be able to sense any threat long before it reached them, but with a shrug of his shoulders, he indicated for her to lead the way. She huffed, but didn't argue any further. They reached her regular parking space and she stopped, eyes wide, and looked around. He watched her rub her eyes and do another small circle, then she rested her gaze on him. He knew he had a goofy smile on his face, but she looked so darn cute with her hands on her ample hips while she tapped her sensible loafers.

"Did you forget where you parked this morning?" Malcolm asked, coughing into his hand to cover his smile.

"No, I did not forget where I parked. Do you think someone stole my car?"

He barked out a laugh. “Why the hell would anyone want to steal your old beater?”

“Bertha is not a beater. She’s the best and most reliable car in the world.”

“You named your damn car Bertha? It’s a wonder it didn’t break down on you for that offense alone.”

When she reared back with her arm preparing to pummel him with her overly large bag, he laughed and held his hands up in surrender.

“You take that back. I love that car.”

“Well, I hope you can learn to love that car,” Malcolm said, pointing at a brand new Mercedes-Benz SL-Class.

“What are you talking about?” She looked truly puzzled and a little upset.

Malcolm didn’t like to see a female of any age cry.

“Happy Birthday Sharon.” He held up a set of keys and passed them to her. She looked at them, and then at the car before finally looking back up at him.

“You bought me a car?”

He shuffled his feet and nodded.

“Where is my old car?”

“Your daughter came and took it. She said you would want to keep it.”

He didn’t know why anyone would want to keep a VW Beetle that was over forty years old, but who was he to judge? He loved classic cars. Hell, his garage was stocked with several. She was looking at him like he was strange again and he could feel heat rise in his cheeks.

“Thank you, Malcolm King. You are a good man,” Sharon said before she burst into tears.

Malcolm dropped his head back and sighed up at the ceiling, and then he stepped forward and folded her into his arms. He knew she was all bluster when she ordered everyone around, but inside she was that motherly sort, who turned to goo when anyone did something nice for her. He held her until her tears stopped and she pulled out a tissue she somehow found in that cavernous bag.

"So do you like it?"

"What's not to like? Oh my goodness, it's beautiful, and you even got the same color as my beloved Bertha."

"Please, please tell me you are not going to name this car Bertha."

"I will have to ponder it, and get to know this girl first."

He laughed when she compared her old clunker to the $200,000 machine in front of her. He showed her how there wasn't really a key, but a push button. After she marveled at the car, he stood back and waited until she familiarized herself and finally pulled off, before he dematerialized.

* * * *

Tamara stood in the shadows undetected by Malcolm and his secretary. She smiled at the interaction between the two. When Sharon got into her new car, Tamara hurried around the corner before they spotted her.

Tamara's mama was always right, and this time was no exception. *Bertha.* She nearly laughed her ass off at the disgust in his tone. Her best friend Selena had a way of naming her own vehicles the most absurd names possible too. The first vehicle she was given at the age of sixteen was a shiny silver jeep, which she immediately named Bullet. Why? Of course because it was silver like a bullet, she'd exclaimed. The girl had no imagination. But Tamara loved her.

Yeah, poor Malcolm was going to have fits with her girl Selena, and she couldn't wait to see the fireworks those two, or three, if her mama was correct. Her mama always was right.

She reached in her bag as she walked out of the parking garage, flagging a cab while she walked. "Hola, Chica. Whatcha doin'?"

Tamara and Selena chatted for a few minutes. Afterward she filled her best friend in on the details of the meeting, minus the parking-garage snooping. There was no reason to give her that information, since Selena tended to be a bit of a stickler against what she called bad manners.

When it came to Selena, Tamara would do everything within her limited power to protect her, even call on her mama. Now, she had real abilities that made the hair on the back of Tamara's neck stand up.

If she was right, and Tamara was always right, then before long her best friend was going to be finding herself between a rock and a hard place. She snickered at her own internal dialogue, causing the cabby to give her strange looks. She gave him her best death stare, the one she often gave her own brothers. He turned back to the road and navigated the busy LA streets.

She had two more days in California, a yellow two-piece that wanted to be covered in sand, and a holiday that she deserved. Sunny days with the windows open at night on the beach, was just what she needed.

The dream that kept returning even in her waking hours telling her it would be her last, made it even more imperative she make it count. Yeah, being right all the time sucked major monkey balls.

So she was taking this time to do just that. Her brand new two-piece bathing suit was going to get covered in sand and ocean water, maybe even some gorgeous man juice. It'd been way too long since she'd let herself be covered in anything man related.

Up ahead the tiny cottage she'd bought came into view. It'd taken over an hour once they'd left the city to get there, with no neighbors close by. Privacy was key.

"You all alone out here, little girl?"

Oh yeah, she knew what the bastard was thinking. "Nope, big guy. My husband is inside waiting for me. Would you like to come in and have a drink?" For the thousandth time she was glad Selena insisted they wore fake wedding rings when they travelled. Of course she had no doubt she could take care of herself, but then she'd have to call the police. Then there'd be a report. Then there'd be a paper trail.

"Oh…No, I just worried about leaving such a lovely lady out here all alone."

Tamara barely stopped the snort from escaping, but the sunglasses hid the eye roll that she couldn't control. "Oh, that's very *kind* of you. Brutus will be very happy to hear humanity still exists."

She hated waiting for him to open her door, but as soon as the bastard lifted the handle she gave him a little help with a shove. He stumbled back a step before righting himself. The saccharine smile didn't quite meet her eyes. At five foot nine and in her five-inch heels she towered over his much shorter frame, giving her the upper hand.

The ringing of her phone distracted her and him. "Hola. Oh are you on the beach then? Si, I'll be right down. Just paying the cabby. His name is Carl. Oh yes, he was very friendly. His cab number? Just a second." Tamara looked at the numbers on the cab. "243. Of course I tipped him well. Geez. Hold on. Thanks Carl." Tamara gave the cabby the required fee plus tip and walked beside the cottage toward the beach. The sound of tires on gravel as he backed out reached her ears while she continued toward the water.

She hit end on the fake call she'd initiated with just a touch of a button on her smart phone. "What a complete dick," she snarled.

He was not the gorgeous man she planned to let see her yellow bikini. The sand under her feet felt good between her toes, warm and soothing, an ache deep within her soul. Goddess, she was going to miss this.

Tamara sat on one of the Adirondack chairs that faced the ocean. She remembered the first time she'd seen Selena Ramos. A smile curved her mouth, and she closed her eyes and thought back to the day so many years ago.

*Tamara had gone out to get fresh eggs for her mama. It was early, but the sun was up and it was only around the corner. They'd only been in Texas for a couple of months, having moved from the bayou that Tamara had loved. She still wasn't sure why her mama wanted them to live there, only that mama Mejia said she'd had a vision. Sometimes Tamara hated her mama's visions.*

*She wasn't really paying attention to her surroundings, just thinking about how she wished she was back home. Not Texas home, but her swamp. She missed the gators, and the people there. Texas was too big, too strange, and the people talked funny.*

*At sixteen she was already taller than most of the boys in her class and had already been asked out by half the football team. It seemed football was real big in Texas. The saying everything was bigger in Texas made her laugh. You'd think she'd fit right in, what with her being close to five foot nine. She hated being so tall. Add in the fact she had a big chest and she hated that more. Boys tended to look straight at her boobs instead of at her face.*

*She stepped off the curb near an alley that was a shortcut to her house and contemplated taking it, but dismissed the idea. Her mama told her to stay on the streets where people were. Before she could take more than two steps a hand grabbed her from behind and dragged her deep into the alley.*

*With one arm wrapped around her waist and one around her mouth she tried to kick out, dropping the grocery bag in the process. She watched in horror as the eggs dropped and broke all over the concrete ground.*

*Tamara fought the man holding her, used all the techniques her brothers had shown her. An elbow to his midsection, heel to his shin, but never did they teach her what to do when another man punched you in the face while an extra held you.*

*They dragged her behind a dumpster where three other men were waiting. The stench, or maybe the knowledge of what they planned to do, made Tamara gag.*

*"Bitch if you throw up on me, I'll make you lick it up before I make you suck my cock. Do you understand me?"*

*Tamara swallowed hard, tears clogging her throat.*

*A hand fisted in her hair. One of the men jerked her head backward, demanding she answer the other man.*

*She couldn't get anything to come out of her mouth other than choked sobs. They were going to do whatever they wanted to her, but she'd be damned if she was going to make it easy.*

*With renewed strength she started flailing. They obviously weren't expecting her to fight back.*

*A scream that wasn't hers pierced the air, and made the men freeze in their attack.*

*Tamara had never been happier to see an angel in all her life. She had fought as hard as she could, but was no match for the men. They had charged her from all sides and gotten her down to the ground, one holding each arm and leg, leaving one man free. He was going to be the first. Just the thought made Tamara wish for death.*

*The angel seemed to fly over the garbage can, knocking the men nearest to her in the head with her feet. She spun, lashing out with her hands and feet. Tamara swore sparks flew from the angel's fingertips. Lying on the cold, hard ground, she heard the crunch of the men's bones as they tried to fight the smaller girl. The angel's long blonde hair was in a braid that whipped around in an arc, looking like a weapon too. A man jumped on her back and Tamara tried to yell out a warning, but the girl merely flung him over her shoulder. There was a loud snap followed by the man's groan, and then silence as the angel punched him in the throat, cutting off his oxygen.*

*The hum of erratic breathing sounded overly loud and Tamara recognized that the young girl was the one doing the heavy breathing. She had backed herself against the brick wall and was covered in blood splatter. She looked about two seconds away from freaking out.*

*Tamara scrambled up and righted her clothes as best she could. She went over to where the younger girl was leaning. "Thank you," Tamara whispered.*

*"Are you okay? My name is Selena." She shook so hard her teeth rattled.*

*"I dreamed about an angel who would save me. I just..." Tamara stopped. She wrapped her shirt together. Both of their clothes were completely ruined.*

Tamara smiled at the memory. After she reassured Selena that she hadn't killed any of the men, she'd taken the younger girl to meet her mama. From that point on they'd been best friends, even though she was three years older than Selena. That day Selena had saved her. Tamara knew it was meant to be that way. She'd dreamt it. But no one could save her this time. She'd dreamt it too. Yeah, it sucked monkey balls always being right.

# Chapter Six

Selena Ramos couldn't wait for Redneck Paradise to open its doors here in Kansas City. The Power and Light District was an extremely busy area that didn't seem to have a down time of year. The seasons went from football to baseball straight into each other and never seemed to lag for customers.

After holding auditions for every aspect of the bar and hand-picking the employees, they were then put through what she and Tamara called *Redneck Hell.* During this time they learned the choreographed dances they were all expected to do. These were mandatory, along with the uniforms. In this business it was all about the tips. Even though they made a good wage, it was all about the tips.

Selena loved her club, loved getting on top of the bar and dancing to the music, and hoped her girls did too. If she or Tamara felt the girls hated their job, or didn't want to be there, they offered them another position. The whole point of the bar was to have fun, make money, and make sure everyone had a good time.

She slipped from her car and strolled toward the front door of the club with a beaming smile on her face. Opening day was just around the corner and this would be the first time she'd been inside since it was completed.

The wind whipped blonde curls about her face, making her shove them aside with an impatient hand. She was almost tempted to cut them off but hated the thought. Her parents had always loved her hair. Even though it had set her apart from the other kids, they'd said it made her special.

"Yes." She pumped her fist up and down at the beauty of the club. It was exactly how she'd imagined it. The bar sat center stage like a huge circle, gleaming with the smell of varnished wood and cinnamon. Behind the bar was the dance floor set up like a huge rectangular area, with every other available space filled with booths, tall bar tables, lower tables, and comfy chairs. Their vision was to have a space where you had a choice of where you wanted to sit.

Although each club had the same name and was similar in design they made adjustments to the surroundings, and this one was no different. With this one they had an upper-level balcony where they had leather couches and tables for a more cozy seating that overlooked the entire bottom level. Her office was also on the upper-level, along with a set of bathrooms for the patrons.

She walked over to the corner where the DJ booth was. They'd interviewed over a dozen men and women for the position, finally settling on one who came highly recommended. She couldn't wait for Tamara to get there so they could celebrate, knowing this was going to be the last club they planned to open. Tamara was a full partner who did most of the traveling, while Selena was the hands-on girl.

Mama Mejia's voice whispered in her head. "*Child, don't go getting too big for yer britches.*" Selena lifted the door and stepped behind the bar to make sure it was fully stocked. The official opening wasn't until tomorrow, but they were having a pre-opening party for some of the local businesses tonight. All the waitresses had been put through the paces at the other Redneck Paradise locations, but tonight was the trial run for this location.

Butterflies began a happy dance in her belly, just like always before something important was going to happen in her life. Thankfully it was a wholly different sensation than the feeling of doom, which she usually had…She shook off the negativity.

She wrapped her hair in a knot and secured it with a pencil before picking up a clipboard, and skipped into the stock room. A smile was firmly on her face as she double-checked the liquor count. She jumped when her pocket began to vibrate and laughed at herself when the song that she had programmed for Tamara began to play.

"Hola, Tamara." Selena locked the store room door behind her as she tucked the phone between her shoulder and ear and pocketed the key.

"Hey there, girl," Tamara drawled.

"Tam, it's perfect. You should see it."

"I know, right?"

Selena laughed at her friend's reply. "So when are you getting here? All the employees are set to arrive shortly."

"Well now, if you would look up, you'd see me standing right in front of you."

Selena jerked her eyes up and jumped, dropping the clipboard on the wood floors. She launched herself at Tamara, wrapped arms and legs around her best friend's waist. "I've missed you. When did you get in? Why didn't you call me?"

Tamara grunted.

"Excuse me, am I interrupting something? I can come back after you two finish," a deep voice rumbled.

Selena's boots hit the floor moments before she was shoved behind her friend's towering form. Tamara had pulled her favorite Glock from wherever she'd had it tucked, and aimed it at the most gorgeous man Selena had ever seen, or tried to see, except her friend kept stepping in front of her.

"Stop right there." Tamara said, pointing the gun at his head.

The man lifted his arms. "I'm Max King."

He answered Tamara, but his gaze snared Selena's. She would swear he looked amused and not the least bit intimidated by the big weapon aimed at his head.

"Tam, put the gun down. This is…" Selena was amazed how looking into his eyes made the feelings from hearing his voice seem lame in comparison, which was saying a lot. Her heart rate kicked up several notches, and a tingle vibrated throughout her body. She glanced at the front of her chest to see if you could actually see the rapid beat of her heart pounding.

Tamara shrugged. "I know who it is. Sorry, you startled me."

The apology was more of an accusation, but it gave Selena a moment to get her emotions under control. She smiled behind her hand as Tamara still hadn't shifted from her protective stance.

With a shove Selena moved around Tamara.

"Oops, sorry."

Selena snorted at Tamara's words, knowing her friend didn't feel bad in the least.

"It's nice to finally meet you, Mr. King." She held her hand out. He gripped her palm in a surprisingly gentle embrace for such a large man. Warmth flew down her arm, centered somewhere down south of her belly button at first contact. The heat turned to a tingle, then a full-out earthquake that only she seemed to be feeling.

"Hmmm…I believe I told you before to call me Max," he rumbled.

His voice added another layer of vibration and his eyes twinkled, for crying out loud. The color was such a brilliant blue they reminded her of the sky. She absently wondered if his brother's eyes were the same, but gave herself a mental shake. His stare was unnerving her.

"Y–yes, you did." Great, now she sounded like a friggin' twit.

"So I will call you Selena, and you will call me Max."

He turned to Tamara, who still hadn't put her gun away, but blessedly it was pointed at the ground instead of at the delectable Max.

"Wow, you guys are like identical," Tamara blurted out.

Selena laughed at the outburst. Her hand still engulfed in Max's, she tried to tug it free. His grip tightened only briefly like he was as reluctant to let her go as she was to be set free. It was like an invisible thread connected them, like a braid missing a piece. She shook her head to clear her mind, then opened her senses to ease into his thoughts.

A marble wall very similar to one she'd been taught to guard her own mind with shielded his. She settled back without disturbing Max. Years of practice kept him from knowing she'd been there.

They all turned at the sound of the door buzzer going off. "That would probably be our employees." Selena looked at the clock.

Both Max and Tamara had puzzled looks on their faces. Selena made a sound of exasperation and rushed to the door. She placed her hand on the latch, prepared to twist the lock, something she'd done thousands of times, but froze at the sight of the large arm locking around her midsection.

"What the hell are you doing?"

"You didn't even look to see who it was," Max snarled.

"That's because I know who it is." She tried to push his arm off, but the man was as unmovable as a concrete wall. "Please let me go," she gritted out between clenched teeth.

With a slight twist of his body he gently set Selena on her feet, turned the lock, and pushed the door, putting himself between her and any unseen attack.

If she weren't so impressed she'd be irritated. "*Grrr*, I think I can handle myself, ya know. I've been doing it for years."

He didn't answer her. He looked at the line of ladies standing outside before turning back to Selena with a lift of an eyebrow. "Are these your employees?" He quirked that damn eyebrow again before he continued. "Have you ever heard of equal opportunity?"

"Excuse me, Mr. King. Could you please move your great hulking form out of the way?" She smiled around his body, inserting herself in front of him with a slight wiggle.

"I do have male employees also, but it's really none of your business. You obviously don't know a thing about my clubs." Shaking her head, she continued, "I have work to do, so please, if you don't mind." She gestured at the women, and flapped her hand in a dismissive gesture toward him. Of course he chose to ignore her not-so-subtle hint to go back inside. The man exasperated and excited her in equal measures.

* * * *

Max couldn't believe his eyes. She was his Fated. Selena was the dream girl and the one who completed him. He rolled her name around on his tongue. *Selena Ramos...*She was also the same woman who starred in his twin's fantasies. *Shit!* Their dream woman and Selena were one and the same. Fucking Fates. They were probably up in the heavens laughing their asses off, he thought with a twist of his lips.

He wanted to give them a double-handed, one-finger salute, but didn't want to tempt them, and besides that was more Malcolm's style than his. *Shit!*

For thousands of years they'd searched. He'd actually begun to give up hope of finding her, what with the world coming to an end soon and all.

The line of employees all took a collective step backward at his scowl, so Max did what he did best. He smiled and turned on the charm. "Welcome, ladies."

By the way Selena's body reacted to his touch earlier she'd felt the power that flowed between them. Oh, she was good at hiding her reactions, but he was so in tune with her every breath, he would have felt her blink those amazing silver eyes without even looking at her.

He kept his palm flattened on the bit of exposed skin of Selena's stomach. The waiting throng of women still had a bit of fear etched on their faces, mixed with awe. "I apologize for keeping you waiting. Please, come inside." He kept his expression warm and inviting.

Selena welcomed each lady by name. He memorized their faces even as he probed their minds as they passed him, only able to relax as the last employee entered and no threat was found.

"Thank you for letting them in, Your Highness," Selena groused.

He laughed. A full-bellied laugh that seemed to irritate her, if the way her shoulders went up along with the narrow-eyed look she gave him over her shoulder was any indication.

She pulled away from his touch, her swaying hips in low-cut, tight fitted jeans with a top so small he could see her muscles flex. Damn, but the woman made him hard.

Tamara watched him with an intensity that, if he'd been a lesser man, would have made him squirm. He met her with a stare that had her dropping her eyes to the gun she still hadn't tucked away.

It seemed like hours had passed, but in reality only moments had, from the time he'd felt a jealous rage at the embrace he caught Selena and her friend in. The other woman seemed to come to a conclusion before the group of ladies was close enough to see her or the big weapon. She tucked it in into her back where she'd had it, adjusting her shirt, and went over to the group.

He still couldn't believe how quick she had drawn the weapon.

Not wanting to delay the one call he needed to make any longer, he walked over to the group. "I'm going to step outside and make a call. I'll be right back."

The blush at his words that stole up Selena's face made him want throw her over his shoulder, and to hell with what the other ladies thought.

His brother's phone rang several times. He was just getting ready to hang up when he heard Malcolm's annoying voice.

"Yo."

"When are you arriving in Kansas City?" Max asked without preamble.

"I'm great. Terrific really, thanks so much for asking."

"Mal, shut the fuck up and answer the damn question." Max growled.

"Dude. What's got your panties in a bunch?"

Max sighed. He really didn't have time for his brother's shit. "Malcolm, really, when?"

"Actually I was just getting ready to board. What's going on?"

"Couldn't you just demat here?" Max cursed at the whine he heard in his own voice. "Never mind, just get your ass here." He disconnected before Malcolm could say something to piss him off anymore. His world had been knocked off its axis while his brother was still completely oblivious for now. He scrubbed his hands through his hair, breathed deep, and tried to get his emotions under control before he started acting like a whipped boy.

Max knew he should just leave and put some distance between himself and Selena, but he couldn't make his feet listen to his mind. With a glance at the sky, he turned and stomped back into the club. Yep, he stomped. He was so whipped.

All eyes turned to him, but the only ones he cared about pretended to ignore him, which just made his inner beast roar.

He walked up to her, invaded her space, making her look at him.

She had on a pair of fire-engine-red cowgirl boots that gave her an extra couple inches, putting her at about five feet six inches. He tried to hide his grin as she stood tall and puffed out her chest, but all the action did was push her breasts out, showcasing her hard-tipped nipples. She tried to act unaffected by his presence, but her body couldn't lie. He turned her on every bit as much as she did him.

"I need to get going, but I'll see you tonight."

He leaned in, brushing his lips across her open mouth. The sound of her gasp along with the way her breath hitched, before she snapped her eyes up to his, had his dick twitching in his jeans and made him want to go all caveman again.

The color of her eyes fascinated him. He wanted to watch them while she came. If his cock didn't become permanently scarred from his zipper, he planned to find out tonight.

With reluctance he let her go. He gave a nod to the other women, a sardonic smile to her watcher Tamara, and then he pivoted and walked out without looking back. A man only had so much strength. Every step he took felt like a battle. She made him feel like a lovesick teenager with his first crush, which was ironic since he'd never been a teenager.

He straddled his Harley and with a quick twist of the wrist had it started, feeling the vibrations shoot straight to his balls as he revved the engine with the custom pipes. He rolled his shoulders and strapped on a helmet before pulling out into traffic and heading home.

He needed Malcolm to be with him the next time he saw Selena. He needed to see his brother's reactions to her. Hell, if he was being honest, and Max always tried to be honest at least with himself, he really needed to fuck her, and if Malcolm didn't hurry the fuck up, he'd do it without him being there.

## Chapter Seven

Malcolm looked at the silent phone and grinned. His brother sounded off, and knowing Max was never off put Malcolm on edge. Out of all the Ravens, Max always had his head on straight, and the goal in sight. He waved his hand toward the pilot and the flight attendant, erasing their memory of their intended flight plan.

He tried to reach Max through their shared link, but hit a wall that meant his brother was blocking him. His stomach clenched, and butterflies took up residence like they planned to stay. *Shit.* He was the twin that wigged out, not Max.

Dematerializing for the Ravens was like breathing. One moment he was on a tarmac in Los Angeles, the next he was standing outside his brother's home overlooking downtown Kansas City.

The mental shields blocking him from Max were gone with an abruptness that staggered Malcolm.

"Why did you shut me out?"

"Sorry, I just had some stuff to take care of." Max took a deep breath. "Where are you?"

"Standing outside your place."

"I'll be there shortly. Listen, there's something I need to tell you about Selena."

Max's husky tone shocked Malcolm. He'd never heard his brother speak a woman's name in such a possessive manor, and it pissed him off.

"What is she to you, Max?"

The butterflies in Malcolm's stomach began doing the mamba, threatening to send the contents back up onto the porch. It would serve Max right to come home to find Malcolm's lunch all over his deck, Malcolm mused. He swallowed down the bile, not wanting to embarrass himself by actually hurling, and waited for his twin.

When Max didn't answer the question, Malcolm slammed his own shields down viciously and hoped like hell Max got a headache.

"Fuck," he muttered.

What the heck was wrong with him? A woman was a woman, as long as she had a pussy, was warm and wet in all the right places and could satisfy him. Right? He nodded his head. His gut clenched like he'd just betrayed someone.

"What the hell is happening to me?"

He could hear the sound of the rumble of a Harley's loud pipes getting closer. As Max brought his bike to a stop Malcolm walked down to meet him.

"You still riding that piece of shit?"

"Up yours. You still riding that thing you call a bike?" Max asked.

They both laughed and eased the tension that was like a live wire between them. With their right arms extended, they gripped each other's forearms and rested their left arms on the other's shoulder. Malcolm peered into identical blue eyes before he pulled Max into a hug, then they each slapped the other's back hard.

Each man grunted.

Max stepped back and said, "You look like shit."

"So do you." Malcolm followed his brother into his home and without being told kicked off his boots. Trailing after Max, he noticed some of his twin's prized possessions filled the walls and shelves.

"You plan on staying here a while, bro?"

"Yeah, I do," Max said.

Malcolm followed into the kitchen, absently accepting a beer. With his head tipped back, he downed the cold beverage before tackling the real issue.

"What's up with Selena?"

"It's her, the girl from our dreams," Max said. He finished his beer and retrieved another, holding up his full one to Malcolm.

Malcolm nodded his head, finishing the last of the bitter brew, and tossed the empty bottle in the trash.

"What now?"

"Fuck if I know. Let's go outside and relax. Maybe meditate."

"Listen, bro…I love you, but I ain't getting nekkid with you unless there's a woman between us."

Max laughed and flipped him the bird. The strain seemed to seep out of the air.

With beers in hand, they sat on loungers next to the infinite pool and watched the sun go down. Companionable silence broken only by the occasional bird followed. Malcolm was loath to be the one to break it. But he needed to know more about Selena.

"So…" He cleared his throat. "What do you think of her?"

The descriptions matched their dream girl exactly. It astonished Malcolm to hear Selena wasn't a petite, brown-eyed, brown-haired woman.

Max's eyes fairly glowed as he spoke of Selena. A light that Malcolm recognized as his twin's inner power seemed to stretch out of his core, searching, calling out, making Malcolm's own reach forward.

A puzzled look crossed his brother's face, a mirror image Malcolm was sure matched his own.

"Did she recognize you?"

"No, I don't think so. Maybe it was only you and I who shared the dreams." Max didn't look pleased with the admission.

That was something neither man wanted to contemplate.

"Go shower and then we will go and meet Selena."

He saluted Max with his bottle of beer then made a bee line for the guest bedroom. A Jacuzzi big enough for six people was in one corner of the bathroom. He pictured Selena sandwiched between Max and him, and decided a cold shower was just what he needed.

Cold water pounded his body from all sides of the state-of-the-art shower. Looking down, he saw junior was still at full mast, and sighed.

"Son of a bitch," he whispered. "I'm gonna go blind if I keep beating off."

Their dream girl on her knees is what he pictured as he reached down and gripped his balls in one hand and fisted his dick in the other. He pictured her mouth opening wide to suck him down, her tongue licking the pearly fluid from the tip. The vision seemed so real his nuts drew up, and before he could brace his feet, his cum boiled up and shot out of the top.

He panted, and caught himself with one arm on the tile wall above his head before he fell on his ass.

At his will the temperature raised enough for him to finish his shower.

When was the last time he'd reacted like this with a female? The more he thought about her, the more possessive he became.

Their *Fated.* The thought should have stunned him.

* * * *

Max was waiting by the door with a stretch hummer running outside.

It amazed Malcolm how without speaking they both tended to dress similarly. He'd donned a pair of loose white slacks and a black button-down top, while Max was just the opposite in a pair of similar pants in black and a button-down white top.

He shook his head at the absurdity.

"What are you laughing at?" Max asked as he settled on the seat across from him.

"Us." Malcolm chuckled.

The trip downtown took forever in Malcolm's mind, and not nearly enough time. A moment of panic lit his insides when they pulled up outside Selena's club. On the radio the song "If You Could Only See" by Tonic was playing, and Malcolm wondered if this were what it felt like when a man's destiny awaited him.

"I'm becoming a pussy," he muttered, following Max out of the vehicle.

"Yeah, well so am I," Max snarled.

They'd both stopped at the door like it was a snake about to bite them. Max quirked his lips then muttered, "You first."

"Age before beauty," Malcolm joked.

"Fuck it…Let's get this over with." Max jerked the door open, taking several steps inside before stopping abruptly.

"What the hell, Max?"

Malcolm looked around Max to see what made his brother stop, and saw an angel standing on top of the bar, swaying her hips from side to side with her arms above her head.

"Holy mother of gods and goddesses alike," Malcolm whispered.

* * * *

The change in the atmosphere was a palpable thing to Selena. One minute she'd been watching her employees go through the different routines on the bar, and the next she was on top the glossy surface and showing them it was okay to do a little improvisation.

With her favorite jean skirt and tank top with the bar's logo bedazzled across the front and a pair of well-worn, fire-engine red cowgirl boots, she started stomping to the beat. By the time the chorus began, she'd shuffled across the bar with her arms up, and the straw hat on her head bobbed along with the words. She stopped abruptly and did an exaggerated hip swivel, facing her bartenders, and smiled. It wasn't a sweet, "aww look how cute I am" lift of her lips. No, as Tamara was fond of saying it was her "girl's gonna do something crazy" look.

Selena raised her left arm in the air and brought her right arm out, swooshing her hand through the air as if she were slapping something. The tempo increased, and with each slap of her hand she moved her ass back and forth, increasing the pace as the beat to the music became faster and faster.

When the last note blared out she stomped first one booted foot then the other, the sound echoing around the now silent bar. She shrugged her shoulders, looked over at Tamara and winked. Not stopping to think, she jumped, flipping off the mahogany surface, landing in a crouch onto the matching floor.

The stunned silence that met her little show was a bit disarming, but Selena was anything but shy.

All eyes had turned toward the entryway and the two men who filled the space with their presence. Both men's eyes glittered with a feral light that sent a shiver of fear down her spine. With their hands fisted at their sides, they looked like warriors who were barely holding themselves in check.

Light and dark filtered through her befuddled brain. Although they were clearly identical outside with dark hair and the bluest eyes she'd ever seen in real life, there was a difference inside.

The vague sense that she knew these two men intimately gave her a start, but she lifted a shoulder and dismissed the crazy images flashing in her mind. Selena couldn't very well meet the two men while having dirty daydreams.

Making her way to where they stood frozen to the spot, she tried to control the full-body shake that ran through her. With her heart threatening to burst out of her chest, she put on a brave face.

All her being wanted to make everyone in the club disappear so she could lay claim to the men whose sole focus was pointed straight at her.

"Howdy, boys," Selena said in her best southern drawl. With her hand extended and smile firmly in place, she reached out to greet the one she believed was Max first.

The first to recover grasped her hand, and with the same ability she'd always had she knew it was Malcolm who gripped her fingers in a gentle embrace. For such a large man he was surprisingly gentle, just like Max had been earlier.

"It's nice to finally meet you, Selena," Malcolm said.

"You must be Malcolm?"

He looked at his brother, then turned a wide grin back to her. "Yep…That's me. I'm the better-looking, smarter and all-around best twin."

A muscle ticked in the other's jaw before he took a deep breath and reached for the hand still enclosed within Malcolm's.

"It's very nice to see you again Selena, you look amazing," Max murmured. "Do you usually get up there and um…dance like that?"

Selena wasn't sure if he sounded angry or jealous, like he wanted to toss her over his shoulder and hide her away. The notion sent a thrill to her core, which worried her. She tugged her palm out of his grasp, tossed her hair over her shoulder to cover her nervousness or whatever she was suddenly feeling for them. Wanting two men she'd basically just met to go all Neanderthal on her ass wasn't her.

She snorted. "As often as I can, yes."

Malcolm nudged Max's shoulder. "Great…I mean you dance really well."

The growl that Max answered his brother's statement with could've been agreement.

"Would you guys like a drink and then a tour? The employees were just getting ready to go grab some dinner before the opening."

They had about three hours before the doors officially opened, giving Selena a little breather.

"How about you give us a tour first? Do you have an office here, too?" Malcolm asked.

The question was asked casually, but the heat radiating off both men was anything but casual.

"Of course."

* * * *

After making sure all the employees had left and the doors were locked up, she walked back to find both men leaning casually against the counter. They straightened at her approach.

"Relax, Selena mine."

Max's deep velvet voice washed over her like a soothing tide.

She took a deep breath.

On the main level the open concept made it easy to see everything. The only doors were the one in the front to get in and one in the back to get out, other than a hallway that led to the restrooms and the large store room. There was a wide staircase on each side to reach the upper level, where more seating and her office sat.

As they walked she pointed out the different design elements, knowing all the while they were checking out her ass. The times she would look back they seemed to have some sort of silent communication between them, making her wish she was part it.

Her skin felt too tight, her mind and body didn't feel like her own. It was like a thousand volts of electricity ran through her veins each time she made eye contact, or brushed against either man.

She felt like a virgin being led to the sacred altar. The picture had her stomping the last few steps to the office suite, thinking she was nobody's sacrificial virgin, dammit.

The key pad on the side of the door blinked green as she entered her code. After the locks disengaged, she stepped inside.

In the corner of the office she had a fully stocked bar, which is where she headed. Nothing like a little liquid courage. Three tumblers were filled with a few cubes of ice before she poured whiskey in her own glass.

Like a frat boy she slammed the fiery liquid, then lifted her head and the bottle to see if they wanted the same as her. Both men nodded their assent.

The men stood shoulder-to-shoulder with identical looks of what could only be hunger. The expression should've scared her, especially when Max boldly leaned back and locked the door.

Never one to show fear, Selena lifted her eyebrow at the action. Wanting to taunt them, she took a sip of her drink. She hid her smile with the glass at Max's scowl. He was the one she referred to as the dark twin, while Malcolm in her mind was the light one. Two halves of one whole.

With predatory grace they stalked toward her.

"What's going on?" Selena wished she hadn't moved from behind the minibar after refilling her drink. Why she thought the insubstantial bit of furniture could protect her she had no clue.

"You, Selena, are our Fated," both men said at the same time.

She shook her head. What they said made absolutely no sense to her.

Were they crazy?

"I'm not sure what that means, but I'm pretty sure it's illegal," she tried to joke.

If her memory served her correctly, you weren't supposed to show fear. Or was she not supposed to look them in the eye? Oh crap, maybe she should just drop into a fetal position. Didn't that usually stop things from attacking?

Looking anywhere but at the two men across the room, Selena nearly wet herself when each man brushed a finger down her cheeks. *How the heck did they get so close without her hearing them move?*

"Don't deny you can't feel it too, Selena. We won't allow you to lie to us or yourself." Max's features hardened, intensifying the blue fire in his gaze.

He leaned in to nuzzle her neck.

His clean, musky scent made her mouth water, and a pulse beat straight through her, aiming for her core.

"You don't want to get brother dear angry, Selena," Malcolm said, nuzzling his nose near her ear.

"Shut up, Mal. You'll scare her." Max growled.

Selena was more aware of her own body than ever before. Everywhere they touched sizzled like heat was surrounding them with the fire of the two men who touched her.

"Oh…goddess…I've never…I mean I've been horny, but nothing compared to this." She slammed her mouth shut to stop the flow of words.

"Don't talk about other men and yourself with us, Selena." Malcolm trailed his hand down her bare arm, leaving goose bumps in its wake.

She bit her lip against the moan of pleasure that threatened to break free as his lips followed the same path, making her nipples tighten.

"Man. Not men. I've only slep—" She closed her mouth at the fierce looks on their faces.

Max's looked like he could've been carved from granite, with his jaw clenched so hard she feared he would chip a tooth.

That wouldn't keep her silent, but the fog of emotion reflected in his eyes had her reaching up to cup his cheek to reassure them, for what she wasn't sure. She just wanted to soothe, to make them…happy.

Max turned his head and pressed a kiss to her palm. A zing of pleasure went through the heart of her that had her knees buckling.

She found herself surrounded by both men as Malcolm stepped behind her, wrapping his arms around her waist, palming her breasts, making her whimper with the extreme pleasure. She stared into Max's eyes. Good lord, she could get lost in their depths.

With both men so close she could smell their individual scents, and moaned at the delicious thrill the dual assault had on her senses. Her hips moved of their own volition, rubbing her body against the two impressive men sandwiching her between them. It all seemed like a dance they'd done a thousand times before.

The reactions her movements caused were more than she bargained for. From teasing and playful to intent in mere seconds, both men groaned as if in pain. Malcolm breathed on her neck before nipping her shoulder, making her shiver in delight, while Max gripped her hips. His lips licked at her closed mouth, demanding she open for him.

She wanted to give them anything. That thought gave her pause, until his teeth nipped at her bottom lip. *Goddess.* She flicked her tongue out over the area he'd bitten. He tasted like the finest wine, and she wanted to savor him.

She wanted more, and Max was obliged to give her more.

With incredible ease he lifted her up, aligning their bodies, guiding her legs around his waist. Their mouths met in a clash of lips and teeth, before gentling. She sank into his kiss, loving the demanding way he held her head as if he'd never let go.

The feel of another set of hands squeezing her breasts reminded her of Malcolm, and Selena was almost shocked out of the sexual haze, but a gentle push at her shields reminded her that something was different with these two. She allowed a sliver of light to flow into her mind that she recognized as Malcolm. He was trying to reassure her.

Instead of jerking away from the invasion she sent a small burst of energy back, still not allowing either man entry into her thoughts.

The action received the desired effect. Malcolm squeezed the tips of her nipples between his thumb and forefinger while trailing his lips along the column of her throat. Max made love to her mouth. There was no other way she could describe it. He ran his tongue over the roof, around the front of her teeth. Who'd have thought that would feel so freaking good? All the while she rubbed herself against Max's rock-hard stomach, knowing she could come at the slightest touch from either man. If Malcolm or Max would just trail their hands down between her legs, they'd find her dripping wet. One flick, or one brush of a finger and she knew she'd fly apart at the seams. The thought should have embarrassed her, but all she wanted was to feel one or both of them touching her.

She was sure Max's shirt and pants were going to be showing a visible wet spot from where she was wrapped around him. Again, she couldn't find an ounce of guilt.

From the size of his erection pressing between her legs, and the one at her back, she'd guess they were in the same situation. She trembled, wrapped her arms more firmly around Max's shoulders, needing his heat. Needing them.

Malcolm's hands disappeared and then Max's mouth pulled away.

They worked together like a well-oiled machine, moving toward the overstuffed leather sofa against the wall in her office. She felt a cool breeze from the central air as first her tank top and then her bra was removed by Malcolm. Absently she wondered how they'd learned to accomplish such a task, but Max reclaimed her lips in a heated kiss. Malcolm's extremely warm hands began kneading her chilled flesh.

"Damn, she feels like silk," Malcolm murmured.

Time seemed to stop. It took several seconds for Selena to get through the sexual fog swirling in her brain. Somehow Max had pried her legs from his hips and laid her on the couch. Two matching blue gazes bored into her where she lay in complete abandon.

What must they think of her?

"Oh God," Selena whispered. She raised her hands to cover her breasts. Even the slight contact with her hands felt erotic with both men watching. She was more than glad Max had the decency to make sure her legs were placed neatly together instead of sprawled out like some sort of…She stopped the absurd thoughts. It took two, or in this case three, to tango and she definitely wasn't the only one who was doing the undressing, she noticed.

Malcolm's shirt had joined hers on the floor at some point and his belt was off with the top button of his slacks open, exposing the black briefs below. Max, on the other hand, was still completely dressed, and to her complete embarrassment he did indeed have a wet spot from where she had unabashedly ground herself against him.

Before she could scramble up, Max leaned down and pulled her boots and socks off in two easy tugs.

"What the hell?"

She truly meant to scramble up. To put up more of a fight. But Malcolm chose that moment to drop to his knees on the floor by her head. The brothers looked so much alike, but were so different. She couldn't explain it or put it to words, it was just a feeling that she had in the pit of her soul.

"You're so beautiful. Perfect," Malcolm said. He captured her mouth in a kiss that stole her breath and her sanity. She raised her hands, not to push him away, but to pull him closer. His muscles bunched under her hands, his skin smooth over the steel hardness. His taste was also different than Max's, but no less of an elixir she could easily become addicted to. Where Max tasted like the sweetest wine, Malcolm tasted like melted honey. She pulled his hair from the binding at the base of his neck, running her fingers through the soft thickness. Another thing that made them different.

The sound of her leather belt sliding and the clang of the heavy blinged-out belt hitting the carpet was overly loud in the room.

A tap on her hips and she was lifting herself up to help them slide her skirt down, leaving her wearing only a tiny red thong. The dang thing was soaked and no longer doing anything anymore. She wasn't sure whose hands were at her waist removing what, or whose hands were touching her breasts. She was lost in a sensory overload of four hands, two mouths, and goddess help her she loved every minute of it.

A puff of air on her soaked thighs had her clit throbbing, aching for one of them to touch her.

"Please," she begged.

Malcolm and Max were both kneeling alongside her. It should have looked ridiculous, only it wasn't.

Max's right hand raised in what seemed like slow motion to Selena's mind. She realized her left leg was raised over the back of the couch and her right was now hanging off the other side. She was completely exposed to them. He trailed his index finger from her belly button straight down to her most intimate flesh, never taking his eyes off of her face. He swirled his finger in and around and under the red thong, but never touched the one place guaranteed to send her over the edge of bliss.

With his gaze still watching her he brought his finger to his mouth and sucked it into his mouth.

*Jesus.* Selena almost came from that alone.

In a graceful move he stood and motioned to Malcolm to switch places with him. Some sort of silent communication took place between the two men. Her clit was throbbing. Her body was shaking with the need for release.

Max unsnapped two buttons on his top then tossed it over his head, releasing his belt and button of his pants in a motion so fast she barely tracked.

A puff of hot air washed over her covered pussy, and she glanced down to see a smirking Malcolm. The man stuck his tongue out and traced his way up and around where his brother's finger had been.

"She's so wet and hot," Malcolm said.

"She's going to smack you if you don't make her come," Selena panted. She reached down to touch herself. Max grabbed her hand.

How did he move so quietly for such a large man?

"I think she needs something, Mal." Max swallowed her next words with his mouth, groaning in unison.

Selena dug her heels into the cushion as Malcolm finally latched onto her clit.

"Shit, Max, she's so fucking sweet," Malcolm murmured from between her legs.

She whimpered, needing more.

"What the hell?" Her eyes flew open when Malcolm tapped the top of her mound with the flat of his hand.

"Stay still, love. We're in charge here. You belong to us," Max answered.

Max's broad shoulders blocked out her view of Malcolm, so she was completely unprepared for the next tap directly over her clit. Max swallowed the scream of pleasure the smack caused. If he made love to her body the way he kissed, Selena thought she'd die a happy woman. He left no part of her mouth unexplored. She'd never been kissed so thoroughly.

Malcolm gripped the sides of her favorite red panties and she heard a rip, just as she lifted her hips.

"Son of a bitch, Max, she's bare," Malcolm groaned. "Do you shave or wax?"

Max raised his head and both men stared as if mesmerized by her. She didn't know how to tell them she'd never had any body hair. When she had been a teenager, it had embarrassed her when all the other girls started shaving. She wanted to be just like them, and even pretended to shave, just to feel like part of the crowd.

Now as an adult and seeing the admiration and the need in both their eyes, she was glad. Selena knew her pussy glistened with her juices, and with no hair to obstruct their view, they would see it, too. Max reached down and smacked the top of her mound and her mouth flew open.

"Malcolm asked you a question."

"N–no…I just…I've never had any, you know…down there," she stammered, but refused to be embarrassed.

They shared another look, that damn silent communication she wished to be a part of. When she met Malcolm's look from between her legs, he had a devilish gleam on his face. He stuck his tongue out, pinning her with his gaze as he leaned forward and licked her. Starting at the bottom of her crack, with one long swipe he lapped up the juices that flowed out of her.

He hummed. The throbbing at the heart of her became more intense, if that were possible. She wanted to be filled. He circled the engorged bundle of nerves and lapped at her like an ice cream cone on a hot summer day.

Max touched her cheek and she turned her head to see him kneeling by her face, completely naked with his extremely large cock in his hand.

"Open your mouth, Lena. I want to feel your lips around my cock," Max said in a guttural voice.

She licked her lips and stared at the milky fluid beading on the tip. She leaned forward and grabbed him with her left hand, opening her mouth to suck on the bulbous head. He tasted like cinnamon and cream.

Selena had had only one lover, but he had tasted nothing like this man. She flattened her tongue on the bottom of his dick and sucked him deep, holding him by the base to control the depth. She wanted to taste more of his flavor. Swirling her tongue back up to the head, she licked the slit and was rewarded with another trickle of the fluid.

She jerked when Malcolm began licking and opened his mouth to suck her folds. The dual assaults of having Max filling her mouth and Malcolm feasting on her had her center clenching. With her right foot planted on the floor, she pressed her pelvis up. Goddess be damned, if the man didn't fuck her soon, she'd kill him herself.

"I think Lena needs something filling her, Malcolm." Max looked down and met her eyes. "She's been such a bad girl, though. What do you think?" he asked Malcolm, but with his eyes on her. She nodded. He shook his head, trying to hide his merriment, until she gripped his dick with her teeth.

"I think she's threatening my manhood, Malcolm." Max laughed.

Selena snarled and scraped her teeth up his length before sucking the tip to release him with a pop.

Malcolm pursed his lips and kissed right above where she needed him, missing the engorged bit of flesh that begged for attention.

"Her little clit is so red and angry-looking," Malcolm said.

They talked as if she weren't there, which pissed her off. She pulled her leg off the top of the couch, intending to stand, but Malcolm cupped her calf and pressed it back. With a shake of his head and a nod to Max, he leaned forward and held her in place with his body, releasing her leg in the process.

He gripped her ass in his palms and raised her pussy up to meet the thrust of his tongue. He stabbed at her opening repeatedly. Her inner muscles squeezed and released so hard, she feared she'd cause him permanent damage.

"She's so tight. I can feel every flutter on my tongue," Malcolm said between licks.

Selena turned at the gentle tap on her cheek to see Max's cock. She opened wide, swallowing as much of him as she could, before she gagged and pulled back. He fisted one hand in her hair and the other held him at the base. His balls slapped her chin as he shuttled in and out. And oh goodness, his cock filled her. She couldn't wait to find out what he tasted like when he came.

Malcolm replaced his tongue with two thick fingers, attacking her clit with vigor.

She squeezed her eyes shut and concentrated on the unique flavor of Max that flowed onto her tongue.

"I'm going to come, Lena, I want you to swallow every drop."

She nodded. When he hit the back of her throat, she breathed through her nose and swallowed on the head. He groaned, rewarding her with a twitch of his dick and the first spurt of his orgasm.

He pulled back and pressed back inside. She lapped and suckled him as he grunted and his strokes increased. Hearing his shout, she swallowed repeatedly, his whole body shook as she drank him down greedily.

Lapping gently at his softening cock, she continued to lick him clean, not wanting to waste a drop of his pearly liquid. He sat back on his heels and looked at her. She couldn't decipher what the look meant, but Malcolm prevented her from doing or saying something stupid with his incredibly talented tongue.

He pressed a third finger inside and stretched her further. She felt ready to explode with his lips surrounding her clit and his fingers filling her. She cried out as he pressed a finger to her bottom hole. His fingers moved in tandem, each stroke over her ultra-sensitive flesh sending her flying higher with each thrust.

His features were so hard, intensifying the blue in his eyes. The sensations reached inside her and every feminine instinct came forth. Everything strengthened, every lick, every breath, every look designed to send her into the most pleasurable place.

"Malcolm. Oh, it's so good. So good," she moaned, and fell apart in a kaleidoscope of colors.

# Chapter Eight

Malcolm watched Selena come apart and waited until she came back down. He stared up her body and saw the flush that covered her rosy nipples, all the way up her high cheekbones. With short, jerky motions he removed his slacks and briefs and climbed onto the couch between her spread thighs.

Her juices coated his face, and he didn't want to lose one drop. With an impatient hand he gathered the evidence of her pleasure onto his hand, before rubbing the moisture into his chest. Poised over her body he waited for her eyes to open. They flared wide when she saw his naked body and he exulted in her appreciative stare.

Rubbing his leaking tip across her smooth flesh had them both groaning. Max had a look that could only be called love blazing from him in waves, the same feeling echoing in Malcolm. His brother leaned forward and captured the gasp of surprise Selena uttered as Malcolm entered her.

She squeezed him so tight he held the first inch of his cock inside, until she relaxed to take a little more. Max's lips traveled down her throat and stopped at her breast.

Malcolm gripped her clit between his fingers and rubbed them back and forth, trapping the swollen bit of flesh.

He felt her body relax and he pushed a couple more inches inside. "She's so fucking tight. I can barely get inside her," Malcolm panted.

Max slapped Malcolm's fingers off of her and replaced them with his own. Malcolm pulled her hips off the couch and rested her ass on his thighs. Her juices coated his dick and dripped down to his balls, making his entry easier with her slickness. He pressed forward, then pulled back, only to slam back inside when she started to come.

"Gods yes, baby. Come all over my dick, Selena," Malcolm said.

He increased the pace of his thrusts as Max continued to strum her clit through her orgasm. Both men were so in tune with Selena's body that when she became too sensitive for his brother's touch on that oversensitive bit of flesh Max removed his hand. He trailed it up to her breast, leaving a trail of wetness in his wake.

Selena's nails dug into Max's arms and Malcolm could see the look of possession on his brother's face when she gave herself to them without a second thought. She lifted her breasts in offering to Max's devouring mouth, and Malcolm wanted to feel her pussy squeezing his dick again.

He reached under her and pressed his thumb to her tight little pucker. With the fluid that trailed down the crack of her ass lubing his finger, he pressed the tip inside. She stilled her movements, but when he pulled out and then pushed inside again, she relaxed and eased his entry.

He wondered if she'd ever had a man take her ass, but decided he didn't want to know yet. They needed to prepare her to take them both at the same time. He pulled his finger almost all the way out as he shoved his cock back inside. His balls drew up. The tingling in his spine heralded the arrival of his own orgasm.

He wanted her to explode one more time before he fell over the edge. Removing his thumb and dick, he inserted two fingers into her clenching vagina. Pulling out, he pressed the well-lubed digits into her ass and pushed them back inside.

Her shoulders lifted off the couch and a scream escaped her throat before Max covered her mouth, taking it inside of his own.

Malcolm aimed his cock for home and slammed back inside. He shafted in and out at the same time as his fingers. Selena burst apart under his assault.

Pumping harder, he answered her cry with his own deep, hoarse shout. He threw his head back, letting go. His cock pulsed deep inside her clenching pussy, milking him of his seed. He looked up to see Selena's eyes had closed, and her body shivered.

Pulling out, he carefully removed his fingers. Selena whimpered. He didn't know if it was from pain or pleasure.

"I'm sorry, baby. Are you all right?"

She opened her eyes and smiled at them with a nervous look. With her arms flung above her head, she looked like a goddess. "I'm so much better than all right. I'm fantastic…"

Selena's phone buzzed from the pocket of her skirt.

He could see she struggled with embarrassment. Malcolm didn't want her embarrassed. He wanted her sated and happy, he wanted to feel her mouth wrap around his cock. *What the hell…*Looking down, he saw junior standing up and ready to play.

"Shit," Malcolm and Max said at the same time, making Selena laugh.

"What are you laughing at, woman." Max growled.

"You guys." Still giggling, she wiped a tear. "You guys look like your mommy said it was time for bed."

"Hmm…I think I agree. It's time for bed," Malcolm said. He could see her lying on top of his bed with her arms spread wide, waiting to welcome them into her body.

"What? Oh no, we can't…I have a club to open in—" She looked at the clock and scrambled up.

Max held her still and asked, "What are you doing?"

"I need to get up."

Selena squirmed so hard Malcolm feared she'd hurt herself. He looked at Max and his brother must've decided the same thing.

"You're right. We'll finish this later." Max used his most authoritative voice, making Selena shake her head. Big brother's man voice didn't seem to faze her. Malcolm wanted to howl with laughter, but knew that if he did Max would retaliate. Malcolm didn't want to fight Max, he wanted to spend the next century or so learning all the things Selena liked.

With a puzzled look, she swung her legs over the side and reached for her panties. Malcolm couldn't help the smirk that crossed his face when she picked them up and shot him a dirty look.

"What?" he asked, trying to look innocent.

"I can't go back down there without any underwear on."

Max opened his mouth and closed it. Malcolm dropped his head back on his shoulders and shoved himself to his feet.

Knowing Max would distract her, Malcolm turned around and walked over to her desk. He hoped like hell she had been too preoccupied when they entered her office to notice anything amiss. With a thought he created a pair of panties for her that covered more than the damn thong she'd worn, and turned with a tiny box in his hand.

Malcolm silently applauded Max's efforts. He certainly had Selena's attention, if the rosy flush covering her gorgeously tanned skin was anything to go by. The way she held his brother's shoulders with her nails digging in, Malcolm knew she'd leave crescent-shaped indents. A pang of envy hit him that he didn't have them too.

"I bought these for you," Malcolm stated, walking back to the kissing pair.

She jerked her mouth away from his brother, causing Max to shoot him a dirty look that Malcolm completely ignored.

"A present for me?" she asked, reaching for the box.

Opening the lid, her silver eyes widened. She pulled out the snow-white, French lace panties he'd made her. She looked at him, then Max, and then at the underwear lying in her palm.

"How? Why?" Selena sputtered.

"I picked them up in Dubai." It wasn't a lie. He had picked them up. He just didn't buy them at the time. But he remembered when they slipped through his fingers, and he'd pictured his fantasy vision of Selena wearing them for him.

Her phone buzzed again. With a snap, she shut her mouth. Looking around, she grabbed her skirt then pulled the phone out. At her groan, Malcolm had a pretty good idea who the caller was.

"Hi, Tam." She listened, and then said, "I'll be right down. Give me ten minutes."

Malcolm could hear the conversation and wanted to laugh at the merriment in Tamara's voice, but didn't want to alert them to his ability. Max started dressing, but Malcolm stood with his arms crossed as he waited for her. Had it really been over two hours? The digital clock on the wall confirmed that indeed it had been well over that.

"I gotta go." She turned and came to a quick stop.

He hid his smile and turned to pick the rest of her clothes up. Max walked out of the bathroom with a warm washcloth and bent to clean her. She stood completely still and bit her lip. Malcolm wanted to replace her teeth with his mouth, but she looked on the edge of bolting.

Max stood, gave her a quick peck on her lips before he turned back to the open door of the bathroom.

She blew out a breath and held her hand out. Malcolm shook his head and stepped forward to help her dress. She slapped at his hands, but finally allowed him to draw the cups of her bra together and snap them in place.

"I don't think I like this job as well as the undressing part," Malcolm murmured. Without making it obvious, he and Max used their ability to ensure nobody looking at Selena would be able to tell she'd been well-fucked. Although they wanted everyone to know, they were smart enough to realize Selena wouldn't.

Max held up her boots. With a huff, Selena sat on the edge of the couch and couldn't hide the wince of pain. Max saw it and shot a look over his shoulder.

Malcolm opened his mouth, but Selena held up a hand.

"I'm not hurt. It's just been a long time since I've…" She bit that damn lip again, and it took every ounce of his control. He wanted to march over to her and begin removing her clothes again.

"Good…" Max said. He folded his arms across his chest.

"Max, why don't you escort our…" Malcolm stopped at the look she shot them. "I mean take Selena back down while I finish dressing and cleaning up a bit."

Selena held her breath as Max reached out and trailed his finger down her cheek. She let out a moan when Max's hand caressed her breast and tapped her nipple through the thin layer of clothes. Malcolm wanted to rip them off her and saw Max's thoughts mirrored his own.

"Listen, I'm a big girl and nobody needs to escort me anywhere. Just because we…um, you know." She gestured at the couch and continued. "Just because we fucked doesn't give either of you the right to go all He-Man on me."

Malcolm burst into laughter at the look of horror on Max's face. They'd been compared to or called many things, but He-Man was not one of them. He wiped at his eyes and crowded into her space.

"Sweetheart, if we went all He-Man on you, I can guarantee you one thing." He growled. "You wouldn't be going back down to your club. You really don't want to push Max on this."

Malcolm saw his brother clenching his fist so hard his knuckles turned white. Neither man wanted to let her out of their sights. When you searched for one thing, for hundreds of years, thinking you'd never find it, only to have it dropped into your life, you could be forgiven for wanting to hold on and never let go.

"Whatever. I'm going down. Maybe you should get dressed first," she said to Malcolm.

To his astonishment, she looked him up and down and licked her lips. He felt his cock jerk and he wanted nothing more than to strip her bare. He shook his head and grabbed her shoulders, jerking her to him before he covered her saucy mouth with his own.

He lifted his mouth and licked her lips, then stepped back and turned her toward the door with a tap on her ass. "Go with Max before we change our minds."

Max linked their hands and headed out the door with her, leaving Malcolm alone to dress and clean up their mess. His body still tight with need, he knew he would never get enough of her. Ever.

* * * *

Max could see the war Selena waged with herself and their demands. He felt sure she'd never experienced what he and Malcolm had just done to her, but with her mind blocked, he couldn't be sure. The only people he couldn't read, unless they allowed it, had been his fellow Ravens. Selena puzzled him, and he didn't like puzzles.

"So how long are you in town for?" Max asked.

"Oh…um…I'm not sure."

"Where are you staying?"

"What is this? Is this the first degree, Max? Just because we—"

He pressed a finger to her lips, stopping her words. "Don't demean what we just did, Selena. You know it was more, just as Malcolm and I do."

She opened her mouth and when he rubbed his finger on the inside of her bottom lip, she licked the tip, making him groan.

"I don't know what you're talking about."

They reached the top of the stairs and in a move she couldn't have stopped, he spun her back to the wall. He gripped her chin, bringing her face up to his, and brushed his lips over her mouth in a soft caress.

"Don't lie to me or yourself, Selena." He kissed her hard, and then stepped back. "Next time you lie, I will spank that delectable ass."

"Kiss my ass, Max."

"Oh I'll do that, too." He laughed at her look of outrage.

"Let's go before your friend storms up here." He grabbed her hand and kissed her knuckles.

Reaching the bottom of the stairs, Max released Selena's hand. He rubbed his chest and ached to touch her again. He met the dark gaze of Selena's best friend across the room as she sidled her way over to them.

"Hello, you two," Tamara said.

"I was just showing…" Selena trailed off.

"Oh, I think I know what you were showing them."

Max pulled Selena into his side, sliding a possessive hand around her waist to hold her close and shield her from her friend.

"Don't even start with me, Tam, I have so much dirt on you, your own mama would turn gray."

Tamara sniffed. "Ha, my mama would never turn gray. We Mejias never turn gray."

Max's face hardened. "Leave her alone, Tamara."

Tamara patted his chest and laughed. He saw the merriment in both women's eyes and realized they'd been teasing him. He really needed to break down the walls both ladies had around their minds. He hated not knowing what others thought.

"I'm just messing with Lena. She's too serious, and it's taken long enough for her to climb back on the horse, or horses, in this case."

Selena shoved her friend and made a slashing motion with her hand across her neck. Tamara obviously had no problem deciphering it. What the hell had she been talking about? Max promised himself he'd learn all there was to know about Selena and her friend.

He needed to talk to Malcolm. Selena had to be their Fated, but they hadn't completed the circle that would combine their souls. He needed to talk to Zeus or one of the other gods, but didn't know how. Zeus said they would know, but didn't say how…Shit. More puzzles did not make Max a happy boy.

He looked up at the ceiling and prayed to the gods and goddesses alike for guidance. He was so lost in his thoughts he didn't feel Malcolm's approach until he laid a hand on his shoulder. Startled, he turned and shoved Malcolm backward.

Selena gasped and covered her mouth with her hand. He opened his mind to Malcolm, and grimaced at the silent laughter ringing in his head.

"Sorry, bro. Did I interrupt you?" Malcolm sounded not the least bit sorry.

"Fuck you, Mal. Let's step outside so we can talk."

They both reached out and took hold of one of Selena's hands and placed them on their chest.

Her eyes flared and her breathing sped up. She smiled up at them, making Max's heart melt a little more. Sharing a conspiratorial look with his brother, he motioned toward the door.

Max bent to kiss her cheek, then strode away, trying to clear his head of one silver-haired angel who was bound to be the death of him.

He shoved the door open and paced. Gripping the back of his neck, he looked up at the sky and wondered for the millionth time if the gods were fucking with them.

They'd kicked them out of Mount Olympus when they had no longer been needed. No goddess wanted to mate with a being the gods created. Sure, they could fuck them and kill for them, but mate with them for life was not an option in their book.

Max didn't mind all that much. They were treated with respect and affection, but he learned early on they weren't good enough for a happily-ever after with one. Shrugging his shoulders, he turned as Malcolm stepped outside.

He stared at his brother, and knew without words Malcolm felt the same way toward Selena.

"What are we going to do?" Malcolm asked without preamble.

"Damned if I know. They didn't give us a manual for this shit."

"I'm not gonna give her up. I don't know how it works, but she's a part of me."

Malcolm raised his hand and rubbed his chest in a gesture that Max mirrored.

"Who says either of us has to give her up?" Max growled.

"Hello…Can you say society?"

"Fuck them. We're immortal. What the hell does it matter what anyone thinks?"

"I feel you bro, but what about Selena? She isn't immortal like us. Which brings me to another question," Malcolm held up a finger. "How does this work?"

"Fuck if I know, Mal. Son of a bitch…Why can't Zeus fucking answer my questions? I've been calling out to him for the last fifteen minutes."

They both stared up at the sky, and then looked at each other and laughed. Malcolm slapped him on the back and turned serious.

"Max, let's just take it one day at a time. I can't imagine they"—he pointed up and continued—"would fuck us over. Zeus said we all would find one woman to complete us. That doesn't mean you and I don't have the same woman. Hell, if I remember correctly, we were intended to be one being instead of two. Of course, Zeus would never admit he fucked up. I mean, I am the smart and handsome twin, while you're the—"

Malcolm dodged the large fist aimed at his head.

"You are such a shit. I should have drowned you when you were a kid."

"I was never a kid."

The reminder of their creation had both brothers brooding in silence. Max turned when he heard the unmistakable sound of a Harley roaring toward them. Max loved the sound of the custom pipes on a Harley that let you know, long before you saw the bike, that it was coming.

"Is that who I think it is?" Malcolm asked.

Max saw the unmistakable helmet of Rafe Blackstone, his second in command. Rafe was seven feet, two inches of solid muscle with a smooth, bald head the ladies seemed to love and dark skin with black eyes. Some would say they were a dark brown, but they were black as pitch.

Rafe stopped his bike next to the curb and kicked the stand down. With a flick of his wrist, he turned the machine off, pulled his trademark helmet off, and shook his bald head.

"Hey, Rafe, what's up? You shake all that hair out of your face?" Malcolm asked.

Rafe tilted one corner of his lips up and lifted his right hand off his thigh to scratch his cheek with his middle finger.

"Nah…I don't think so, dude. I love you, but you are just not pretty enough for me," Malcolm joked.

"Max, can't you control your baby brother?" Rafe asked.

"Nope…So what are you doing here?" Max asked.

"I've just rode up from Texas following a lead. When it dried up here, I thought I'd look you up."

The Ravens had a connection and could sense when another was near. Max must be losing it, because he hadn't sensed Rafe until he was almost on top of him. So not a good thing, when Max knew they were not the only immortal beings on Earth.

"You have a lead on the goddess or is it something else?" Max asked.

He sent a thought to Malcolm, wondering if he felt as uncomfortable as him. A shake of his twin's head gave him his answer.

"I'm not sure what it is. How about you guys?"

Shit…Not good if neither of them could sense Rafe. Looking over his shoulder, he looked at the closed door to the club and inhaled. He needed to center his thoughts and check for other threats. Not that he thought of Rafe as a threat, but if he hadn't sensed him, maybe he'd missed another.

With his mind focused, he didn't find anything other than Rafe and Malcolm. He knew Selena was inside, but there seemed to be a blank space surrounding her. He promised himself he'd knock down the walls protecting or hiding her. The thought of her being hidden popped into his mind, and took up a more sinister twist.

"Max, did you hear me?" Rafe asked again with a puzzled look.

"We heard you Rafe, and the answer is negative. We haven't heard anything, or found anything for that matter, on the missing goddess. Shit man, the way it's going we won't know until the end of time. Or if Zeus is correct, in a few short months when his baby girl explodes."

"Fuck…" Rafe rubbed his hands across his bald head and Max smiled at the gesture.

There were only two of the Ravens that had bald heads and they looked almost identical, except Rafe was much bulkier and about two inches taller than Vin. Both had the same snapping black eyes and dark skin, but they were not twins like Max and Malcolm.

"Where's Vin?" Max asked. Usually where there was one, the other was close by.

Rafe shrugged his shoulders. "Somewhere in the Middle East. He said he was following a lead."

Max shared a look with Malcolm, and then made a snap decision. "We found our Fated."

"What? Wow, congrats to you both. What are their names, where are they?" Rafe asked, looking around.

"Her name is Selena Ramos," Max said.

"What's your lucky lady's name, Mal?"

"Selena Ramos."

Max already had his hand balled into a fist, expecting his friend to say something stupid, except Rafe took him by surprise when he flashed his white smile, threw his head back and laughed. Max shared a puzzled glance with Mal while they waited for Rafe to calm down.

Max stepped forward, prepared to kick the bike over with his friend still on it. Rafe snapped his black eyes open and with a nod tossed his leg over the bike. He reached out and grabbed Max in a bear hug, then releasing him grabbed Malcolm. Rafe slapped Malcolm's back a little too hard and laughed when his brother slapped Rafe on the back of the head.

"Did you guys think I'd judge you or her? Fuck me, man. I'm happy you guys found her. Now we just need to find Zeus's daughter and all's good."

Max grimaced. He wished it could be that easy. But finding the golden girl Cronus had stolen and hidden somewhere here on Earth was proving close to impossible. Rafe averted his gaze, but not before Max saw the look of envy cross his friend's face. He knew the feeling. Many times over his long existence, he had seen a couple in their late years holding hands, or sitting next to each other. He'd felt their peace and love flowing through them and would get a pang of longing.

Malcolm seemed to be less fucked in the head as he spoke in low tones, explaining to Rafe how they each met Selena. He skipped the office details. Thank the gods! He'd hate to have to kill them both.

"When do I get to meet her?"

Malcolm looked at his watch. "She officially opens in about a half hour. The local radio stations should be here shortly. They're going to broadcast live. Selena's a smart businesswoman."

Max nearly choked on his spit when his brother puffed his chest out like he had something to do with her achievements. Silently he agreed with him. Selena was everything he ever wanted in a woman. He just never dreamed he'd find her, and share her.

"Let's go inside and I'll introduce you to her," Malcolm said, taking the lead.

Rafe pocketed his keys and followed Malcolm inside, while Max took another long look around. He noticed the streets were filling up, and more people were walking up and down the sidewalk.

Selena's club already had a line forming behind the red rope, which was being manned by a large man Max had checked out earlier. With a thought, he lifted the shield that kept others from overhearing their conversations. To onlookers, they would've heard three men standing around discussing football or some shit. He followed the others at a slow pace, and with one last look up, he asked for guidance.

# Chapter Nine

Selena couldn't help but stare at the tight asses of the two men she'd just shared herself with. Damn, but they were fine. She waited until the door shut off her view before she focused on the amused gleam in her best friend's eyes.

"What?" Selena asked, placing her hands on her hips.

"Hmm...Let's see." Tamara tapped her chin. "Did you fuck them both or what?"

Selena swallowed hard. She didn't know if she should laugh or hit Tamara. "Shut up, you be-otch...*Grrr*."

"Don't growl at me. I'm just asking."

She covered her cheeks with her hands, trying to hide the blush she felt creeping up her body. Tamara had a way of making her feel like a teenager all over again. Her pulse fluttered, she ran her tongue over her swollen lips.

Tamara followed the gesture, making Selena groan at the knowing look.

"Let's just say I kinda sampled them both, but I didn't have sex with both of them."

Selena consoled herself with the fact she hadn't lied. She just omitted a little truth. A smile crossed Tamara's face, and she patted Selena on the arm.

Damn. Double damn. Thank the goddesses, Tamara let the subject drop. They walked over to the bar in the center of the room. She listened to the rundown of stock, and checked the girls to see they all had on the matching tank tops and denim bottoms.

"You ladies look awesome. Thank you all for working so hard to learn the steps to all the songs. I know you're probably nervous, but as long as you smile, you'll do great."

"Yes…Just what she said and to the bouncers." Tamara turned wide, innocent eyes to them. "If someone steps out of line, ask them to stop, but be polite. If someone starts a fight, ask them to leave. But be polite. If someone…"

Selena slapped her hand over Tamara's mouth. "Are you quoting Patrick Swayze, from Road House?"

"What did I say? He was great, and it worked, didn't it?"

"Did we watch the same movie, Tam?" Selena couldn't help but laugh, and wiping the tears from her eyes, found herself staring at the door to the outside. With a look at her watch she noticed the time. Clapping her hands, she motioned everybody to their stations.

"Heads up, girlie, here come your men," Tamara began, and stopped with a gasp.

Selena had already spotted Malcolm and his long-legged stride being followed by one of the largest men she'd ever seen…*Shit*…He had to be well over seven feet tall.

The door shut behind them, blocking the light and temporarily blinding her, but she continued looking at the entryway trying to see Max. She released a breath when he strolled in at a much slower pace. His whole demeanor had changed. She watched as he scanned the place, and if she didn't know better, he also seemed to look into their minds.

She met his gaze, and a jolt of recognition flooded her body. She had the overwhelming urge to run across the room and climb inside his body. *What the hell?* She tore her eyes away and found herself being jerked into the arms of Malcolm.

He bent and pressed a kiss to her cheek like a butterfly's wings' caress. Her arms wound around his neck, and she kissed him back, skipping his cheek, aiming straight for his mouth. He groaned and took control of the sweet caress, kissing her fiercely.

Malcolm lifted his head with a ragged groan. "I missed you too, Lena."

Hearing a deep rumble, she turned and met the amused stare of the overly large man. She tried to unwind her arms from Malcolm and put some distance between them. Malcolm pressed a possessive hand to her rear and held her in place, letting her feel the massive erection straining the front of his pants.

She felt an answering wetness between her legs and squirmed. "Malcolm, let me go."

Stretching muscles still languid from her earlier romp with Malcolm and Max, she stilled when she felt another body press into her from behind.

Looking over her shoulder, she shivered at the look in Max's eyes.

"Lena, this is our friend, Rafe," Max said.

"Nice to meet you." Rafe nodded.

Selena noticed his eyes were black as night and he seemed riveted in place, staring as if transfixed at Tamara. She turned her head and watched as Tamara backed away with a look of horror.

She tried to mind-talk with Tamara, but slammed into a brick wall. Wincing, she raised her hand to her head and stepped back into Max, whose arms came around her.

"Rafe," Malcolm growled. "You are scaring our woman."

He shook his head and with reluctance turned those eerie black eyes back to her. She didn't know if she should stick her hand out or run screaming like a little girl for the nearest exit.

Good manners almost lost, but then he stepped forward with a grin that lit up his face and flashed the whitest smile. He gripped her bicep in a surprisingly gentle squeeze and pulled her from between her two men and into his body.

She saw a wicked glint pass over his face before he pulled her from Max. He turned her, bending her over his arm, and shocked them all when he blew a raspberry on her neck.

She giggled…Freaking giggled…*What the hell…First I almost ran screaming like a gawd damn girl, now I'm fucking giggling? Next I'll be fainting into a swoon like a maiden in one of my fairy tales.*

He released her almost as quickly as he grabbed her and laughed, before pushing her into Max's arms again. Okay, so the man was truly hot in a scary kind of way, but what the hell?

Malcolm and Max had matching scowls on their faces that gave her an overwhelming urge to comfort them. Reaching out, she held Malcolm's hand in her left and placed her right on Max's thigh. She felt the tension leave their bodies and wondered at their response to her touch.

Rafe stilled in his movements and focused on the retreating form of Tamara. "Who is that?"

"Tamara Mejia. She's my best friend and business partner," Selena said with a bite of steel in her voice.

"Easy, kitten, I would just like to meet her."

She sputtered. "Did you call me kitten?" Turning to look at the amused smile on Max's and Mal's faces, she asked, "Did he just call me kitten?"

Rafe's eyes followed Tamara as she fled to the stock room. Selena's cheeks heated as she saw the speculative gazes of her employees, looking at her in Max's and Malcolm's arms.

Taking a deep breath, she met each gaze with a fierce look. She held her head up and watched as her men stepped beside her and presented a united front. Every woman in the room smiled and most of the men seemed uninterested.

Shrugging, she raised her hand to her mouth and whistled a high-pitched sound, getting everyone's attention.

"Okay, people. It's almost show time. If you have a problem with anything, please come see me or Tam. If you can't find either of us—" she stopped as Max held up a hand.

"If you can't find them, come to me or Malcolm."

His tone brooked no argument. She marveled as everyone nodded and turned to their stations. With a bounce, she headed toward the door. A slow smile slid across her face, before she moved directly in front of the opening.

Max pulled her up short. Swallowing the small bit of fear, she opened her mouth to object. He stopped her with a groan and leaned down, pressing his lips to hers, and murmured, "I just want you to slow down, baby."

"What do you mean? It's time to open the doors."

"I am aware of this, but you need to take a breath. You look ready to faint."

She giggled and slapped a hand over her mouth and tried to block the sound. They must have thought she was a Barbie doll twit giggling like a friggin' loon, dammit.

"I always get this excited on opening day. Usually Tamara and I share a shot or two before we fling the doors open."

"I'll buy you a shot just as soon as we—and I do mean we," he said, looking over his shoulder at Malcolm, "ensure your safety."

Pushing at his chest, she grunted when he didn't even pretend to feel it. "Listen you two, you are not my…my daddy, so just back the fuck up. I can take care of myself."

"Oh goody, Max, our woman is feisty. Do I get to spank her first, or do you?"

Selena let her eyes flutter closed and prayed for patience. Opening them, she pinned them with a glare. Their eyes opened wide in surprise when they looked at her, and stepped back. A strange sensation wracked her frame, as a thrill of power raced through her, making her hair feel as if it stood on end.

She felt sure she resembled Drew Barrymore in that show where she started fires with her mind. Selena laughed at the image, and some of the energy dissipated, leaving her shaken.

"Don't fuck with me, boys. I'm not your little lady to be tucked away. Now step aside so I can open my club."

She didn't wait for them to move. With a lightning fast move and more force than they were obviously prepared for, she shoved at their shoulders and glided between their hulking forms.

She bit her lip, and held the laugh she felt bubbling up at the stunned look on their faces. With a flourish, Selena flung the doors open and walked out. Coming to an abrupt halt, she beamed, seeing the line of people waiting to get inside stretched all the way down the block and across the road.

Grabbing the bull horn her bouncer Alan handed her, she brought it to her mouth. In a clear voice, she welcomed everyone and said she'd see them inside. People didn't want to hear a speech from the owner, they just wanted to party, and her clubs always gave them what they wanted.

She rocked back on her heels when she felt two sets of strong bodies surround her and lead her back inside.

Malcolm leaned down and whispered, "Selena, you are in *so* much trouble." He nibbled the lobe of one of her ears.

His breath was hot next to her ear. She shivered at the promise of retribution reflected in his eyes.

"I'm not scared of you or your brother." She was happy her voice didn't shake.

"Good," Max said in a guttural voice.

She walked inside. How could these two strangers make her feel so much? She'd been with Tim, her high school boyfriend, for two years before they did the deed. Once they did the deed, he seemed to think it should be done every day. Looking back, she realized she had never really wanted Tim the way he did her. If he hadn't died, she knew they probably wouldn't still be together. Why the hell had she not tried having sex with a normal man before tonight? And to think she gave up her celibacy to not just one man, but two of them.

Exasperated, she ran her hand through her hair and let out a huff. She didn't really want to be working right now, which was another first. She wanted to grab hold of her men…*Whoa…They are not my men. They are just…*"Grrr."

"What's the matter, baby?" Malcolm asked.

Startled, she spun around and came to a stop in the middle of the dance floor. How the heck had they ended up there?

"Do you want to dance?" Max turned her toward him. His eyes seemed to light up from within. They blazed a trail of heat down her body, soaking her brand-new panties.

She pressed her legs together and tried to stop her knees from shaking. "I don't understand what's happening."

Max's brow furrowed. She could see his confusion. Selena needed some space. She didn't like this uncontrolled hunger they created when they closed in on her.

"I can't dance yet. I need to…" She peered behind her and saw the worried expression on Tamara's face giving her an excuse. "I need to check with Tam and make my presence known."

Spinning on her feet, she weaved her way through the already crowded floor. She talked and laughed with the people who stopped to say hello. She eased her way toward the bar, shaking hands without missing a step, and even paused with a smile for a picture with a group of men celebrating a bachelor party. One of the men placed his hand on her ass, and she quickly grabbed it and settled it on her hip.

He beamed down at her, flashing a smile with two dimples on his cheeks. He probably got away with just about anything with that look. Maybe if she'd met him yesterday it would've worked on her. Now, all these men looked like boys to her.

By the time she reached the end of the bar and managed to extricate herself from more prying hands, she was pissed at herself and the two men who did that to her.

"Are you pissed off about something, or two gorgeous men?" Tamara asked.

"Try myself. What the heck am I thinking?" She grabbed her hair with her fist and tugged. "I need to focus on the club, not on men."

"Yeah, but what men," Tamara said, but looked across the room on the opposite side.

Selena heard the beginning beat of Sugarland's "Stuck like Glue" blare through the speakers, and with a smile, stepped up to the bar and hauled herself on top. Within seconds, she had the attention of the room and her Coyote girls joined her. They began with a stomp to the right and a slide and repeated it. By the time the song reached the semi-rap beat they'd turned sideways and strutted around the circular bar.

She heard the clapping and the howls from the crowd as they started shaking their asses, facing the bar. Stomping their boots, they swished down, slapping the bar with their right hand, before popping back up and rocking back and forth, finally ending with a booty shake until they'd turned to face the crowd again.

Selena felt like a rock star and smiled until her jaw ached. She absolutely loved the rush of dancing for a large crowd and gave herself a mental pat on the back. One of the bartenders handed her a microphone and the DJ stopped the music.

"Good evening, Kansas City. How is everyone doing?" Selena asked in her best southern drawl.

The room exploded with cheers and catcalls. Holding up a hand, she waited until it settled. "I would like to thank y'all for coming. I ask that you please respect your bartenders and waitresses, and don't grab them when they're up here dancing." She indicated herself on top of the slick surface.

"Now, without further interruptions, please everyone have a good time and thanks again for coming out tonight."

She turned and handed the microphone to Alicia, one of the bartenders, and felt a set of arms reach up and help her down. Her boots hit the floor and she looked up into Malcolm's face that was set like stone. What did she do to piss this man off? With a quick glance around him, she looked for Max.

"Max had to take care of something." Malcolm growled.

"What is wrong with you?" Selena crossed her arms under her breasts. Malcolm eyed her like a wolf ready to take a bite of his prey.

"Oh, I don't know. I like watching men fondle you. Not!"

"Dear lord. Are you jealous?"

"Duh, Lena…" Malcolm tugged her closer to his body. "I hated seeing them put their hands on you. I had to physically restrain Max, or that fucker who grabbed your ass would've needed surgery to remove his arm from his own ass."

Selena unwound her arms and wrapped them around Malcolm's waist. He was so much taller than her that even in her boots, she had to look up, and up some more. Resting her chin on the center of his chest, she felt his heartbeat.

"I'm glad he didn't do that. I'd hate to have to bail him out of jail," she joked. Malcolm's expression didn't change. "Mal, he can't get upset and neither can you. This is my club. I can take care of myself. That is why I have security."

"We know that, but that doesn't mean we have to like it."

She couldn't think with his body touching hers. In an attempt to put space between them, she stepped back and bumped into a barstool.

"You guys don't have any right to like or not like anything I do. Just because we…" Looking around, she leaned forward. "I'm sorry if I gave you both the wrong impression. I've never, you know, done that before."

She could feel heat climb up her chest, but continued. "I mean, I've had sex, but never with two guys, and actually I've only slept with one other. I'm not sure what the protocol is, and honestly I'm a little freaked, because what I did is just not me and who I am." She spoke so fast, the words seemed to trip over themselves.

He cut off her words with a kiss that made her toes tingle. His mouth descended to the side of her neck. Her fingers gripped his arms, meaning to push him away, but he suckled that bit of flesh beneath her jaw, and she pressed closer to his heat. She should have been upset with him and his brother for their overbearing attitude.

The sudden shove to her body brought her back to their surroundings. A little bit.

Malcolm lifted his mouth and she missed his sucking. “We can’t do this here.”

“We can’t?” she asked, uncertain if she agreed or not.

“Don’t tempt me, baby. I would love to lift that skirt and fuck you here, but I think you might get pissed at me.” He smiled, and she noticed he had one dimple on his right cheek. Damn the man.

“Go get a drink or find your brother. I need to circulate, and no, I do not need a guard dog.” She made a waving motion, hoping he understood, and then walked away. The heat of his stare practically scorched her retreating form. She swore he growled when she added some extra swing to her walk.

# Chapter Ten

The woman was trying to kill him. His dick felt so hard it no longer ached, it throbbed. He couldn't walk around with a tent in his pants. Malcolm focused on breathing and counted to ten. When that didn't work, he counted to fifty, and then a hundred. Finally he felt like he could walk without injuring junior, and looked around for his twin.

He spotted him near the back of the club on the second floor balcony talking to Rafe. He headed toward the stairs and avoided the women who tried to get his attention.

"Hey, gorgeous, you can put your hands on me if you want."

Malcolm stopped midstride to look into the heavily made-up eyes of a young girl, who couldn't be more than legal.

"Thank you for the offer, but I'm taken."

She sniffed. "That bitch doesn't deserve you, honey. I can make you feel really good."

She trailed her long, skinny hands down his chest and tucked them into his waist band. Junior didn't even stir. Yep, his woman had ruined him. He grabbed the girl's wrist and pulled it free. He tilted his lips up, and with a shake of his head he released her.

"Thanks for the offer, but no thanks."

Side-stepping the pouting female, he took the stairs two at a time. He needed to talk to Max and find out what Rafe knew.

Now that they'd found their Fated, if they didn't find Zeus's daughter, they wouldn't get to enjoy her for long. The god believed if she reached her twenty-fifth birthday without an anchor here on Earth, she'd destroy everything around her, and that included *everything*. *Shit, what a fucked-up time to find Selena only to lose her.*

"What's up, Rafe?"

He listened as Rafe and Max filled him in on Rafe's journey, and how he came to be here. Seems he ran into a voodoo priestess who told him his destiny lay in Texas and the one he searched for. Malcolm never discounted a seer and their talents. Many gods and goddesses had found pleasure on Earth with humans and left behind a part of themselves inside the ones they'd touched.

The Ravens had fought many wars, and come across more than he could count, of the descendants from these couplings. Most were good people with extraordinary talents, but lately there seemed to be an uprising of the bad ones. They'd even begun banding together and calling themselves Cronites. They were a vicious lot with an aversion to the sun. Some called them vampires like in the movies, but Malcolm had a suspicion they had something to do with Cronus. Hence the name Cronites.

"So you ran into over a dozen of those leeches and came away basically unscathed. I'd say they are not so tough. What do you think they're after?"

"Max, is your brother really that dumb?" Rafe asked.

"Hey, I resent that remark," Malcolm said, and dodged the slap to the back of his head.

"Shut up, Mal. This is serious."

"No shit, man. I was just joking, you both need to chill."

He could see his brother fought the urge to deck him and tried to tamp down the urge to make him. He needed to expel some energy, and it didn't look as though it would be in Selena's delectable body for a few more hours. He checked his watch and grimaced.

"This is nothing to joke about."

Rafe poked him in the chest, and Malcolm grabbed the bigger man's wrist and twisted, holding it out to the left of his body, keeping his right hand free. Malcolm seethed, "Don't fucking put your hands on me, boy, or I'll rip it off and you'll be left with only one hand to jack off with."

Malcolm jerked as Max stepped between them and spoke into his mind. "*You need to release Rafe now. You do not want to upset Selena.*"

Malcolm looked over Max's shoulder into the pitch black eyes of Rafe and released his wrist. He knew Rafe could have broken his hold, but was glad one of them had kept their anger in check.

"Dude, I'm sorry." He raked his hands through his hair and thought of cutting it. Looking at Max and his short hair, he changed his mind.

"No problem, Mal. I shouldn't have pushed you. I can literally feel the energy pouring off you both. You need to go find your woman and get laid."

"No shit, Sherlock, but I don't see her leaving the club until closing time."

Malcolm saw Rafe's nostrils flare and his pupils dilate. He watched as Rafe swallowed and averted his gaze before Malcolm could see what had caused the coldest man he knew to react that way.

Rafe slapped Max on the back and stuck his hand out toward him. In a strong grip, they grasped forearms and bumped chests. Malcolm was glad his friend had forgiven him. He had no doubt if they were to fight, it would be bloody and he wasn't sure who'd come out the winner.

When they'd been training, all the elite twelve sparred against each other to hone their skills, but each man had similar powers and strength. Any time he came up against Rafe or Vin he always felt they held back, like they needed to hide their true strength.

"I'm going to do a circuit of the club, find me some pussy, and get laid."

Malcolm laughed. Rafe didn't need to do a circuit. All he needed to do was crook his finger and he'd have half a dozen women lined up to suck or fuck him right there.

Thinking of sucking and fucking, he scanned the bar, looking for Selena. He found her with a glow surrounding her. He blinked his eyes and opened them again. "*What the hell is that?*" He asked Max mentally, whose eyes had trained onto Selena and the man crowding into her personal space.

Malcolm saw his brother grip the railing and prepare to launch himself over the fifty-foot drop. He grabbed his arm and stopped Max before he could leap.

"Yo, bro, you can't act like Spiderman and jump."

"That's not Spiderman, Mal. Do you see that dumb prick touching our woman?"

"I see him, but I also see our girl taking care of herself."

The glow surrounding Selena seemed to get brighter with her anger if Malcolm could guess. He didn't want to stand and wait to see what the asshole did. He took off at a fast pace and hit the stairs at a jog. By the time he reached Selena, she'd extricated herself from the dumbass and had moved up to the bar again.

He groaned when he realized it was time for another performance on top of the bar. He really didn't think he could stand to see her gyrating again for all those people. He wanted a personal dance just for him and Max.

Malcolm pictured her wearing nothing but his top as she strutted to the fast beat of a song. He could see her swinging her hips and starting to unbutton the top covering her naked flesh. He was brought up short when a group of drooling men bumped into him from behind.

Max gripped his shoulder and squeezed, helping him focus on Selena here and now instead of his fantasy.

He laughed when the women raised their arms, touching their shoulders with a hand, and the first one did a breakdance move where her right hand rolled all the way up her arm, then her chest, down to her feet, and jerking the motion back up and down her left arm until the next woman did the same.

He didn't expect that, and there was no denying Selena looked sexy when she did the same, only adding a swivel of her hips. He wanted her to swivel her hips like that when he had his cock buried deep inside her. The song ended and he stepped forward to help her down, startling her.

"You look hot up there." He indicated the counter.

"Thank you. I love it. I feel like a rock star, ya know?" Her eyes sparkled and blinded him from everyone else in the room.

Max elbowed him aside and wrapped his arms around Selena. He pulled her up onto a stool and stepped between her legs. Malcolm watched as Max leaned forward and murmured something in her ear. He saw Selena's tongue peek out, licking her lips. He wanted those lips wrapped around his cock.

*Son of a bitch.* He needed to get his emotions and his hormones under control, before he pulled Selena from his brother's arms and fucked her right on that stool.

"Do you have to stay and clean up when the bar closes, or do you let your employees take care of it?" Max asked.

"Oh, I usually take the money up and count it before I put it in the safe. By the time I finish, the cleaning is usually done." She looked into Max's eyes. "Why do you ask?"

"Will you come home with us?"

She looked startled and pressed her hand to her chest. She opened her mouth and closed it again. He didn't like the deer in the headlights look she had. He crowded into her side and cupped her jaw.

Turning her face toward him, Malcolm pressed his forehead against hers. "Don't be scared of us, Lena. We would never hurt you."

He looked into her eyes as he spoke and saw the gray eyes turn liquid silver, with an eerie light that had him stepping back. He released her jaw and trailed his hand down her neck and tapped her nipple that stood up, begging for their attention.

He and Max blocked the view of anyone stupid enough to try and look at them. Max stood close to her body while Malcolm pushed her thighs wide open. Malcolm could see her skirt touching her hips. He screened their actions and blurred their presence, so anyone looking would see the three of them, but wouldn't be able to make out what they were doing.

He didn't want anyone else, other than Max, to see her legs spread and her nipples so hard they stood out like two twin points. He could feel his mouth watering, and had to remind himself they couldn't fuck her right here in the middle of her club. She would hate them for that, and how could he explain to her that nobody would see?

He didn't think she would believe the truth. *Selena, honey, nobody saw us fuck you senseless because we aren't human. We are creations of Zeus.* Nope, he was not gonna go there with her yet.

"I can't think when you guys are touching me. Let me get through this evening and then we'll…" She swallowed and continued, "I'll let you know, okay?"

Malcolm saw his brother open his mouth to protest. "Okay baby, just try to enjoy yourself. I'm going to take Max out back for a chat."

She nodded and smiled. The action wiped the hard expression off of Max's face. Malcolm wanted her to trust them, but in reality, she'd just met them. Sure they'd spoken several times, and every time he'd heard her voice, junior stood up and saluted. He'd taken more cold showers than he cared to count, and had tried slaking his lust with other women, but the little man between his legs had other plans.

He should've realized then that something was happening. "Fuck me," he muttered.

"Me too," Max agreed.

Malcolm raised his hand to slap Max on the back of the head, but Selena's laugh stopped him with his arm raised.

"You two are trouble with a capital T."

She squirmed, and Max stepped back with a look of reluctance. "We'll be around if you need us."

"Okay." Selena smiled.

Damn, her smile made him feel good. She hopped to the floor with a shimmy of her hips and brushed past him. He stopped her with a hand to her arm and brushed his lips on the corner of hers. Happy to hear her breath catch, he patted her ass and let her go.

She twitched her behind with an exaggerated swing and smiled over her shoulder. He clenched his fists at his side and gave her a fierce look, mouthing the word *later.*

He continued through the back door with Max right behind him. The buildings were connected in a U shape, creating the sense of an alley between the next block of buildings. He turned and kicked a can toward a dumpster against the far wall. When no rats scattered, he raised his brows.

"It's not like New York, bro. Hell, I mean we'd have to kick rats and bums out of the way to even get through. This place is really clean and classy."

"There are some places like that here, too, just not in my area." Max looked around with his hands on his hips.

Malcolm opened his mouth to ask Max a question, when he was slammed in the back. He grunted and ducked the next blow. "Fuck me," he roared when he saw over half a dozen men circling them.

"I told you I don't swing that way."

Shit, they must be in trouble, Max never joked.

He and Max stepped into the middle of the men, if you could call the ugly sons of bitches surrounding them men. Opening a link to Max he said, "*I don't think these guys are normal.*"

*"What made you think that? Could it be the unnaturally long claws, or the half beast look they got going on?"*

Yep...they might be in a bit of trouble. Well shit, he was no pussy. With that, he lashed out with a butterfly kick and knocked the biggest of the six flat on his back. He reached down and snapped his neck with a hard twist. Someone jumped on his back and sank their fangs into his shoulder.

"Dude, your breath is rank," Malcolm said, flipping the creature over his shoulder, before his arm was grabbed and twisted behind his back. He slammed the back of his head into the attacker's face, hearing a satisfying crunch, and something wet flowing down his back. The thing released his arm. Malcolm jumped to the side, sucking in his breath as the other guy slashed at his gut.

He heard fist connecting flesh and could smell the acrid scent of blood. Not the copper scent of humans, but a stench that smelled like sulfur and rotten flesh. A thick, hairy forearm wrapped around his throat from behind, cutting off his ability to swallow. He planted his feet firmly on the concrete ground to prevent the thing from toppling him backward.

Reaching his arms behind his back, he gripped the big beast's head and jabbed his thumbs into its eyes. He heard an eerie yowl as the thing released him. He turned and punched the fucker in the throat, and with a quick twist, jerked its head off, before he tossed it toward the one he could see in his peripheral vision.

"Motherfucking bastards," Max yelled.

Malcolm didn't take his eyes off the mountain of a beast in front of him. It was wielding a knife with serrated edges on both sides. From the way he twisted and turned the piece of steel, Malcolm had no doubt the thing knew how to use it.

The throbbing of the music from inside the club, along with the sound of flesh being struck by fists, could be heard. The door to the bar opened, making the music blare louder. The door shut with a bang, muffling the noises from the alley. He didn't need to take his eyes off the knife to know Rafe had just entered the fray.

"What's doin', boys?" Rafe shook his head. "Damn, I guess I'm gonna have to kick some ugly motherfuckers' asses now."

Malcolm smiled at the excitement in the other man's voice. Rafe sighed loudly and cracked his knuckles before he stepped out of Malcolm's view.

Malcolm curved his hand and motioned to the man-beast. "Come on, pussy. What're you waiting for, an invitation?"

The thing roared and lunged forward. Malcolm grabbed his wrist and snapped it backward. Hearing a satisfying scream, he continued squeezing until the knife dropped. He twisted the arm up and around the guy's back and palmed the back of its head as he slammed it into the brick wall. The big beast went slack in his hold, but Malcolm held him up and continued slamming until the wall was no longer separated by the head.

Looking down, he saw bits of brick had broken off and the ugly thing no longer had any shape to its head.

"You can't protect her forever," the smallest of the creatures snarled.

"Protect who?" Malcolm advanced on the thing that was close to his own size, and looked more like a man than an animal.

The thing flashed his fangs and gave them a parody of a smile. "Fools who follow gods that don't even care if you live or die are stupid," he spat.

Malcolm cleared the space separating them, grabbing the knife the other one dropped as he flew at the cretin. The thing disappeared before Malcolm reached him. He jerked to a stop and looked around in a battle stance, prepared for an attack. He backed up to the wall and saw Max had killed two of the beings, and Rafe had his arm wrapped around the neck of the last one.

Max had his hand on the chest of one of the beasts, and within moments it disappeared in a cloud of dust. He squatted next to the other, and did the same thing while Rafe snapped the neck of the flailing one in his arms. He didn't drop it like Malcolm would have. Instead he inhaled, and there was a flash and a bang as the thing exploded.

Rafe and Max turned toward him and quirked their brows. "What? I killed two," he said, pointing at the bodies.

"Did you find out anything before you bashed their heads?" Max asked.

"Dude, should I have taken them out for a drink and asked what the fuck they wanted?" He stood up and looked at the blood covering his body and grimaced.

Selena would not want to see brain matter on him and blood that made him gag. He coughed and with a thought, wiped all traces of the blood and gore from his body, and then replaced his clothes with clean ones.

"Did you see that pussy? He looked like he was gonna hurl," Rafe said.

"Up yours, dickhead." Malcolm smirked.

Max stepped up to the two on the ground and shook his head when he looked at the faceless man. Malcolm met his gaze and lifted his shoulder. He wasn't going to apologize for smashing the thing's face in. He probed its mind, but all he saw was a red haze inside with the command to get the girl. The other one didn't even have that much thought going on.

"I couldn't get a single thought out of any of the ones I fought. How about you? Did you get anything from your guy?" Max asked Rafe.

Rafe shook his head and Malcolm watched as his body blurred, and then he stood looking immaculate in his black cargo pants with chains, a black muscle top, and a black leather jacket covering his broad shoulders. The dude looked scary as fuck, but somehow he pulled more pussy than his fair share.

Malcolm raised his hand and got their attentions with the wicked-looking knife fisted.

"Did you guys see the one who disappeared?" When both men looked at him like he'd gone nuts he continued, "He kinda stood off to the side watching us. He said something about not being able to protect her all the time, flashed some fangs, and poof."

"Damn…they've never been able to poof before," Rafe said.

"Shit," Max yelled and paced. "This can't be good. Nope. Not good at all. First we find our Fated and now these, what the fuck are they called?" Looking around, Max rubbed the back of his neck.

"I'd say a cross between a grizzly bear and a man who really needs a shower. Those things stank," Malcolm said.

"They call themselves Cronites. When I met up with them in Texas, they sneered that we were called Ravens but were nothing but dogs. How the fuck do they know anything about us?"

"Cronus," Max and Malcolm answered in unison.

## Chapter Eleven

Max stopped pacing and looked at his two top enforcers. He tried to swallow around the burning in his throat. He refused to admit the first being might have damaged him.

"What are we going to do?" he rumbled.

"Hey, I'm the one who got a hickey from one of them. Why do you sound so messed up?" Malcolm said.

Max's nostrils flared and he spun around in a loose-limbed stance, prepared to attack, but nobody was there. "I'm jumping at shadows. I need to go check on Selena. Can you two make sure there's no evidence left for anyone to find?"

"Sure, but I'm keeping this." Malcolm indicated the knife.

"Look at the designs on that, Max." Rafe pointed to the blade.

Max gazed at the patterns and tried to figure out what the symbols meant. He had a niggling in the back of his mind what they stood for, but an overwhelming urge to rush inside and check on Selena coursed through him. He had learned over his long existence to listen to that inner voice.

"Malcolm, flash that blade into the safe at my house. Until we know what those symbols mean, I don't want it out in the open."

He didn't wait to see if they agreed before he jerked the door open and scanned the interior for Selena. He let out a breath when he found her strolling through the crowds. She seemed totally oblivious to the appreciative glances she received from the men, and the jealous stares of some of the women.

"You are making the other women jealous with your beauty," he whispered in her ear.

She jumped and spun in his arms. She looked up at him, and he felt his heart melt under her gaze. She smelled like strawberries and honey. His mouth watered, wanting a taste of her essence. He could smell her excitement, and watched her nose flare like she could scent him too.

"Where is your brother?" she asked, and looked around his body.

"You smell like heaven. Will you dance with me?" Max asked, steering them to the dance floor without answering her question.

She smiled when he backed her further across the floor into a secluded section where the lights didn't reach. He made a mental note to talk with security about the lack of lighting. Even though he could see perfectly they couldn't, making it a hazard.

With the single thought of tasting Selena, he placed her hands on his shoulders, forgetting about everything except his woman. Trailing his hands down her sides, he wrapped his arms around her ass and lifted her up.

His mouth descended and captured hers into a melding of lips and teeth and tongue. He heard a groan and wasn't sure if it was his or hers, or both of them. He thought he might die if he didn't feel her wet heat surrounding his dick.

"Wrap your legs around me, baby," he said in a guttural voice he didn't recognize.

Selena inched her legs up and locked her ankles behind his back. She might be only five feet and a stone, but her legs were long and muscular and they gripped his hips. He thrust his pelvis forward, letting her feel his hardness at the apex between her thighs.

Her hands crept up his back and held his head as her tongue peeked out and licked his lips. He met her tongue with his own, and nearly dropped her when she sucked his into her mouth like she had his dick earlier.

"I need to be inside you, Selena. Will you let me?" he asked, rocking his erection against her dripping panties.

Her legs squeezed spasmodically each time he pressed forward and up, hitting her clit each time. She gasped and reached between their bodies and fumbled with his belt.

With one step, Max had her back against the wall and released one butt cheek to help her open his fly, freeing his erection before tugging her panties aside to test her readiness.

"Oh yes. Yes. Touch me Max," Selena wailed.

He slipped one finger inside her. At the feel of her inner walls gripping him, he added a second digit, pumping in and out of her wetness. He placed his thumb over her hard little nub, and pressed down as he pushed in a third finger. She clamped down and tossed her head back, hitting the wall with a thunk. He continued fucking her with his fingers and rubbing her clit until he felt her vaginal walls flutter.

As she rode out her orgasm, he covered her mouth and swallowed her cries. Feeling the tension leave her, he pulled his fingers out and she whimpered. He didn't give her a chance to object before he shoved his dick in, sheathing himself in her tight heat.

"Damn. You feel so fucking good," Max said.

"So do you," she panted.

She opened glazed, passion-filled eyes, amazing him with the silver lights glinting from within. He cradled her head in his palm to protect it from the hard wall behind her. Bracing his feet on the floor, he bent and shoved up and out, and then up again. He continued in a slow, easy rhythm until her body started moving with his.

She squeezed her inner muscles, and he could swear she cut off the blood supply to the head of his dick. He couldn't help but think it wouldn't be a bad way to go, fucking his Fated as she squeezed the life out of him with her pussy wrapped around him like the tightest, sweetest vise.

He pulled back out, swiveling his hips as he pushed back inside and bumped her clit with his pelvis. Her eyes flew wide, and her mouth opened in a silent scream. He leaned back, changing the point of friction to her and where their bodies connected.

His strokes became frantic and shallow, his groans low and guttural. His hands gripped her ass cheeks, moving her up and down as he continued to fuck her. He thrust his hips hard, holding himself deep inside her.

"Don't move, baby, just hold still for a minute." He rested his head on her shoulder.

She grinned, grinding her hips in a circular motion, clenching and releasing her inner muscles around his throbbing flesh. Gods, he loved Kegel muscles. There was nothing sexier than a woman who liked to fuck. She worked hard to make him come, but he wanted to feel her come all over his cock before he let go. Her pussy relentlessly tugged at him. She raised herself up and slammed back down, squeezing and relaxing, trying to milk him.

Max closed his eyes and tried to count backward, but kept losing count. Finally, he gave up and reached between their bodies to stroke her clit. He stilled her movements with a tighter grip and ground his pelvis into hers, trapping his hand on her quivering flesh.

"Are you trying to make me come?"

"Don't you want to?" she pouted.

"I think we should come together."

"Yeah," she nodded. "We definitely should."

He rubbed his chest against the rock-hard pebbles of her nipples and cursed the clothes separating them. He pounded into her as she worked his body like no one else. She fell into another orgasm and surprised him with the force of her contractions as his seed erupted, filling her with his essence. He pumped into her, continuing to fill her, and felt her body respond with another mini-orgasm.

The pleasure was intense, the spasms that rocked his body incredible as he twitched, embedded deep inside her. He groaned and held her down, his muscles contracting as he floated in a place between agony and heaven.

Taking a deep breath, he collapsed, pinning her body between his and the wall. "Oh damn, I think you killed me," he gasped.

"Max, I can't breathe," Selena pushed at his shoulders.

"Oh, baby, I'm sorry," he muttered as he lifted his weight off her body but kept his dick buried inside her. They stayed that way as they tried to find their bearings.

"Let me down. I need to go to the ladies room."

"Don't want to," he whined. *Freaking whining like a baby.*

She shook in his arms and he raised his head from her shoulder.

"Did you just cry like a little boy?"

"If I did, does that mean I get to stay right here?" he asked, pumping his hips, and his newly awakened cock, inside her.

"Ha ha…Let me down, big guy. I have an hour before the club closes."

He wanted to convince her to stay right where she was, but one look at her face told him she wouldn't agree. He didn't want to piss her off. With a huff of a breath, he gave a sigh of disappointment.

"Can you stand?"

"I think so."

He held her hips, started to pull out until he saw her wince. He groaned, taking it slower, and rested his hands on her sides. She stroked his cheek, offering him comfort.

"Are you okay?" Max asked.

"Shut up!"

Stunned at her outburst, he dropped her legs. She wobbled and he reached out to steady her. "Did you tell me to shut up?"

Laughing, she pulled her skirt down and grimaced. "It worked, didn't it?"

He must've looked like a goof. She beamed at him and he felt his lips twitch. "Yeah, it did."

When she started to walk past him, Max stopped her with a light touch on her arm. Her eyes jerked up to his, and he bent down, rubbed her nose with his, and kissed the side of her mouth. "Next time I get my dick in you, I won't be alone. And we won't be leaving your body until all three of us are so exhausted we can't move, let alone walk." He patted her ass.

She stood with her mouth open while he tucked himself back into his pants, fixed his shirt, and fastened his belt. "Let's go. I'll walk with you."

She opened her mouth, but he pressed his fingers to her lips. She bit the tip and he groaned. "Don't start, Lena, unless you want me to carry you back to that corner. Speaking of corner, you need to have your security add some lighting back here."

"I'm kinda glad there wasn't any. I could barely make out your face, so I knew nobody could see us. Maybe I'll add a table back here with a circular booth."

"Wrong kind of club." Max tapped her nose and led her back onto the dance floor.

They skirted the crowd and she headed toward the closest restroom. He waited with one foot on the wall across from the door, unable to avoid the women who stopped to talk to him. A redhead in a too-tight, strapless top that barely restrained bowling-ball-sized tits approached him. She trailed a bloodred nail down his chest, and made circles around the last visible button on his shirt. He grabbed her finger and held it in one big fist.

"Sorry, but I'm taken."

"Mmm…" She licked her lips. "We can have a party. Your girl will never have to know."

Selena stepped out into the hall, banging the door so hard it hit the wall with a resounding crash. Max still had a hold of the viper's hand, amazed when she didn't seem to notice the sound the door made.

He had a sardonic smile on his face as he shook his head. "My girl knows."

Selena grabbed the taller woman by the back of her hair, yanking her away from Max's body.

"Get the hell away from him, you fucking whore. He said he was taken," Selena yelled. She dodged the fist the other woman aimed at her head as she twisted in her hold.

Max crossed his arms and watched in amusement, as a hunk of hair came out of the mass of red locks Selena still held in her fist. She threw the screaming woman down the hall and tossed the hair extensions into her face.

"You're a crazy bitch," the other woman spat.

"Yep, and I got the shirt that says it, too. Now go to the bar and I'll buy you a drink, but make no mistake, little girl, I catch you touching what's mine again, and I'll do more than yank your fake hair out."

"Fuck you."

"Shit…Did I miss the cat fight?" Malcolm asked, passing the other woman as she stomped down the hall.

Selena covered her face with both hands and trembled.

Malcolm wrapped his arms around her shoulders and cuddled her close. "How come you're crying?" he asked in a soothing voice.

Selena looked up, and Max saw tears of mirth light her eyes. "Whew! That was fun."

Malcolm looked at her like she might attack him at any moment, and Max couldn't control his chuckle.

"Come here, woman." Max tugged her out of his brother's arms.

"Uh, Max?" Malcolm asked.

"Our girl has claws." He hugged her back to his front. "I promise you, I didn't enjoy her touch. You are all I can think about." He plucked her nipples until they stood erect.

The music in the club quieted and they heard the DJ announce last call. Selena wiggled out of his embrace and pointed a finger at him, and then Malcolm.

"You two are trouble." She spun on her toes and stomped back toward the bar.

"I love you too, sweetheart," Malcolm quipped.

She didn't pause in her angry stride, but with her hand raised high, she twisted her wrist and flipped him the bird.

"Oh yeah, baby, I definitely swing that way!" Malcolm said

Max slapped him on the back of his head and prepared to block a blow. His brother laughed, and they both turned to watch, until her twitching little behind disappeared behind a wall of bodies.

"Did you and Rafe see anything out of the ordinary, or find any clues as to who the Cronites were looking for?" Max asked.

He looked through his brother's mind and followed the path he and Rafe had taken and cursed when he saw they couldn't find anything.

"That's it, no trail? Hell man, there had to have been hundreds, if not thousands, of females wandering around through all the clubs down here," Malcolm said.

"I need to call the Ravens here. If I'm right, and those things were created by Cronus, we're going to need all our men to defeat them."

* * * *

Cronus sat on his bloodred throne while one of his slaves sucked his cock and another his balls. He gazed across the stone floor littered with bodies, writhing in ecstasy and pain, and closed his eyes.

"Harder. Suck me harder." He growled, and both women hollowed out their cheeks. The one with his dick took him to the back of her throat, and they both hummed in pleasure, sending a pleasurable shock down his shaft.

He scooted closer to the edge of his seat, spreading his legs wider, and grabbed the hand of the woman tonguing his balls and pressed it to his ass. She knew what he wanted. With a finger slick from her saliva, she worked two fingers into his ass and played his prostate like a pro.

"Yeah, that's it. I'm going to come," he warned them as he shot his load down a greedy throat, feeling it tighten around him until the one with her fingers up his ass pushed her head off and finished sucking him through his orgasm. They both licked him clean and rested their heads on his thighs, looking up at him with love in their eyes.

He rubbed the heads of both women and heard a bellow from below. “Go to my chamber and wait for me. I’ll be there shortly, but don’t touch yourself or each other.”

Watching the naked forms of his two newest lovers, he sighed. His latest creations were getting better every day at pleasing him. His female creations were perfect. His males, not so much. Hearing a commotion outside the great hall, he slung his right leg over the arm of his throne and waited for his guards to open the door.

Cronus looked down in disgust at the lack of attention his other creations paid to a possible threat. He flashed them out of his sight before he killed them. Tapping his long, black claw on the arm, his patience worn thin, he jerked the doors open with a thought and in stumbled dumb, dumber, and something even worse. He sighed in exasperation, wondering what the hell was wrong with them.

Balky, his smallest but most cunning soldier, recovered first. He quickly fell on both knees, bowing low with his arms stretched out and his forehead resting on the stone.

Cronus waited until dumb and dumber followed his actions. Finally, bless the goddesses, the dumb shits got down on one knee and then two.

“Enough,” he roared. With a thought, he had both idiots in a position that was sure to make them resemble a pretzel, instead of road kill, and motioned Balky to him.

Realizing the fool still had his head down, Cronus jerked him to his feet, and enjoyed the way the man—if you could call him that—walked like a puppet with strings attached. At the image, strings appeared on the other man’s hands and feet, and for amusement, he had Balky dancing like a fool.

He loved the power he had over his minions. They followed without question, unlike his son and the other morons on Mount

Olympus. He had plans for the traitors, and couldn't wait to put the final piece of his surprise into action.

Stealing his granddaughter had been easy. Zeus and his arrogance made it like taking candy from a baby, or maybe more like taking a baby from a baby would be more appropriate.

He rubbed his hands together, and looked up to see Balky suspended from strings with his eyes bulging out of his face. Fear was etched on every feature. He should be scared. He could see the events leading Balky back to his compound, and the failure of securing the woman he'd been sent to retrieve.

It should've been easy. Cronus had given Balky the vicinity, even had it narrowed down to a small location, and sent some of his best soldiers to take with him.

"Where is my granddaughter?" He asked in a deceptively calm voice.

"We…we were ambushed, My Lord," Balky stammered.

There was no need to ask by whom. He saw the twin Ravens fighting the soldiers through Balky's eyes, and looked on in distaste as the one with long hair tore the head off of one man, and then pounded the head in of another. They were so barbaric in their fighting. Cronus enjoyed spilling blood and dismembering those who opposed him. He loved exerting his powers, but he was a much more hands-off kind of ruler. He would have, and could have eliminated them with a thought. A niggling notion that he couldn't actually do it with the creations of Zeus tried to push forward, but he squashed it just as quickly.

"I gave you my fiercest warriors. You outnumbered their two." He growled.

"Yes, Sire, but they…"

Cronus silenced him with a wave of his hand. "I don't want excuses. Did you find out anything useful? Did you locate the goddess?"

Cronus had a few allies on Mount Olympus, and it had been easy to get one of them to open a door for him, to enter the baby's room and steal her right out from under her parents' noses. They'd been so arrogant in their assumptions that he couldn't harm them anymore. Stupid fools couldn't even keep track of their offspring, and they thought to banish him to this hellish place. He smiled, a sardonic twist on his lips.

He'd showed them though, hadn't he? Now, if he could just locate the damn girl before her twenty-fifth birthday, he could reclaim his throne on Mount Olympus. He thought back to that night. How he'd escaped with their precious child and grimaced at having to leave her in a dumpster.

Not a fitting place for a goddess, but he'd had to improvise. The damn elite twelve had been called, and they didn't quit until they won their battle. Zeus had created them, and empowered them, with all the strengths of the gods, but with humanity thrown in, giving them a soft underbelly that Cronus had no problem using to his advantage.

Flicking his wrist, he released Balky and pinned him with a glare. "You will find my granddaughter and bring her to me or let them kill you, because if you come back without her I will take care of you myself. Believe me when I say what happened to the others will look like a love story compared to what I will do with you." Another flick of his wrist and he sat alone in his great hall.

He looked around at the bloodred walls, coated with things better left unsaid, then pictured his throne room on Olympus and cursed. The walls shook and debris fell, coating the filthy floor littered with a mix of food, blood, and other bodily fluids. Grimacing, he sighed, and with only a thought the room shone like a ruby, instead of blood, and glowed with a myriad of colors reflecting back at him. Nodding, he flashed himself to his bed chambers and the pleasures awaiting him there.

# Chapter Twelve

Selena followed Malcolm as he led the way out of the club. It took longer to close the bar since it was the first night, but she couldn't help but smile at the amount of people who'd shown up. Tamara usually stayed and helped, but before the last patron had left, she said she didn't feel well and left. A frown pulled at her brow. Tamara never left early.

Malcolm turned with a grin tugging at his lips. She gave an answering smile as she looked into his too-handsome face. Thoughts of Tamara vanished with the knowledge of all the naughty things the two brothers had promised her and done to her. A flush she was glad the darkness hid had to be covering her body.

Although she had only just met Malcolm and Max face-to-face, she already knew they held a part of her soul. Her mind turned to mush, and her bones like jelly, just from the searing looks they gave her. She could feel her heart pounding in anticipation of the night to come, and an answering throb at the heart of her. It was maddening to want them so much when it had taken Tim two years to get into her pants.

She tried to bring up a mental picture of her ex, but no matter how hard she tried, she couldn't see him. It had to be unnatural to want two men so desperately. Especially ones she hardly knew. Hands sliding up her sides, caressing her breasts, brought her back to the present.

"What put that look on your face?" Malcolm asked, tapping her nose and running his finger between her brows.

"Nothing," she lied.

"What did we say about lying to us?"

"Don't threaten me, Mal." She pushed him away, blinking her eyes to dispel the threat of tears. She dipped her chin to hide her emotions.

"Oh, baby, please don't cry. I'm sorry. You know I would never hurt you, and neither would Max. We've been searching for the one who would complete us for years." He lifted her face up to his with a finger under the chin. "You complete us, Selena. There is nothing we wouldn't do to ensure your happiness and wellbeing."

"How can you say that? You just met me." She swiped angrily at the tears leaking from her eyes.

"Because every time I thought of you or heard your voice, I got hard and my heart would thud. I swear I have never had that reaction before."

She sniffed and wrapped her hands around her bare arms. Malcolm's eyes seemed to glow in the lights from the street, and she shivered seeing the truth in those blue depths.

"I'm scared, Malcolm. I'm not sure how this will work." She gestured between the two of them, and waved a hand toward the building where Max was still holed up with Rafe. "A relationship with one person is hard enough, but the three of us? Won't there be jealousy or anger if I spend time with one of you and not the other?"

"Did I look pissed when I met you and Max outside the ladies room?" She looked at him with a puzzled look and he continued. "I knew you and he had recently fucked. You both smelled like sex, and before you ask"—he placed his hand over her mouth—"I didn't see you two, nor did Max tell me. We would never kiss and tell. Sweetheart, there are going to be times when you are with one of us alone, and I can guarantee you we won't be angry. Jealous maybe, because we weren't there…but never angry."

She closed her eyes and rested her head on his chest, listening to the beating of his heart. The steady beat calming her own racing one.

"Take me home, Malcolm."

He grunted and leaned down, capturing her lips in a fierce kiss, pressing his cock into her lower stomach, awakening a hunger in her only they could satisfy. He pulled back with a lick to her lips, their breathing labored as they struggled to take in a breath. She relished the effect she had on him.

"Let's go." He grabbed her hand. "Do you know how to ride?" He gestured toward his Ducati sitting next to the curb.

She stared, wide-eyed as she looked at the sleek machine that shouted his name. "I think I can handle it." She raised her chin and took a step toward his bike.

He gave her a small pink helmet, and she smiled at the girlie thing and then frowned.

"I bought this just for you, Lena. I have never taken another woman riding with me." He laughed. "You are so transparent I could see you were about to refuse to put it on. I love that you feel possessive of me and Max. Hell, if I'm being honest, it makes me hard when you get all pissy."

"Did you just say I'm being pissy?" She pinned him with a glare and the dumbass laughed even harder. Didn't he know that she could do some serious damage to his family jewels? She eyed his growing package and smirked.

"Don't look at junior like that, or he's likely to jump out and bite you," Malcolm said, snapping his teeth together.

"Let's go, big boy. I'm tired of standing here all night, and if you keep it up I might bite you."

She placed the helmet on her head and watched as he snapped his into place.

He swung his left leg over the bike and patted the seat behind him. Strolling forward, she grabbed his arm and straddled the seat as he sat looking over his shoulder. Selena leaned forward and wrapped both arms around his waist. The muscles of his stomach jumped at her caress. She rubbed up, and then down all the way to his thighs, lightly trailing her fingers over the erection straining to get out.

A growl came from him, followed by his hands grabbing hers, placing her tingling palms on his flat belly. She loved the sexy sounds he emitted. With a turn of a key, and a twist of his hand, he fired the bike and smoothly flowed onto the road.

Releasing a breath, she rested against him and let her body go lax. Knowing Malcolm would never allow anything to happen to her, she let her mind drift.

By the time they reached Max's estate, she was a quivering mass of need. Having her chest pressed up against Malcolm as he expertly drove them through town to the winding roads leading up to his brother's home felt so good. With the machine throbbing between her legs and her skirt pushed up to her waist, she wouldn't be surprised to see a damp spot on the leather seat. Good lord she was becoming a right hussy. She unhooked her helmet, handing it to Malcolm, who hung it on the handlebars.

She let her hand wander down Malcolm's front, happy to see she wasn't the only one affected by their drive. She wondered if he got a hard-on every time he rode or if it was from being close to her. She hoped it was the latter.

The silence finally broke into her erotic musings and she got her first view of their location. She heard Malcolm chuckle and jolted at the sensuality the noise held. With a start, she realized her hand cupped his dick through his jeans. It seemed to twitch in her hand.

He twisted in the seat, making her grip loosen and maneuvered her around his body so she sat facing him. With her legs draped over his thighs, that rigid pole between his legs now throbbed against her core, soaking her already wet panties. At the rate she was going, she would need to carry a backpack full of fresh undies or walk around with damp ones all day.

Malcolm tugged her tighter against him. "I always get excited when I feel the purr of an engine under me, whether it's a motorcycle or a car, but having you ride bitch almost made me come in my pants."

His words stunned her, leaving her speechless, not that he gave her a chance to answer before he swooped down. His face was the only thing she could see. In a clash of lips and teeth, he claimed her mouth in a kiss so erotic she melted into him.

Wrapping her legs around his hips, she rocked forward, hitting her clit on his shaft with the press of their bodies. She trembled as a mini-climax took her completely unaware.

He jerked his mouth away, his face like granite. He stood with her wrapped around him like a monkey and maneuvered them off the bike, amazing her with his strength.

She didn't take the time to inspect her surroundings as he walked them into his brother's home and up the stairs. She barely noticed the calm, neutral colors as he nearly jogged them down a long hallway and into a room. A huge, king-sized bed with a canopy sat in the middle of the space. She inhaled the fragrant breeze that blew through the open curtains, floating like ghosts in the wind.

Gasping, she opened her eyes as he threw her on top of the big bed. He stood with his legs braced apart and his chest heaving like he'd run a marathon.

"By the goddesses, I have dreamed of seeing you like this."

She looked down at her skirt that had ridden up past her hips. The panties he'd given her were completely exposed to his gaze. She shimmied and tried to push the fabric down to cover her exposed flesh. He placed a big hand on her thigh and trailed it up the inside of her leg, stopping at the juncture in the middle.

He rubbed his thumb back and forth over her mound, and she saw his eyes glow an eerie blue. She was sure the strange effect had to be a trick of the moon or light filtering through the curtains. He shut his lids and pulled his hand back, bringing it to his nose, and inhaled her scent.

"Malcolm," she whispered. His actions stunned her and turned her on.

"You smell so goddamn good." He shucked his clothes with no care to the fabric as he tore his shirt off. The rest didn't fare much better.

She sat up, prepared to take her top off when his big body pounced on top of her, pinning her to the bed. With a shake of his head, he held her hands above their bodies and his tongue licked over her lips. He nipped his way down her jaw, stopping at the bit of flesh on her shoulder that drove her crazy.

Sitting up, he pulled her tank top off and unhooked her bra, leaving her bare on top as he gazed down at her breasts. Her nipples stood up in tight little points as he raked his gaze down and scooted backward, unsnapping her skirt. He maneuvered her out of the denim and her panties in mere seconds.

His cock looked so hard and painful. She sat up and reached for him, wanting to taste his unique flavor on her tongue again. She swiped her tongue over her suddenly dry lips and leaned forward, engulfing the plum-shaped head in her mouth.

She hummed at the exquisite taste that leaked from the tip, and dipped her tongue into the slit at the top.

He stood on his knees, rubbing her ass as she sucked him with one goal in mind, and that was to taste him as he came down her throat. He pulled her off him, and brought her face up to his, devouring her mouth. His eyes smoldered darkly as his hand tugged her hair. The little bite of pain sent more of her juices down, coating her thighs.

She rubbed her legs together to alleviate the ache centered at the heart of her. He seemed so attuned to her needs. With a growl, he reached down and plunged two fingers into her core, sending shockwaves of pleasure through her.

She shivered as he let her ride out her climax. Her head fell to the side, and his mouth moved over her cheek and nipped her lobe. She felt every movement of his lips, from the soft brushes to the slow glide of his tongue and the sexy nips of his teeth.

"That was number two."

She looked up and opened her mouth to ask what he meant, only to snap it shut when he pressed on a spot inside her that had her moaning, and her eyes rolled back in her head. She'd never had multiple orgasms before, but as Malcolm worked her body, she felt herself climbing toward another one. His head hovered above her nipple and his hot breath feathered over the taut peaks. He engulfed as much of her breast into his mouth and lashed the tip with his tongue. He pulled back with a hard suck and bit the tender flesh. She felt the shock all the way to her toes and fell into a hard, fast climax, squeezing the fingers he held inside her vagina.

"Mmm. That's three," he murmured.

She wanted to ask why he was counting, but he didn't give her a chance to speak. She squeaked and moaned as he laid her down, biting at her tender breasts, and soothed the little hurt with his tongue and a sweet kiss.

She ran her hands through his hair, marveling at the silky texture that brushed across her flesh as he moved down her body on a leisurely journey. She gasped a little puff of air as his tongue dipped into her belly button, before he continued lower. His hair added an extra stimulant that brushed over the areas he caressed with his lips and tongue.

She drew in a sharp breath as he parted her folds with his fingers. He gently opened her to his gaze and his tongue brushed against her engorged bit of flesh. He repeated the motion again and again, leading her internal beat one lash at a time until she exploded on a silent cry. Gripping his hair in both hands, she held him to her until the flick of his tongue became too painful to bear on her oversensitive flesh.

Her whole body shook in shameless pleasure as he crawled up her, kissing the tops of her breasts and claiming her mouth in a sweet, gentle kiss, and entered her in one smooth lunge. It was so tender, tears formed in the corners of her eyes and left a wet trail on her cheeks.

His head snapped up, and she mourned the loss as he pushed himself up with his hands. The only part of their bodies that touched was where they were still joined.

"Why are you crying?" he asked.

She swallowed a lump in her throat and tried to reassure him as more tears fell. She swiped at them and smiled at the confusion in his voice.

"They're happy tears, Mal. I just felt a little overwhelmed for a minute. I've never felt so cherished."

He beamed, and with a wicked smile pulled out and pressed forward with a swivel of his hips, hitting her clit on each downward stroke. She gripped his shoulders and scored his back with her nails, digging her heels into his buttocks to hold him tight as he moved faster. She felt every ridge of his cock as he stroked in and out, her inner muscles urging him on.

Her skin rose in goose bumps of sheer delight and he took her on a journey of passion and pleasure with no limits.

"Faster. Harder," she urged him.

"I need to slow down or this will be over way too soon." He growled.

"I have great faith in your ability to recover quickly." She gave him a sultry look from beneath her lashes.

He brought his mouth down on hers hard and pounded into her furiously, grinding his pelvis on her exposed clit. She lifted her hips, meeting his downward strokes, her pleasure climbing higher and spiraling out of control, until finally she broke apart in spasm after spasm.

"Five," he said against her neck.

He expertly rolled them until she lay on top of him, trying to catch her breath as he stroked her back in a soothing motion.

She raised her head, pushed herself into a sitting position, and rocked her hips from side to side. He twitched inside her. His face looked so hard, but he still didn't let go.

"Why haven't you come? Don't you want to?" she asked.

"I want to see how many times I can make you come before I do."

"Do you have a personal best you're trying to beat?" She slapped a hand over her mouth. "Oh god, don't answer that."

He grabbed her hand and brought her fingers to his mouth, kissing her palm and licking up to the tip, before sucking it into his mouth. He released it with a chuckle.

She wanted to smack the man in the face, barely suppressing the overwhelming need to do just that very thing.

"I don't remember any woman before you, Lena. They were all just practice so I could get it right with you."

She jumped when a naked chest cuddled up to her back and hands reached around, tweaking her breasts and pulling on her nipples, making them stand at attention. She swiveled her head and met the amused look on Max's face.

"Is Malcolm upsetting you, baby?"

She rested her head on his shoulder, marveling at the utter perfection of the two men. Selena licked her lips and saw a glow light the blue depths of Max's eyes. Her pussy clenched on the cock buried deep inside her. She heard a groan and tore her gaze away from Max to see Malcolm with a pained expression.

"Ignore him and come here," Malcolm grunted.

She was shocked she hadn't heard Max enter the room. He knelt on the bed between Malcolm's legs, completely naked, rubbing her back with his front like they did this every day. Maybe they did. She suddenly felt shy and confused. What did she truly know about either of them? Thoughts swirled in her head of two women surrounded by children.

"Are you guys married? Do you have kids? Shit, I don't know anything about you guys, and here I am fucking you both. You must think I'm…" She swallowed and took a breath. "You must think I'm a whore."

She yelped in pain as Max swatted her ass, and not a love tap. He rubbed the slight pain, holding the heat inside.

"I never want to hear you talk about yourself that way. Neither of us is married. Neither of us has kids. We definitely don't think you're anything but an amazingly sexy woman. Our woman!" Max stroked her overheated skin with each word, awakening sensation with his rough fingers.

"Sweetheart, look at me," Malcolm said, forcing her to look at him with a bite of steel in his voice.

She shivered and looked down into his amazing blue depths and lost herself in the sensation of being sandwiched between two men. She drew in a sharp breath and reached behind her to wrap her arm around Max's neck. She broke eye contact with Malcolm and kissed Max, wanting to be connected with both men.

* * * *

Max stroked his tongue over Selena's lips, coaxing them to open. He brushed his hands down her sides, palming the perfect globes of her breasts, lifting them and squeezing her cherry-red nipples between his thumb and forefinger.

She made the most amazing sounds that had his balls drawing up, begging for release. Not yet. He wouldn't allow himself to come until they reached at least ten orgasms for her, for their one. He'd watched the strain in Malcolm's eyes as he counted out the number five and couldn't help but smile.

His brother had a competitive streak a mile wide. Malcolm had been so focused on giving Selena pleasure, he hadn't noticed she had the shields down that blocked them from her thoughts. Max marveled at the complexity of her brain.

He felt her shudder against him. He released her breast and tugged her head to the side. "I'm going to take your ass, Lena." He made it a statement.

"I've never, I mean…" she croaked, undulating her hips, causing Malcolm to groan.

"Do you trust us?" Max asked.

Max had watched her bite her lower lip, holding his breath until she answered. When she gave a small nod of her head, he exhaled, relaxing his muscles that had tensed up waiting for her to answer.

*Thank you gods above, she said yes.* He couldn't have walked away from her any more than his brother could, but they would've had to adapt if she wouldn't allow them complete access to her body. He needed to fill her at the same time as his brother, to complete the connection that had been missing his whole life.

Max didn't know how the act of the three of them, being connected intimately, would seal the bond he already felt tying them together forever worked. He learned early not to question the fates and their gifts. She was a gift from the gods meant only for him and his brother.

"I'll go as slow as you want. Just don't tell me to stop." He pressed her forward to rest on Malcolm's chest, desperation lacing his voice.

Malcolm ran his hands down the lovely line of her back. Her flesh glowed as she hummed in obvious pleasure at the sweet caress.

Max knelt between their legs and squeezed the firm mounds of her ass, running his thumbs down the crack, across her little puckered hole and then down to where she was joined with his brother. He gathered some of her moisture, trailed his fingers back up, and rubbed in small circles.

He slipped the tip of one finger inside her ass until she moved, trying to take more of him into her. Malcolm's legs went rigid as she slid forward and back on his cock, making Max wish he could be in both places at once. With a thought, he entered his brother's mind and was shocked at the thoughts tumbling around in his little brother's head. He threw his head back and laughed. Selena tensed, and he rubbed her back in a soothing motion. Speaking directly to Malcolm, he told him to quit counting backward from a thousand. The laugh that threatened to escape was hard to suppress when Malcolm gave him the image of his middle finger, raised high in their mind link.

"Are you two talking?" Selena asked, and both brothers stilled.

"What do you mean?" Max asked.

"Duh, you both got all quiet and focused on each other. I felt a little left out."

"Um, Selena." Malcolm cleared his throat. "Can you communicate with people without words?"

She squirmed and Max spoke directly into her mind. "*Can you hear me, Lena?*"

She shocked him, and by the look on Malcolm's face, he obviously heard as she opened up a path connecting the three of them.

*"If you two don't quit talking and start doing, I'm going to have to take care of myself."*

Max was amazed at the beauty of hearing her in his head. Although he's always been able to talk to his brother and the other Ravens, having his Fated mind-speak was a miracle, one he never thought to have.

He wanted to take time to prepare her before entering her like a rutting bull, but her words were like a red flag being waved in that bull's face. Taking a deep breath, he grabbed a bottle of lube out of the drawer before spreading a generous amount down the crack of her ass, and then coated two fingers.

Snapping the cap, he laid it next to him and concentrated on opening her up for his cock. He entered one finger in and out several times and then two, repeating the process, adding the motion of moving them together and apart. She purred. A low humming sound he wanted to hear again and again, every day for the rest of his life.

With only a thought, he poured more of the gel onto his hand and pushed a third finger into her incredibly tight hole. She tried to take over the pace he set by thrusting backward, but he swatted her left butt cheek in warning.

Malcolm pulled her down for a deep searing kiss, preventing her string of curses. With all their minds open he wasn't just experiencing what he felt, but what his brother was feeling along with Selena.

He could feel how incredible her inner muscles felt as they squeezed Malcolm. He could feel the fullness she felt with Malcolm's cock in her pussy and his fingers in her ass. She transmitted her need to be filled by both of them without words. To a man who compartmentalized his life it was almost too much, but for once in his long life he decided to accept it.

"Selena, I need you to push out when I press forward and try to relax. I don't want to hurt you baby," Max said.

She jerked her head away from Malcolm long enough to look over her shoulder and pinned him with liquid silver eyes that looked eerily familiar. He stared at her face, but she dropped her head with a moan and flexed her inner muscles.

He coated his cock with more lube and removed his fingers before placing the head of his dick to her opening. Malcolm wrapped his arms around her, holding her in place as Max worked the first inch of his erection inside her.

Her inner walls contracting around him was both pleasure and pain. It felt as if an eternity had passed before she finally relaxed enough for him to press another inch inside. He pulled back out only to push back in, burying another couple inches inside her incredibly tight sheath. He was ready to explode with only half his dick inside her ass, but refused to lose control. The urge to shove the rest of his cock all the way inside Selena was pushed aside until he knew she was ready.

He mentally sent a stream of more slick liquid inside her back passage without breaking stride, easing his way so he could bury his full length inside in one final stroke. He blocked the feelings of his brother and Selena, knowing he'd lose all semblance of control if he felt their emotions too.

"Oh Max, it's too much…Don't move," Selena gasped out.

"It's all right, baby," he stroked her back. "You have it all. I'm not moving until you're ready."

He waited and swore he might die if she didn't get ready soon. He squeezed the muscles at the base of his cock in a tight fist, fighting his release, and considered counting backward from a thousand like Malcolm. Just when he thought he was going to pass out, she moved her hips from side to side.

He groaned and spoke directly into their combined minds. "*Are you ready Lena?*"

"Yes…Oh…I feel so full," she whispered aloud.

"You're doing great babe," Malcolm reassured her.

Max couldn't have said a word to save his soul. He felt her heart beating against his chest and the echo of Malcolm's matched. He focused his mind, and all three hearts began beating the same rhythm.

He moved out and Mal moved in. They set up a slow pace, keeping Selena trapped between them. Her hums became moans, telling them to hurry or slow down. But they would not let her dictate how they made love to her.

She felt so hot and tight, squeezing his cock in a viselike grip. The same emotions crossed Malcolm's face.

"You are an incredibly amazing woman, Selena. Gods but you feel so fucking good." Max growled. "Yes, baby, squeeze my cock. Look at Malcolm's face, Selena." He punctuated each word with a firm stroke, before he pulled back only to slam back inside.

His balls were on fire, as sparks of lightning streaked down his spine. Max moaned when he felt another orgasm claim Selena and counted out six through their mind link. In complete accord, Max and Malcolm held themselves deep in her body and waited for her to come down before they started moving again.

Malcolm wrapped his arms around her back and she arched like a cat. "Our kitten has claws," he bit out between clenched teeth.

Selena snapped her head up, almost whacking Max in the face, and removed her nails from Malcolm's shoulders. Max could see the moon-shaped indents and wanted a matching set on his own arms or back. Hell, he'd love to have them permanently tattooed on his ass.

The little minx laughed, letting him know she was firmly in his thoughts.

Max flashed his brother a look, and within seconds Selena flew into another orgasm as Malcolm manipulated her clit.

"Seven," Malcolm gasped out.

"You're going to kill me," Selena whispered.

Her body continued to twitch. Max looked down and saw a soft glow encompassing his brother and Selena. He sat back on his heels and gripped her hips. He pushed her up his brother's chest, almost bumping Malcolm's nose with her head, and then pulled her back, slamming her back onto his cock.

"You two just lie there. I'll do all the work. I always do anyways." He laughed, until Malcolm and Selena both slapped him upside the head with an invisible hand.

"Shit! I was just kidding, you two."

His muscles strained as he moved her faster on both their cocks. She screamed their names as she crested another peak that almost had Max coming with her.

Malcolm counted again and she fell forward, breathing hard. Max could feel her inner muscles tighten and relax, and wanted to join her in a mind-blowing orgasm.

Max jumped when she growled an animalistic sound and bit down on Malcolm's chest. He felt the pain like it was his own body that was stinging from the slight hurt. Malcolm retaliated with mental nips to her breasts. She released him with a yelp and squeeze of her pussy that had Max's eyes rolling back in his head.

His cock swelled even further and he pulled Selena up and turned her head toward his, kissing her with all the pent-up emotions he'd yet to express. He captured her tongue between his lips and sucked on her like a favorite treat.

She jolted in his arms. He looked down to see Malcolm rubbing at her little bundle of nerves with a wicked smile.

Pumping his hips, he watched as Malcolm manipulated her into another hard orgasm.

"That was nine, Malcolm. I think we should all go over the edge together next time." Max wanted to let go now, but the goal his brother had set shimmered in his mind like a finish line in a race.

Malcolm nodded his head against the pillows, a painful grimace on his face.

Selena went lax between them. "I'm done. Really," she panted. "You two go ahead and I'll just lie right here."

"Oh no, sweetheart, you've got one more to go." Malcolm pulled her down for a kiss.

Max mourned the loss of her tits in his hand, but consoled himself with the thought of the pleasure to come.

They waited for her to stop squeezing their cocks before they set up a pace ensured to drive them all to the stars and back.

He pulled back to the end of his cock and looked down at the vision of her opening to take him back inside. He could see the flutter of her pink flesh as it contracted around the head of his cock. Placing his hand on the center of her back, he slammed inside and held her down when she would have sat back up.

"Shit, man, I can't take much more," Malcolm wheezed. "She's so tight. Fuck…"

Max pounded into her back entrance in tandem to Malcolm. His balls drew taut and streaks of white-hot pleasure traveled up his spine and back down. Max opened his mind and shared what he felt with his twin and Selena. He heard them groan and mirrored their sounds with a deep growl.

"Let go, Selena. Feel what you do to us," Max murmured, sharing the pleasure he felt at the same time as Malcolm shouted his pleasure.

"Yes. Yes. Oh yes…" Selena screamed.

Keeping his eyes open and focused on Selena, Max saw a yellow ball of flame shoot out of her body and surround the three of them in a circle of gold. He pumped his hips, emptying his seed deep within her body, and convulsed as spurt after spurt continued to flow from him into her.

Malcolm had his head tipped back, his mouth open on a silent scream, but Max could see he too had his eyes focused on their woman. Her screams echoed around the room and amplified in volume as the golden glow flared out, stretching throughout the room and in a shocking wave, powered back into them.

Max held Selena by the hips and rolled them all to their sides, keeping them connected. He looked over her shoulder and met the stunned gaze of his brother. *What the fuck?*

# Chapter Thirteen

Malcolm watched as Selena's eyes snapped open, and those silver orbs swirled with power and an unnatural glow radiated out, before they fell closed and a soft moan passed her lips. She went completely lax and her breathing evened out.

They fucked her into a faint and Malcolm didn't feel the least bit exhilarated. If he was being honest, then he would have to admit he was a little freaked. He and Max never considered the ramifications of what their combined power would do to a mortal woman. Even one who had special abilities like Selena.

Malcolm closed off his mind when Selena began to stir, lest she see the turmoil raging through him. Max gave him a little shake of his head over Selena's shoulder, and in agreement, they gave her an order to sleep into her subconscious.

Slowly he waited for Max to pull out and Selena twitched, but thankfully kept her eyes closed. He eased out of her incredibly tight sheath that continued to twitch long after that final orgasm. He watched as Max strolled into the adjoining bathroom and returned with two warm cloths. They could have easily cleaned her with a thought, but he understood the significance of doing the job with their own hands.

He rolled her to her back and brushed the hair from her face, marveling at the fact she hadn't even worked up a sweat from their intense lovemaking. He understood why he and Max hadn't. Hell, none of the gods did, and when they'd created the Ravens they gifted them with that ability. He and his brethren could be in a battle in the middle of summer with the sun beating down on them, and they would all be able to control their internal body heat, keeping them cool even when every man, woman, and child around them stood in a puddle of their own sweat.

Shrugging his shoulders, Malcolm accepted the damp cloth and brushed it over her golden skin. He jerked his eyes up and saw Max staring at her body.

He opened his mind and asked the question he knew Max was thinking. "*What the fuck is up with that?*" he nodded toward the golden glow still covering her body.

"I have no clue," Max answered out loud.

They quickly worked the warm cloth over her skin and watched the light surrounding Selena like a halo of gold. Once they finished wiping her down and ensured her comfort, they flashed outside to Max's veranda overlooking the city that seemed so far away.

"There isn't a rule book, Malcolm. We don't know what has changed about Selena since our joining her, but something did." Max raked his hand through his hair, making it stand on end.

"Do you think we hurt her?" Malcolm asked the only question he wanted Max to answer. Everything else would fall into place as long as their Fated wasn't hurt.

"I don't think so. It could be the ten orgasms we put her through, and then having both of us join her in release that triggered her reaction. Maybe we changed her, and now she's more like us," Max said.

"I hate not knowing what's going to happen."

Malcolm saw Max's lips twitch and swore he'd punch him if he so much as uttered a word about how the mighty have fallen. They were so focused on Selena they didn't sense the attack until it was almost on top of them.

He saw Max fall back in a total *Matrix*-like move, bending his body backward until his head touched the ground and he grabbed the sword that tried to separate his torso from his legs. He didn't have time to watch Max battle, because he saw three more abominations shuffling toward him with gleaming red swords.

A light flashed, and he had two short swords in his hands and battle armor covered his own torso. The biggest of the three lifted his blade and tried to slash his head off with a powerful swipe. Malcolm dodged and met the next cretin in mid-swing. He leaped over its taller frame and swung his blade as he cleared its head with a well-aimed slice, but didn't have time to watch the head slide off the body.

They circled him, one to his back, and one in the front like a well-trained unit. He tilted his head to the side and looked into the mind of the one staring at him with a single-minded intensity. Entering the thoughts, he found a mass of swirling red mist and a picture of Selena in chains strapped to a blood-coated stone table.

Malcolm let out a battle cry and, jumping up, he kicked out with his right leg, connecting with the jaw of the one in front, then turned in midair, slashing with his swords in a double assault. He flipped over the body that now lay in three pieces and faced another creature.

He looked over and saw Max raise his hand, and lighting flashed out, incinerating another creature as another jumped on his back. Malcolm knew Max would be able to handle them and thanked the gods Selena still slept. Before leaving the room and sending her into a deep sleep they put up safeguards only Zeus himself could penetrate.

A hot blade sliced across his arm and he flashed away, disappearing only to reappear behind his newest assailant. His blades disappeared and he turned the man's head around without the body moving. Another turn and the body slumped. He let the head go and stepped around him, stalking the two who were trying to get into the house.

"Excuse me, boys. Can I help you?" Malcolm flashed them a smile, and raising both hands, sent power surging into their bodies. He didn't wait to see if they exploded, but heard the screams and felt their presence fade.

Flashing over to Max, they faced another half dozen of the beings, each one uglier than the next.

"What the fuck are they?" Malcolm asked.

"Ugly motherfuckers," Max answered.

"That they are, bro. That they are for sure, but where did they come from?"

"I can answer that for you."

They both turned and faced the being that got away from them in the alley outside of Selena's club. Max made a movement of his hand behind his back and Malcolm mirrored his movements. They let their powers combine and incinerated the creatures behind them as they tried to sneak up on them. They didn't usually combine their powers like that since it could either wear them down or lift them up. They prayed it would be the latter this time.

Malcolm knew the real threat was the strange half man, half beast standing tall in front of them. He nodded his head and gestured for the thing to continue.

"My name is Balky. I am here to get the girl."

"Why do you want Selena? She's a human," Max, the calm one, asked.

"Cronus wants his granddaughter, and what Cronus wants I get him." Balky shrugged.

Malcolm opened his mind and searched for answers in the mind of Balky who stood tall in front of them. He slammed into a wall and watched the other man stumble back as if he got hit. Interesting…

"Okay," Max said slowly as if he were speaking to a child. "What does that have to do with Selena?"

"You can't be that stupid." Balky's eyes flashed from red to blue, and back to that eerie red again.

Malcolm stumbled when he felt his and Max's power surrounding Selena being ripped open by the force of a god. Looking over at Max, he saw his brother's eyes widen in disbelief a moment before he disappeared, leaving Malcolm facing a threat they'd yet to figure out. He heard his brother scream and flashed to his side to find the bed where they left Selena empty and the aura of power still pulsing throughout the room.

"What the hell? Selena," Max roared, shaking the thick walls of his estate.

Malcolm opened his senses and saw the faint trace of power that felt very similar to Zeus, and closed his eyes at what he knew it meant. He turned to Max and winced at the tortured look on his brother's face. He laid a hand on Max's arm and felt the heat pouring off his skin.

"We will find her, and get her back."

Max jerked and seemed to slam back into his body, and that was when Malcolm realized his brother had let his essence follow the trail that was too faint for them to physically trace.

"What did you see, Max?"

"Shit, this can't be real."

Malcolm saw a bead of sweat form on Max's brow and grimaced at the physical proof of the strain he felt. He scrubbed his hands over his face and through his hair, and gripped his neck in a tight vise.

"What did you see?"

"He saw Cronus with your Selena," Balky said.

Both brothers spun on their feet and shot a blast of power toward the intruder, amazed when he only stumbled backward before he righted himself.

"What the fuck do you mean? And do we know you?" Malcolm snarled.

Balky shook his head like he was dealing with a couple children, and Malcolm lost it. He reached out with his right hand and slammed the being into the wall, making the room shake from the force. He felt a little satisfaction at the alarm reflected in the other man's eyes.

"Don't play with me, boy, or I'll tear you into so many pieces, they won't be able to make dog food out of you. Before you say anything else, I suggest you think about it, because I swear by the gods and goddesses, I can and I will kill you." He waited a beat and squeezed the man's throat with his hand and his heart with an unseen force.

Max stepped up beside him and added his power to the viselike grip he had on the lesser being. Just when they thought he would talk, a bright flash of light lit up the room and they released Balky, turning to face the newest threat.

Malcolm looked into the glowing silver orbs of the god he hadn't seen in more years than he could remember. He swallowed and went down on one knee, showing his respect. Looking up, he saw Max staring at Zeus and realized they were communicating without him. He felt a little left out, and then Max blinked and shared the conversation with him.

The gods looked at speaking out loud as primitive behavior and seldom lowered themselves to the level of mortals. Malcolm was stunned when Zeus turned to him and focused his intense gaze on him. He tried not to squirm under the pressure of his stare, but seeing the twitch of the god's lips, knew he failed.

"Where is my daughter?" the god asked out loud, shocking him and Max so much they both stumbled forward. He wrapped his big palms around both their throats and lifted them up to eye level with their feet hanging several feet from the ground.

Malcolm gripped the arm that held him and couldn't reach around with both hands. He opened his mind and tried to communicate, and that was when he saw who Zeus was talking about. His daughter, the missing goddess and Selena were one and the same. He tried speaking, but the god didn't seem to care what they had to say. He showed Max what he had just seen in the god's mind, but received a shock when Max shared what the god had just done to him.

Malcolm hated the feeling of someone invading his mind and would have sworn nobody could have penetrated his brother's blocks. But they weren't dealing with a normal mortal, or even those humans with special gifts. They were dealing with the Lord of the Sky and a very pissed-off god at that. Malcolm felt his consciousness begin to fade as the god held them with a death grip.

Zeus released them as quickly as he snatched them up and seemed to shrink from the ten-foot, seething being to a larger-than-average man, but neither Malcolm nor Max could move. They both rubbed their throats, and Malcolm saw Max cough and spit blood onto his pristine floors.

He watched the god pace back and forth, if floating could be considered pacing, then he turned, and both men were lifted up and the severe pain he felt constricting his throat was gone.

"I am sorry. I may have overreacted," Zeus said.

Malcolm, never the smart one according to his brother, just nodded. He may usually be the one who opened his mouth and inserted his foot, but this time he knew that foot could grow to unusual lengths and he liked his pretty-boy looks. *Thank you very fucking much.*

"Shut up, pup." Zeus growled, pinning Malcolm with a look.

Malcolm swallowed and straightened to his full height, trying to imitate the military stance Max had.

"You have no reason to apologize, my Lord. I think you know we had no clue that our Selena was the same as the goddess of the moon."

"Do not call her your anything," Zeus said in a low tone.

"My Lord, you must understand what she means to us. I know you could see and feel what we felt. I'm sorry, Sir, but she completes us and without each other…" Max let his words sink in before he continued. "Now that we have completed the joining, to separate her from us will destroy her and us."

"Silence," he roared.

Malcolm couldn't believe the god was speaking in the primitive way he so despised, but he saw when Zeus realized that Max spoke the truth. People thought the gods and goddesses didn't need anyone, and he supposed that was true to an extent. What people didn't realize was that just because they had unbelievable power and immortality, they also needed companionship and love, just like everyone else.

When a god or goddess loved, it was stronger than a normal human. They hurt with more pain along with every other emotion the gods felt, everything so much more.

* * * *

Zeus especially had stronger emotions because the freedom of his people depended on his ability to rule them, and having lost his youngest child to his father he tried even harder to protect them. When he'd banished his father to Hell and stripped him of his godly powers, he had no clue the man could still somehow enter Olympus and slip away with his baby girl.

He saw the battle his Ravens had fought here on Earth and the recent attacks they endured protecting the woman they called their Fated, but Zeus couldn't wrap his mind around his baby being mated to two men. Not that he had a problem with the prospect in itself, but he didn't like the picture of the three of them completing their bond that made them whole. He could still picture her as a tiny thing with white-blonde, curly hair and liquid-silver eyes. Eyes so like his own.

He grimaced, and if he didn't know better, he'd say he just threw up in his mouth, but that couldn't be right, because he had never been sick a day in his extremely long life. He heard his wife's amused laugh through their link. He sent her the image of him snapping his teeth that looked more like a wolf's jaws into her mind.

*"Honey, you have to realize our baby has become a woman in the twenty-four years she has been hidden from us. You can't blame Max and Malcolm for loving her. I mean did you see her? She is so beautiful and such a tiny thing."*

Zeus heard the catch in her throat and knew she was fighting her tears, trying to stay strong until they could finally hold their baby girl. He brought the picture he caught of her through the minds of his two enforcers up and smiled. She really was a tiny little thing. He then pictured her sandwiched between the two larger men and felt his temper flare up again.

With only a notion, he slammed the two men into the wall and heard a satisfying crack as their backs landed against the hard surface.

"*Sweetheart, stop it and fix what you just broke, and do not deny it,*" Hera said.

Zeus sighed, releasing the two deflowerers of innocent baby girls. He heard the laugh of his wife and sent her a vivid fantasy of what he planned to do when he returned. Turning, he pinned the two men with a glare and waited for them to speak. As the silence lengthened he threw his hands up in the air, pleased to see the men didn't flinch.

Zeus prided himself on his forgiving nature, sometimes. A burst of feminine laughter interrupted his thoughts. "*Shut up, Hera.*" His lips twitched at the continued merriment. Gods but he loved that woman.

"*I love you too, Oh Great One.*"

"*You need to work on your respect,*" Zeus said.

"*Yes, yes I should. I mean you are my elder and everything.*" *Hera laughed. "I'm just kidding. I'm worried about our girl and you know how I get.*"

"*Hera, sweetie, give me a minute to deal with these two and see if I can find her.*"

"*Be nice. If you have to kill someone just remember to be nice when you do it. Now, if you find your father, then you can be mean. In fact, I order you to be really mean.*"

Zeus sent a mental hug to his wife, and feeling her arms wrap around him, he let himself bask in their love before he snapped the door closed on their communications. His wife didn't understand you couldn't always be nice even when you killed someone.

"My wife said I need to be nice," Zeus snapped.

He watched the younger twin nod his head and his brother slapped him before snapping to attention. Grudgingly, he admired the way they stood facing him as a united front. He sighed and came to a quick decision.

"You two will find my daughter and you will do right by her." He held up his hand. "Foolish one, do not open your mouth."

"My Lord, I vow I will. No, I mean we will do everything to bring Selena home to you and to us," Max said.

"Don't test me, pup. Now here is what you need to do. Cronus is a god. When I defeated him, I stripped him of all his godly powers. How or who helped him get some back I do not know, but I can tell you he is not as powerful as me. The problem is that I cannot detect him or her. I do not admit this easily, and if you repeat this I will dismember you with a smile."

Tired of all the speaking, he forced himself into their minds and yep, he threw up in his mouth at the memory of the two men and his daughter together. Good goddess, no father should ever have to see that. Surely there was enough bleach he could wipe the vision from his eyes?

# Chapter Fourteen

Cronus strolled into his throne room satisfied from the bout of amazing sex. He was stopped short by what he saw lying on the large stone slab he had his followers erect to offer sacrifices in order to get his powers back. The small woman radiated power. He could smell the unmistakable scent of the demigods he hated more than any others all over her.

He flashed to the table and was happy to see he'd shocked the little goddess who had been strapped down. She turned her silver eyes toward him, eyes that were so like his son's he wanted to snap her head off and remove them with his bare hands. A little primitive perhaps, but the urge to kill her passed with the knowledge that he'd get to it soon. He'd learned very quickly to be ruthless in order to survive.

"Hello, sweetheart. How are you this fine evening, or should I say morning?" Cronus said.

"Who the hell are you, and why am I here?" Selena snapped.

"Ah yes! You still have no clue, do you?"

"Quit talking in riddles, old man, and get on with it."

Cronus narrowed his eyes, unable to believe the way the little bitch talked to him. He sealed her lips with a thought and smiled. He enjoyed how her eyes flew up and collided with his and the fear reflecting back gave him a jolt of much-needed power. Fear was exactly what he wanted to see. He couldn't wait to see how she looked when her intestines lay outside her body and her blood soaked his floors. He planned to watch it all so he could be sure and send a mental picture to her traitor father, and his whore of a wife.

"That is much better." He nodded at her sealed mouth. "I will tell you a little story. It's about a boy who betrays his father and sends him to the one place he thought would hold him. This boy thought he was so smart, but the father will have the last laugh."

Cronus told Selena how he snatched her from her gilded cradle, right out from under her parents' noses. He smirked when her eyes widened and tears leaked from the corners of her closed lids. He fed off the misery of others and her misery fueled him like no other.

"You see, my dear, your father banished me to hell, but he never thought to make sure I was secure. He assumed in his *almighty* greatness, that he had defeated me and wiped his hands clean. He turned his back on me and pretended I didn't exist. Those were the first of many mistakes the ungrateful weasel made. However, the biggest…" Cronus stopped and trailed his bloodred fingernails down her torso, popping the buttons on the man's shirt she wore, and continued. "The biggest mistake was sending me to Hades's realm. Now he is a true god, and smart, too. Hades, or son, as I like to call him, knew from the start we couldn't coexist in the same place. So here I am," he spread his arms wide.

"*Why are you telling me all this*?" Selena spoke directly into his mind.

Cronus jerked at the voice in his head. "I see you have some of your powers, but not enough to save you." He nodded in satisfaction. "I have no fear of you or your father. You will be dead long before you can spill my secrets."

Turning, he focused his red gaze on the man hiding in the corner. "Balky, come," he snapped, watching as Balky shuffled forward a few steps and waited until he spoke.

"I just wanted to make sure I wasn't needed before I left," Balky said.

Cronus tilted his head to the side, and with only a thought brought Balky to stand before him. "Were you listening in on my intimate conversation with my granddaughter?"

"No, Sir."

"Hmm. Be gone then." He flicked his finger and sent Balky flying backward and out the doors. He smiled when the man cursed.

"Where was I? Oh yes, I remember. Hades helped me get here," he gestured at their surroundings. "I found out really fast that being over seven feet tall, people fear you. I fed off that fear. It took me a long time, but I am finally almost at full strength. When I finish with you and I suck your essence out, I will be as strong, if not stronger than before."

"*I am not scared of you, old man. Where are you going to get the fear to help you power up or whatever*?"

"Ah, my dear child, you are so foolish." He waved his hand. A mass of people on their knees quaking in fear appeared in the once-empty space. "You see, goddess of the moon, I do not need your fear, when I have all of these people who love and fear me in equal parts. Stupid humans will follow any false god in their quest for salvation. I've been feeding off their fear by showing them my powers in little bursts. It's amazing how people will shake and piss themselves when you rip out the heart of a loved one in front of them."

"*You are a sick bastard*," Selena said.

Cronus snarled and jumped on top of the table. The solid surface didn't even shake at his large frame. He straddled her nearly naked form and whispered, "I could fuck you right here, in front of all these people, and not one would raise a hand to help you."

Gods help him, but his granddaughter had balls. She didn't even flinch as he trailed his claw down her stomach and slashed the top completely open. She stared up at him with a defiant look that made him smile, showing her his fangs in the process.

He made sure she saw the image of what humans thought the devil looked like, the way he now looked thanks to her father. With the deep red skin and his black eyes, he made the horror movies look tame. His once long blonde hair had also turned charcoal black, but he let it all feed his hatred. He could change his outward appearance to look however he wanted, flashing from a golden-haired young man to a silver haired old man the next, and still she didn't show any fear.

"I have no taste for women who reek of the abominations my son created." Cronus hopped off the table and faced his congregations.

"Welcome, my children. Tonight, you will all be a part of my victory and will reap the benefits of being true to me. Now bow your heads and pray."

"*You are such a coward. You make yourself look like the devil and make those people believe you will save them. You make me sick.*"

Cronus had enough of her and her disrespect. Who the hell did she think she was? He raised the table and as it floated in the air he strapped her wrists and ankles to the corners. He looked on in satisfaction and watched her blood bead up and run down her arms and into the bowl below. His followers gasped at his show of power. Fools, all of them! Their blood and their fear would be raising him up and giving him back what his offspring took from him. If he'd been as strong as before he'd just devour her like he'd done his own children, like he should have done her father, but their time would come. Oh, yes, he'd feast on them all.

He turned his back on his followers. They were all alike, lambs being led to the slaughter. Show them a little miracle, and poof, they panted after you. He held their leashes in the palm of his hand, just as he held their souls. They didn't know the only place he would be sending them was to hell with Hades. That was the deal, and when Cronus made vows! Well, sometimes he honored them.

He flashed to his bedchamber and saw his creations slept on. They were almost perfect in their physical appearances. It was too bad they were all so stupid. He tapped his chin and reconsidered. No, mindless minions are so much better, he thought, and rubbed his hands together.

* * * *

Selena seethed as the giant spoke of her and her father, or who he said was her father. She couldn't wrap her mind around what he told her, and if it were true, then she wasn't just a girl with special abilities. She was a goddess for crying out loud. She tried to stay still and not panic, which was a little difficult since she'd been strapped to a stone table that was now floating over a large freaking bowl collecting her blood.

If she truly were a goddess, then maybe she could get herself out of this mess. Where the hell were Max and Malcolm? With a shudder, she realized they'd probably been killed. She sniffed and willed her tears away. There would be plenty of time to mourn them after she killed the man who claimed to be her grandfather.

Sending a small burst of healing power into her wrists, she sealed the wounds on the inside but left the blood trailing down her arms. The chains bit into the flesh at her ankles, sending jolts of fire up her legs. She concentrated, trying to find her inner strength and relieve the weight on her wrists. Cronus believed she hadn't come into her powers, and she was glad he seemed to be as arrogant as he accused her father of being. Thinking of her real father, she brought up a mental picture of the god called Zeus. Maybe she should've studied him more, but she'd always felt a stronger connection with the goddesses. She thought back to her joining with Max and Malcolm and the yellow glow that had surrounded them. At first, she'd thought it was the lighting from outside or possibly the bursts of lights exploding behind her eyes. Now, she realized they'd awakened the powers within her.

Opening her eyes, Selena looked over the crowd of kneeling people. She wished she could talk, but the big bastard had left her mouth sealed. Several women eyed her with what could only be called envy, and she silently offered to trade spots with them.

"*Hello, Goddess.*"

Selena jolted at the soft voice in her head. She twisted her head back and forth, looking for the speaker, and belatedly realized it was spoken directly into her mind.

"*Don't look directly at me. I will tell you where to look and what to look for, but don't let on that we are speaking*," a lilting voice said. "*I am in the very back with red hair. Don't look,*" she yelled.

Selena winced at the high-pitched scream and realized she couldn't lift her eyes to see who spoke anyway.

"*Who or what are you*?" Selena asked.

"*It doesn't matter who I am, but my name is Jaklyn. I will try to help you, but I fear it is too late*."

"*Am I still breathing*?" Selena questioned. "*Then it is not too late*."

Centering herself, she concentrated on breathing and giving the appearance of being defeated. She let her body sag from the chains, nearly screaming at the pain that stabbed into her wrists, but she blocked it. She left her physical body and sighed at the immediate relief of pain as she floated toward the back of the large room. A glimmer of power emanated from a woman surrounded by men, a lock of red hair peeking out beneath the hood of her robe. Selena probed her mind and found the one she had been searching for.

"*Very good, goddess, I see you have control of some of your abilities*."

Selena barely prevented her immediate retreat when the woman spoke into her mind again. "*Do you know how to get out of here*?" Selena asked.

"*We wait.*"

"*What the fuck. That is your plan?*"

"*Yep, that is the plan.*"

"*What are we waiting for*?" Selena strained to hear as the silence stretched. She was so focused on listening, she didn't hear or see when her hair was jerked back and a demon licked the blood from her arm.

"*Get back to your body now, goddess,*" Jaklyn yelled through their link.

With a thought, Selena opened her eyes to see one of the ugliest things she'd ever seen in her entire life. The man-beast had to be at least seven feet tall with knots of flesh all over his body that looked like open wounds. She gagged when he breathed directly into her face, and then inhaled her scent. She wished Cronus would have sealed her nose along with her mouth.

"You smell good," the beast said.

Too bad Selena couldn't say the same. The man smelled like ass. Not just ass, but ass that hadn't been washed in years. Okay, so maybe she'd never actually smelled ass like that, but really, he smelled awful.

She pinned him with her laser-like gaze and waltzed into his tiny little mind. What she found amazed her. He had no thoughts, just orders to capture, hurt or kill. Digging further into his cavernous mind, she found what she'd been looking for. In a far corner she saw him bowing before Cronus, accepting all the god offered, and judging from the size of that thing, her grandpa offered a lot. Gah! A girl should never have to see her grandpa's manly bits. She fast-forwarded the vision, knowing there wasn't enough power in the world to scrub her eyes clean.

Through this beast's eyes, she saw Cronus spend himself all over the beast, which lapped it up like a treat, and then left the man kneeling on the stone floor. Cronus turned and walked over to a large bowl in the center of the room. She couldn't see what he looked at, but from the satisfied smile on his face that had nothing to do with what he'd just done all over the beast, she assumed it couldn't be good.

Selena watched as Cronus slapped his hands together and rubbed them in glee like a little child. She wished she could've been there with him and shoved his face into the water, or whatever the bowl contained. Fantasizing about what she'd do to the god, she jerked when her chains tightened further. She pulled out of the beast's mind to see Cronus had returned, and by the looks of him, he had just spent himself again. He shoved the beast away from her, and honestly, she wanted to weep at the fresh air she inhaled.

"*You need to buy that thing some toothpaste, Gramps. His breath is so foul. I almost died from the stench alone*."

"Silence, you unworthy child." Cronus growled.

Nobody had ever accused Selena of having a death wish, but a girl had to do what a girl had to do and Selena was definitely a girl. "*Okay, so if you don't want me to call you Gramps I won't. But what do I call you?*"

"My Lord will do."

Blinking her eyes, Selena tried to control the automatic response of an impressive eye roll, and barely succeeded. She didn't say another word, but felt him trying to probe into her mind. She pictured the wall she'd seen in Max and Malcolm's minds and imitated its structure behind the wall she already had in place. He powered through her wall, but slammed into the new barrier.

"Ah, you think you can keep me out of your mind?"

"*I guess I do. How is it working so far*?" Selena tried to smirk.

Cronus didn't raise his hand to strike her. He just smiled a parody of a smile that sent a bit of fear down her spine. His chest swelled, and she knew she'd fed his powers with her fear. She banked down the instinct to crawl away in fear and raised her head, meeting him stare for stare. That seemed to enrage him. The blow came without any warning, and she gasped at the fiery pain. A quick look down revealed a jewel-encrusted dagger impaled in her right side.

More blood leaked from her body into the bowl. She didn't dare send out a healing thought to the new wound and alert him to her ability.

"*If Zeus is my father, aren't you afraid he will punish you more than just banishing you from Olympus for hurting me?*"

"Let him try. Your father is a pup, and I'm going to be the pit bull that rips him apart."

Selena didn't say any more. He seemed to relish in his daydream, giving her a moment to stop the internal bleeding. She wished Max and Malcolm were there to hold her. Her men would've done anything to protect her, and she found that amazing. They'd just met her, but the love she sensed they felt for her had been true.

Selena didn't have many regrets, but she really regretted not telling them that she loved them. Her mama who raised her always told her that sometimes love came slow and steady, like what she had with her father. But sometimes, it came fast and hard. Selena decided her love for her two men went far beyond fast and hard. It was supersonic.

Thinking of Max and Malcolm coming to her rescue made her shudder. They may be big and willing to die for her, but she was glad they wouldn't. If she was going to die at the hands of the crazed thing before her, just knowing they still lived gave her peace. She sighed, and then silently screamed when another lance of pain shot through her system.

She vowed not to show the bastard the pain he inflicted. There was no need to look down at the cause of this newest pain. She could see more of her life's blood flowing from her body. Surely, if she were a goddess, then she wouldn't bleed to death…right?

# Chapter Fifteen

Max paced as he waited for the rest of the Ravens to arrive. Rafe, Vin, Coltrain, and Grayson had already shown up. He'd heard from Garrick and Thantos, but Blade, Uri, Dimitri, and Dion were still not answering his call.

"Where the fuck are they?" Max asked. He spun on his boot and stomped from the room only to return a few moments later. "Okay, let's go. If they show up while we're gone they can follow us."

"How they gonna do that, boss?" Rafe asked.

"I'm leaving a trail, so to speak. Let's go!" Max linked with the men and they flashed out, reappearing outside the mausoleum Cronus called home. He still couldn't believe Cronus had not only clawed his way out of hell, but was smack dab in the middle of the Arizona desert. Add in the fact he was able to hide something that could easily fit three football fields inside was a testament to the god's powers.

"What the hell is that monstrosity?" Grayson asked in a gravelly tone.

"That, my friend, is going to be the final resting place of a god," Malcolm answered.

With only six Ravens, Max planned an attack that was less brawn and more stealth. He didn't want to alert the beings—be they human or other—inside the temple to their presence until they had a chance to get in. He'd been trying to speak with Selena for the past hour and every time, he ran into a wall she'd obviously mimicked from his. Smiling, he scaled the imaginary wall and sighed when he penetrated her mind.

"*Thank you, gods above, I found you. How are you, baby?*" Max whispered.

"*Max! Is that you?*"

"*Don't make any move to alert them we are talking. I'm going to look through your eyes to see what you see. I need you to take a slow look from side to side.*" Max continued to tell Selena what to do, taking in all she saw. "*Good job, baby. Leave this line open and I'll keep you informed of our plans.*"

"*Max, I need to tell you and Malcolm something.*"

"*Hush, sweetheart. You can tell us face-to-face in a few.*" He surrounded her with his love and embraced her body, trying to warm her. "*I need you to be strong just a little longer, and then we'll get you out of there and with us, where you belong.*"

Max could feel the strain she was under and vowed he would rip Cronus and his people to shreds with his bare hands. With a little burst of power he stopped the flow of her blood, but left the illusion for the people watching.

He could see Cronus holding court to the hundreds of humans kneeling at his feet. The humans didn't concern him—much. It was the army of half men, half beasts that surrounded the bowed people. Through Selena's eyes, he focused on a group of people who had an aura of power near the back of the room. He saw the communication between the two women and knew these people would be allies in the battle to come if needed. He hated using humans with their fragile lives, but had learned early that not everyone survived in wars.

Shrugging his shoulders, he broke his link with Selena to face his brothers. He replayed what he'd seen through Selena's eyes and saw Grayson's eyes widen at the picture of the bowed redhead. He didn't have time to wonder what caused that reaction in the usually stoic man's expression. He felt a flash of pain and knew it was from Selena.

"Son of a bitch, we can't wait any longer. He's hurting Selena. Malcolm and I will immobilize the humans with an order of paralysis.

If any are strong enough to resist then we will take care of them. Rafe and Vin, I want you to take the back wall and spread out. Colt and Gray, you take the front and do the same. Malcolm and I will take the middle, but our main focus is going to be Selena. Understood?"

He didn't wait to see if they all agreed. That was one of the best things about the Ravens. They were a unit first and foremost. He flashed inside the temple with Malcolm right beside him. Cronus floated above the ground looking more like the devil, with bright red skin and horns longer than those he'd seen on bulls in Texas.

Max shook his head at the image. Cronus was so focused on his people and the newest wound he'd inflicted on Selena, he sucked up the fear and pain of others. The crowd gasped and stared wide-eyed in awe at the pool of blood, giving the Ravens the leverage they needed.

Malcolm reached up to break the chains surrounding Selena's right wrist when a bellow from behind them sounded. Max didn't have time to wonder what happened. Cronus turned his head in a completely grotesque imitation of *The Exorcist*. Obviously, the man's neck couldn't be broken. As if that wasn't bad enough, Cronus smiled, showing a full set of teeth that looked razor-sharp, and several rows of them.

"Holy shit. That must be the offspring of Satan and Jaws," Malcolm said. "Dude, how much are your dental bills?"

Max wanted to smack his brother until he realized he'd moved away from Selena. Malcolm was trying to keep the god's focus on him, giving Max a chance to free Selena. Gods were known to be very vain, and Malcolm hit him right at the heart of his vanity.

"I know of a really great plastic surgeon who could help with the um…Well let's just be real. You are so fucking ugly even Dr. Ray couldn't help you. However, I hear Dr. Drew has an opening at *Celebrity Rehab*."

Cronus roared and lunged for Malcolm.

Max tracked Malcolm's movements out of the corner of his eye and worked on freeing Selena.

"Hold on, baby. I just have to break these chains," Max said.

"You can't break them," Jaklyn said next to his side.

Max spun and grabbed the smaller woman by the throat. He felt several things poke his sides, but didn't take his gaze off of the stunning creature in his grasp. She smiled, showing cute little dimples in her cheeks.

"You are the one who spoke with Selena?" He didn't give her a chance to answer. The swords he knew pointed at him didn't deter him. "Do you know how to break these?"

She nodded, and he carefully set her back on her feet. He noted she had on sturdy black combat books and that smile still graced her mouth.

"Of course I do. My name is Jaklyn. Now step back," she waved with one hand to make a space for herself. "I will not hurt the goddess."

Max gave a simple nod and allowed enough room for her to stand beside him. The sharp swords became more like a mosquito, in the desert sun, and he tired of their poking. He sent a small shock from the point of their blades, to the hands and up the arms of the ones holding them. They gave a little grunt, but held still. Amazed, he let them have their little victory. If he truly wanted to hurt them, he could've incinerated them. But they seemed to want to protect his Selena, so for that, he gave it to them. That didn't mean he was going to allow them to stab him or Selena.

He watched as the human ran her palms over the steel holding Selena's wrist and barely restrained the gasp he felt when the chains fell away. He caught Selena to his chest and held her as Jaklyn did the same to the ones at Selena's ankles. He sent a blast of healing warmth through the wounds and pushed the blades out from the inside.

Selena's smile lit up her face, but he didn't have time to bask in her glow.

"Yo, Max. Can you quit fondling our woman and help with the fighting?" Malcolm panted.

Max turned to see Malcolm suited up in his favorite armor, fighting off a very pissed-off Cronus. He looked to the group of humans surrounding him and Selena and asked one thing. "Will you protect Selena with your life?" He watched as they all nodded without missing a beat, and hugged Selena.

"I had a dream several years ago. It's led me here, and hasn't let me down yet. I think you can trust me. If we wanted her dead we wouldn't have helped." Jaklyn held her hands out. Her two companions that looked very similar tilted their heads in agreement.

"Baby, I need you to be safe. But I can't leave Malcolm to fight that thing alone." He nodded to the battling pair. "I don't know how much you know, but you are a goddess, the youngest child of Zeus and his wife Hera. Until you come into your powers you are at risk. I'm going to transport you all out of here. I need you to promise me you will stay safe and be careful."

* * * *

Selena smiled at the authority in his tone. The poor man had no clue she'd already come into her powers, if that was what this excess energy zinging through her body was. She felt like bolts of lightning kept striking her flesh, a really pleasant feeling that made her hum in pleasure. Max and Malcolm were such overprotective men they had no clue she equaled them. Bless their hearts. She couldn't wait to show them what she could do.

She realized he waited for her answer and the longer she held off the more danger Malcolm faced, alone. Not wanting to lie, she nodded. "I promise I will be safe and very careful. Go help Malcolm."

He kissed her hard and leaped down, obliterating the beings in his way. Her heart fluttered and then turned over at the sight of her two men standing side by side with shiny armor covering their torsos and swords raised. Good lord but they made her freaking hot with a capital *hot*.

"Don't even think of it, goddess. He hasn't forgotten to get us out of here," Jaklyn said.

Selena's eyes widened as a burst of light flashed all around her. She blinked her eyes and stared in awe at her new surroundings. Jaklyn had her mouth gaping open until one of the men next to her tapped the bottom of her chin. She almost smiled at the snarl Jaklyn let out, until she realized she had no clue where they were.

Closing her eyes, she followed the faint trail that would lead her back to Max and Malcolm. Damn the man, he'd sent her and the others to California. Opening all her senses, she could smell the ocean, and if she listened carefully, could actually hear the waves crashing on the beach. With her mind open, she realized they stood in Malcolm's California home. Knowing they were in a safe place, she latched onto the essence of Max, and with a thought she followed, leaving Jaklyn and the others behind.

Selena cautiously entered the compound on the astral plane, not wanting to alert any of the occupants of her arrival. She nearly stumbled when she saw Max lying in a pool of blood and Malcolm not far behind. An ungodly roar split the air, and Rafe, followed by a man very similar in looks, covered the space separating them from her men.

She watched in horror as Cronus turned, huge teeth snapping and ten-inch claws extended, beckoning the newcomers closer. He swatted them away like flies, not even blinking a glowing red eye. Her hand flew up to muffle the scream she felt bubbling up her throat.

Selena raised her arms out to her sides and swung them up in an arc, bringing them in front of her in a fighting stance, and screamed. The walls shook, and she heard the shattering of glass.

"Bastard," Selena yelled, and flew across the room. She didn't have time to wonder at the ability, but made a mental note to do it again.

"Oh how sweet. You've come back to save these worthless creations. I knew I smelled the stink of something on your body. Had I known it was these two"—he spat at the bodies on the floor—"I would have dipped you in a tub of acid."

"I love you too, Gramps."

Selena never let the smile slip from her face. She wanted to keep his focus on her, giving Max and Malcolm a chance to heal. She'd gotten a glimpse of their abilities when Max healed her earlier and knew they needed a little time. She wouldn't allow her mind to think they wouldn't survive. She dodged the first strike Cronus threw at her.

"Is that all you got, big boy?" She curled her fingers. "Come on then, bring it." She laughed again and danced backward. She started flipping head over heels, landing in a crouch. One minute he was hovering over the forms of her men and the next he slammed into her from behind. She stumbled forward and barely kept from landing on her face.

"Nice, we call that a sucker punch, or being a bitch." Selena taunted him and turned, facing him again.

Cronus swiped his arm out, hitting her in the face, knocking her off balance. Rolling with the fall, she came up and sent a bolt of lightning toward his head.

"Fuck," she muttered as he disappeared.

"Is that all you got, little girl?" he sneered.

Selena tracked his voice and without raising her arm, created a bolt of energy and struck at the open space where she gauged him to be located. She heard a roar and felt bits of the roof hitting her head. Her cheekbone throbbed like a son of a bitch. Swiping angrily at the blood she felt running down her face, she grimaced at the sting. What the hell did he have his claws tipped in, anyway? She wanted to take the time to heal herself, but he was a dirty fighter.

He proved it with his next move. He didn't reappear and gloat in her face. Oh no, the big man had to go and grab her by the throat, bringing her up to meet his angry look. She reached up and tried to push his gaping mouth away, but his stench made her gag. She felt her lunch coming back up to make an appearance and instead of fighting it back, she let it loose.

"You bitch," Cronus tossed out before launching her across the room.

When she landed in a heap of bodies, she thanked the goddess they broke her fall. If only something wasn't stabbing her in her back, Selena was pretty sure she would've jumped right up. Knowing every moment counted, she expended precious energy healing her face and probing the thing in her back. She smiled. A sword with an extremely sharp blade and yep, rubies in the hilt, had been tossed aside like garbage. *Well, you know what they say? One person's garbage is another person's treasure.*

Trying not to let Cronus know she'd recovered from her injuries, Selena twisted around, removing the blade from her back and freed it from the grip of one of the beasts. With her back to her grandfather, she knelt on top of the bodies that lay in a pile, waiting for him. She heard him stalking toward her over the pounding of her heart. With every step he took, she breathed in, centering her energy, infusing the blade with her essence. Knowing him in all his arrogance, Cronus probably thought he'd bested her, so she let the wound in her back continue to ooze blood.

She gripped the hilt of the sword and rolled forward off the pile, putting a mound between them. He flicked his wrist and the bodies disintegrated into a cloud of dust. She almost lost her nerve at his show of power, but hearing a groan come from the direction where Max and Malcolm lay gave her strength.

Selena didn't take the time to look around and see if the other Ravens were faring any better. From the sounds of it, they still continued to fight off the baddies, giving her hope of a rescue. Focusing on her gramps, she raised the sword in her right hand and slashed forward. With each arc of the blade, lighting flashed out, hitting her target and forcing him back. She jumped up and spun in the air, slashing down with the blade, connecting with his shoulder and slicing through the thick hide of his flesh.

His angry growl made her smile, but she didn't stop her pursuit. He started jumping back, trying to avoid her blade, but she'd paid attention when he flashed out and in. She focused and was able to block his abilities. She knew when he realized she held him semi-captive with her mind when his eyes seemed to become thin slats. Her blade continued to arc and swing as she lunged and jumped. She kept trying for a killing strike, but decided to weaken him with more wounds.

Lighting shot out of the blade, making the small slices on his skin burn and smoke. Her arm began to feel heavy and shake from the exertion of swinging and hitting the rock-like surface of Cronus. He fell over another pile of bodies, landing with a loud *thunk*. She hoped to take advantage and leapt over the mound, raising her sword high, and aimed for his heart, but she was stopped in midair by an unseen force.

She gasped and looked down to see Cronus holding his own long sword. She dangled like a skewer of meat from the blade. "Shit," she mumbled between gritted teeth.

## Chapter Sixteen

Malcolm King couldn't believe his eyes when Selena stormed in like an avenging angel and engaged their greatest enemy. The little fool taunted the big-ass beast with words a child would use, and by all appearances, it worked like a charm to divert Cronus from killing him and Max. He waffled between beating her ass red and kissing her senseless. He decided he would do both, just as soon as they finished this fight.

He looked over to see Max rolling to his side, pulling the numerous stakes Cronus had thrown at him that made him look like a porcupine out of his body. Deciding he needed to get on with the healing and quit gawking at the train wreck, he groaned and wobbled on his feet.

"Damn I feel lightheaded." Malcolm rubbed his head.

"I think our girl might have come into her powers."

"Gee, ya think?"

Malcolm laughed at Max, who flipped him the bird. He looked around the large room, assessing the collateral damage, and was happy to see his brothers still fought. If he and Max could just get their lazy asses back into the battle, they could save their girl and make it back home before sunrise.

"You are so projecting right now and I so don't need a hard-on while I battle that thing." Max growled.

"Sorry, but fuck…look at her move. She is fan-fucking-tastic, for real dude."

"Are you ready?" Malcolm asked.

"As I'll ever be, I guess…"

Malcolm and Max both gasped as they saw Selena advancing on Cronus with bolts of lightning flying out of her blade. They watched in horror as the big beast fell on his back and Selena jumped in the air with a battle cry to finish him off. Time seemed to stand still as they saw Cronus raise a blade and stab into her stomach.

Both brothers flashed to the pair, and Malcolm focused on Cronus as Max grabbed Selena by the waist and dematerialized out of the hall. She dropped her sword and with a roll, Malcolm picked the thing up, amazed at the weight and the power he felt pulsing through it. He raised the sword and aimed it at the head of Cronus.

The bastard smiled, his shark-like teeth covered in blood, and swiped at the spittle dripping from his chin. Malcolm wanted the god to pay for the pain he'd caused Selena. He pictured skewering him on a pike like he did to Selena. Cronus wavered and seemed to shrink right before Malcolm's eyes.

Blinking, Malcolm stared at the man who looked so much like Zeus it shocked him and he didn't finish with the strike aimed at Cronus. He barely missed the blow aimed at his own head. Malcolm channeled Keanu Reeves and dodged several more strikes and kicked out, hitting Cronus in the chest.

Rafe stepped up on his right with Vin on his left and they all raised their blades, ready to strike at the same time. Nobody could ever charge Cronus with being a stupid man. Arrogant yes, but stupid not so much, and he proved it in the next moment.

Cronus flashed out, leaving the battered and bloody Ravens staring at the space where he'd been.

"Fuck," Rafe and Vin said in unison.

Malcolm turned in a circle, holding his blade in front of him, and spotted Balky who had come to steal Selena from them. "You," Malcolm snarled, and flashed across the room and grabbed the ugly son of a bitch by the front of his shirt. "Where did he go?"

Malcolm saw the smaller man lift his shoulders, but he didn't raise his arms to protect himself. Shaking him like a rag doll, he heard the approach of the rest of the Ravens.

"Do I know you?" Something seemed familiar.

Balky shook his head and opened his mouth. "I am Balky," he said.

Like that meant shit to Malcolm. He brought Balky closer to his face with one hand and snarled, "Start talking or I'll start dismembering." He grabbed the other man's arm with his free hand and twisted. Hearing a satisfying crack he let off the pressure. The other man's arm hung by his side, useless, and right before their eyes the being's arm started healing itself.

"What in the hell are you?"

"I'm not sure," Balky said.

"I don't have time for this shit." Malcolm looked to Rafe. "Take care of him. I need to go to Selena."

He watched Vin open his mouth, but didn't wait to hear what he said. He followed Max and Selena's trail back to his home. Flashing inside, he came to an abrupt halt at the sight that met his eyes.

Max was straddling a bloody Selena with his hands pressed over the gaping wound of her belly. He saw the glow emanating from Max's hands and heard his brother speaking softly to Selena.

"Selena, baby, I need you to focus and help me heal you," Max said.

She raised her hand and rubbed at his brother's cheek, and Malcolm could see the effort that small gesture took on her body. "It's no use, Max. I can't do it," she gasped. "I need to tell you and Malcolm something." She placed her palm over his mouth. "I love you both."

Malcolm watched as a trail of blood trickled out of her nose, and when she coughed, more of her precious fluid came out of her mouth. Malcolm kneeled beside her and placed his hand over Max's.

"Yes you can, Selena. Just concentrate and feel me and Max inside you." Malcolm prayed and sent up a silent cry to the gods.

He blinked the tears away, but let them fall down his cheeks. He heard Max sniff, but neither let up the healing pressure on her wound. Closing his eyes, he flowed into her mind and soothed her even as Max entered the wound. He could see what Max was doing through their link and was startled at the lack of ability they had. It seemed whatever Cronus had done to his own blade caused a wound they couldn't heal.

He heard Max snarl a silent warning and continued to shield Selena from the pain. He feared they were losing her when her eyes fluttered closed, only to snap open again when a bright light lit the room up.

"Oh, my baby," Hera whispered, dropping to her knees and placing her hands on each side of Selena's cheeks.

* * * *

Selena gasped and tried to speak, but choked on blood. She knew who was looking at her with such love and longing. If she weren't dying she'd talk to her mother and give her a hug to soothe the heartache emanating from her. But oh god, she hurt.

She couldn't feel the pleasant buzz of lightning flashing through her body. Instead she felt fire scorching her from the inside out. Damn Cronus!

"Mom?" Selena croaked.

Another flash of light, and Selena saw the god called Zeus. The look in his eyes mirrored hers, and she felt a flutter of hope. She watched him shake his head and he smiled at her. She tried to smile back, but knew it looked more like a grimace.

"Hello, my child," Zeus boomed.

Selena would've laughed at the looks on her two men's faces, but Zeus didn't give her time to answer. One minute she was lying under

Max in California and the next she was surrounded by several, larger-than-life people. She knew, without asking, she was on Mount Olympus and the people surrounding her were all gods and goddesses.

* * * *

"Ah, you are finally awake," Zeus said.

She turned her head and saw her father seated next to her bed in a rather uncomfortable-looking chair, appearing a bit ruffled. She looked to the other side and saw her mother slumped forward, resting her head next to her leg. "What the hell is going on?" She didn't realize she spoke her question out loud until she heard an intake of breath. Turning back, she faced Zeus.

"You have been out of it for a few days and we feared it might have been—" He swallowed. "We feared it might have been too late. Cronus poisoned that blade with his own blood before he impaled you on it."

"That man is such a coward," Selena whispered, and rubbed her throat. She felt like she'd swallowed a thousand shards of glass.

Her father reached his hand out and waved it over her neck, and she swallowed without any pain. Smiling, she reached out and grabbed his arm before he could pull it back. She flowed into his mind as naturally as she did her own, amazed at the vast knowledge and the lingering pain he felt at her loss. She watched in slow motion the things he'd done and how he tried to find her to no avail. She marveled at the absolute love he felt for her. Surrounded by warmth, she closed her eyes and slept.

The next time she woke up, she looked over and saw Hera sitting next to the bed knitting. It was such a domestic and normal sight, she giggled.

"Oh my, you are awake. How do you feel?" Hera reached over and poured a glass of water in a short, golden tumbler.

"Fine." Clearing her throat, Selena continued, "I feel much better. What time is it?"

"I suppose if you were going by Earth time, you would say it is past midnight."

"Shit, I slept through the whole day? Max and Malcolm must be going crazy. When can I see them?"

Her mother had such a strange look on her face, Selena thought she wasn't going to answer her, but finally she opened her mouth, and then closed it. Selena had gathered from her father's mind the gods and goddesses didn't normally speak out loud. They considered it too primitive, but she could see her mother tried to make the effort for her.

"Selena dear, you have been asleep for over two weeks." She gestured at the pile of knitted items littering the floor around her feet.

"What? Oh, I have to go," Selena said, throwing back the covers, and attempted to stand. She gasped at the lightheaded feeling that almost had her doing a face-plant on the marble floors.

Her mother moved so fast, or maybe she didn't actually move. One minute she was sitting in the chair and the next she grabbed Selena and cradled her in her arms like a baby. Selena knew she was small, but being held in the other woman's arms, she felt like a baby. She watched as Hera's eyes closed and a golden tear leaked out of each of her mother's eyes.

She reached up and wiped away the tear. When Hera placed her back on the bed she mourned the loss of her mother's arms. What the hell? She was a grown-ass woman wanting to be held like a baby? What was next? Maybe she needed a fucking pacifier or something. Her mother laughed, and she realized she hadn't blocked her thoughts.

"No, my baby, I don't think you need a pacifier," Hera said.

"Thank the lord. I don't think I had one when I was an actual baby." Selena regretted her flip words when Hera's face scrunched up. "I'm sorry. I didn't mean to upset you."

"It is all right. I know what you meant. It is just, really…" She took a deep breath. "It is just, really wonderful having you here and having the ability to hold you. I cannot even express to you how long I have waited and hoped to find you. Now you are here, and it is all I can do not to wrap my arms around you and never let go."

Selena smiled, feeling the same love pouring from her mother that Zeus had shown. The Ramos family had adopted her and given her all the love a child needed, but she had room for another set of parents. She opened her arms and Hera stepped forward. They hugged and cried until they heard a gruff voice being cleared. Hera pulled back first and tucked a lock of hair behind Selena's ear.

"Are you two done with the girl chat? I have two imbeciles who keep battering my mind, and I am this close"—he pressed his thumb and index finger together—" to eliminating my top two Ravens."

"Oh hush, you know you love them boys."

Selena looked between her two parents and wondered who they were talking about. Her father grimaced and rubbed his temple.

"Dammit, they are yelling in my head again."

"Who are you talking about?"

"Who am I talking about?" Zeus looked at Hera. "Did she really just ask me that?"

"Yes, honey, I do believe she did and I do believe you should probably let them come to her," Hera said.

"But we just got her back." Zeus growled.

"Are you whining like a baby?" Hera asked.

Selena couldn't help but laugh at the look her father shot her mother until he shot that laser-like gaze in her direction. She raised her hands, saying without words she didn't say anything about him being a baby.

"You do realize, as soon as I let them up here they are going to try and take her away again?"

Hera glided over to Zeus, and Selena was amazed at the affection her parents didn't try to hide. She felt like a voyeur when her mother wrapped her arms around Zeus and laid her head on his chest. Zeus rested his chin on top of the smaller woman's head, and Selena saw him take a deep breath with his eyes closed. She looked away, not wanting to intrude on their moment.

"You could never intrude, Mikroula."

"What does that mean?" Selena asked.

"It means little one." Zeus explained.

"I think I need to work on not projecting my thoughts a little better."

"Okay, I hear you," Zeus muttered.

"They cannot take her away from us, she is always going to be here," Hera said, pressing a hand over his heart.

Zeus covered her hand with his larger one, and Selena couldn't help but smile at their show of affection. She really was a very lucky woman to have had such great adoptive parents and now these two who obviously loved each other very much. The books she read didn't portray them as such loving people, but then again, you can't always believe everything you read.

"I'm going to let the King brothers come to Mount Olympus, but I swear to all that is holy, I will slay them if they try to take her away from me—I mean us!"

Hera patted her husband's cheek, and it was all Selena could do not to giggle at the astonished look that passed over the big man's face.

"Ah, you are such a big softy, my love."

Selena did roll her eyes at that one. Softy! Ha, what a joke.

"Oh, believe me, Selena, this man is a teddy bear at heart. Hard as a stone on the outside, but inside." She tapped his chest. "Inside he is like a big marshmallow."

"Oh yes, I think he looks just like the Stay Puft Marshmallow Man," Selena joked, not letting them see the image of the thing as it looked in the *Ghostbusters* movie.

"I see that, young lady, and I resent that remark." Zeus smiled.

Selena laughed, feeling almost complete.

"Okay, I will let them up, but I will speak with them alone before I allow them in to see you."

"Dad," Selena whined.

"That has a lovely ring to it, Mikroula," Zeus said. He let go of Hera and floated over to the bed. Leaning down, he pressed a kiss to her forehead, and then her cheeks.

Selena closed her eyes and enjoyed the first show of affection her father had given her. She felt him stand up, and then he disappeared. She looked around and met her mother's amused gaze.

"You father and I love you very much. I think you just wrapped that man around your finger with one little word," Hera sobbed.

Selena climbed out of the bed, amazed at the strength her body had. She floated. *Yeehaw!* She friggin' floated, just like her father, over to where her mother stood and embraced the woman in a hug.

"I love you, Mom," Selena said with meaning.

"Thank you, Selena. I love you, too."

# Chapter Seventeen

Max King prowled the gilded room they were shown to after they'd been zapped from Malcolm's home. He didn't spare a glance at the opulence of the room, or stare in awe at the beautiful people who walked past. It had been two weeks since they'd had Selena snatched away from them. He knew why the god had taken her, and for that, he was grateful. Truly he was. Now he was prepared to beat the man senseless.

"You can try, pup," Zeus said from behind him.

Max spun around and pinned the man with all the pent-up emotions he had held in check for weeks. He heard Malcolm's intake of breath, but didn't break his hold or his gaze. He learned never to show fear or emotions in battle and he made no mistakes. This could be the biggest battle of his life.

"Where is Selena?" he asked between gritted teeth.

"Release me, boy," Zeus said.

The authority the man wielded had no effect on the half-crazed demigod. Malcolm laid his hand on Max's shoulder and spoke directly into his mind.

"*Max, you need to chill, dude. This is not the way to ask a father for his daughter's hand in marriage*," Malcolm said.

"You two think you are good enough for my baby?" Zeus asked.

"It doesn't matter what you think. We bonded with her and her with us. If you try to keep us apart we will all suffer."

"I would never allow my child to suffer. Now you two"—he flicked a glance between them—"I am willing to allow it."

"That is just too fucking bad, we won't allow it. We love her more than life itself, more than our next breath." Max snarled.

"Zeus, you have to understand, we love Selena and we know she feels the same. You need to give us a chance to explain and..." Malcolm stopped.

"Oh, you want to explain how you both claimed her? Or maybe you want to tell me how you plan to share her and make her your plaything?"

Max widened his eyes as Malcolm raised his arm and a bolt of lightning flashed out, slamming into the wall next to the god's head.

"You will never speak of Selena like that again, or, god or not, I will hurt you." Malcolm growled.

Zeus flashed a pearly-white smile, nearly blinding them with its brilliance. Max stumbled back and released his hold on the bigger man.

"Good. You two have passed." He rubbed his hands together.

Max looked at his brother, and then the god. Malcolm shrugged his shoulders while the god looked very pleased with himself.

"What the hell is going on, Zeus?" Max asked.

"I wanted to see how far you both were willing to go to claim my daughter. By the looks of it, you both were prepared to die for her."

"Well, duh," Malcolm said.

Max reached over and slapped his brother in the back of the head. Malcolm looked up with what could only be described as a petulant look.

"Mal, you do not say 'duh' to a god."

Malcolm rubbed his head and glared at Max. "It was a really stupid thing that he said. What was I supposed to say?"

"Oh I don't know, maybe something a little more appropriate. He says 'duh.'" Max rolled his eyes heavenward.

"Ya, well you just hit me. What are you, a two-year-old?"

Before he could pummel his brother, Zeus clapped his hands. Max turned to see the god had glided over to his large desk and sat behind it. It was such a domestic-looking scene, except the man had on a short white gown and sandals. Not to mention the gold bands around his head and arms. Some things were best left unnoticed, like your future father-in-law in a dress.

Max saw Zeus steeple his fingers and rest his chin on them. He looked at Malcolm, and then Max, seeming to judge them. He didn't flinch as the man invaded his mind. He did, however, cloud over the lovemaking he shared with Selena and Malcolm. A father really didn't need to see that.

"You are a little late, pup," Zeus said in a gruff voice.

Max winced.

"What do you want us to say, Zeus?"

"Nothing," Zeus shrugged.

"What the hell does that mean? You take our Fated away from us, and then you bring us here to do what? Can't you see we are suffering without her? How would you feel if you were separated from Hera?" Malcolm asked.

Max watched his normally laid-back brother pace back and forth, pulling at his hair in a clear sign of frustration. He tilted his head side-to-side, hearing a satisfying pop, then shook his hands out, trying to relax to no avail. Max knew what Malcolm was feeling.

"Calm down, boys. I do believe your little avenging angel is on her way here as we speak..."

* * * *

Selena barreled into the anteroom to her father's office and scattered the people inside with a flick of her wrist. She didn't stop to apologize. She raised her hand and watched the large door fly off the hinges. Hearing a more-than-satisfying thud, she stepped over the threshold, and sparing a glance in her father's direction, she focused her gaze on the two loves of her life.

"Where have you two been?" She raised her hand and they both fell silent. "I don't want to hear a word from you." She pointed a finger at Zeus.

"Oh gods, Selena, are you okay?" Malcolm asked, rushing to her side.

Selena brushed his question aside with an impatient shake of her head. When she woke up and found it had been weeks, and neither of her men had been there to hold her, she was saddened. Now here they were in her father's office, and still, neither man had come to see her. She was beyond pissed.

"Am I okay? You ask if I am okay? I am not okay. As a matter of fact, I am so fucking pissed at you two." Her eyes pinned both men.

"Gods but you are gorgeous when you're mad." Malcolm dropped to his knees and wrapped his arms around her waist.

Max shook his head and smiled.

Selena saw that look and stomped her bare foot. The pain that shot up her leg let her know she probably shouldn't throw a tantrum on marble floors.

"What are you smiling at?" Selena asked Max, running her hand through Malcolm's hair.

"He is correct." Max motioned to his brother with a tilt of his head. "You are truly magnificent when you're spitting fire."

"*Grrr*…you guys make me so angry. Just answer the question. Where have you guys been? Why haven't you come to see me?" Selena sniffed. She hated to cry, but her emotions were so out of whack.

"We've been trying to get to you, but it is really hard to get here from Earth, my love," Max said.

Malcolm nodded his head, but didn't loosen his hold on her waist. She couldn't help but smile at the purring sound he made as he nuzzled her belly. She heard a noise that sounded suspiciously like someone choking and saw her father with his finger in his mouth making gagging sounds.

"Please, spare me. You three are making me sick with your lovey-dovey stuff." Zeus looked at Selena and smiled a charming smile that almost made her forget why she was so pissed.

"Daddy…"

Selena saw her father's smile widen and she gave him a smile in return.

"I had to make sure they were worthy of my girl," Zeus said with a little bite, looking at Max and Malcolm.

"What do you mean?"

"What your father means is, he loves you and wanted to protect you. He was only doing what any loving father would do. He had to ensure your health and safety first and foremost." Max turned to Zeus. "Isn't that correct, Sir?"

"Oh now you show respect, when not five minutes ago you vowed to kill me if I didn't let you see Selena?"

She gasped. "You tried to kill my father?"

"No, I didn't try to kill your father." Max looked at Zeus with a look that could only be described as outraged.

"I beg to differ, Max. I clearly remember you slamming him against the wall, and if memory serves me correctly, you had pictures of him in pieces floating through your mind…Ow…Why did you do that?" Malcolm rubbed the back of his head.

"Because you are fucking stupid," Max snarled. He raised his hand again.

Selena reached out and grabbed Max with an invisible force and brought him closer to her. He dug his knee into Malcolm's side and Selena laughed at their antics. Malcolm released his hold and fell to the side as Max took his place in front of her. He placed his hands on her hips and brought her up to his eye level. She gasped at the raw cmotion shc saw in his cycs.

"I missed you," Max said.

She wrapped her arms around his neck and brought his mouth down to kiss her. He let her lead for all of two seconds before he swooped in and took control. He plundered her mouth with his tongue and wrapped one big arm around her waist, twisting his other hand in her hair, never once breaking contact with any part of their body.

He had her pressed so tight to his body. She lifted her legs up and around his sides, squeezing him with her thigh muscles. She wished they were alone and naked, but reality intruded in her fantasy with a loud banging on a hard surface that shook the walls.

"Enough! You may not, and I repeat, you may not molest my daughter in my own office." Zeus slapped his hand on his desk again.

Selena pulled her mouth back from Max and licked his full lower lip before turning her eyes toward her father.

"Selena, I do not say this easily, but it was I who kept these two from you. I just…"

She watched the man who was the king of gods rub his neck and look upwards like he was seeking help from the Most High. He then turned his piercing focus back to where she stood wrapped around one man while the other had snuggled up to her back and wrapped his arms around her waist above his brother's. She felt almost complete. She decided to take mercy on her father.

"I understand, Daddy, but you can't keep me from them. They are my life, don't you see that?" She smiled to lessen the blow. She knew her parents had searched for her for over twenty-four years and knew they'd suffered every day that she'd been gone. Selena also knew she had brothers and sisters she had yet to meet, but that fell way down on her list of priorities at the moment.

"I am aware of that, but you can't blame a father for wanting to make sure the men who mated with their youngest child were worthy of her."

Sighing, Selena tapped Max's shoulder. He nodded and she felt Malcolm's loss of heat as he stepped back and released her before Max followed suit.

"Thank you." What else could a girl say when her father got all protective of her?

* * * *

Zeus closed his eyes and when he opened them, his office was empty. He rubbed his chest where his heart lay and realized the ache he'd felt for over twenty-four years was gone. Now he had a little twinge of loss.

"She is not gone forever," Hera whispered in his ear from behind.

Zeus twisted and pulled the love of his life onto his lap and ravaged her lips with a kiss. He closed his eyes and relished her familiar taste of berries and sweet cream. He flashed them out of his office and into their bedroom, where they created magic each and every time they came together. He growled at the smooth feel of her bare flesh rubbing against his semi-clothed body. Within moments, he too lay completely bare and open to her caresses.

Between one second and the next, he rolled her under him and entered her in one fluid stroke. She welcomed him into her body like a glove made just for him.

"Just for you, my love." Hera breathed.

Zeus stopped her words with a soul-searing kiss. She opened under his assault, meeting his tongue and sucking it into her mouth. Goddess but the woman drove him insane with her talented tongue and roaming hands. She gripped his ass in a firm, steady embrace and wrapped her legs around his thighs, urging him faster with her movements.

He wanted to stay inside her welcoming heat forever, but could feel his body preparing to release. They made love almost every day, sometimes several times a day, since they'd met. He couldn't get enough of her, and thankfully she felt the same. He didn't want to leave her behind and with that in mind, concentrated on squeezing the muscles at the base of his cock. He pumped in slow and pulled back an inch, only to slam back inside her tightening sheath, his balls slapping the sensitive area between her back hole and her pussy. He buried his incredibly hard shaft deep and held still, feeling her walls begin to flutter.

"Move, damn you," Hera screamed.

"Are you ready, my love?" Zeus asked wickedly with a twist of his hips.

"Gods yes…"

He pulled out to the tip, not giving her a chance to complain as he pushed forward, setting a frantic pace that Hera matched with a raise of her hips. She smiled up at him with the look he'd come to crave. It transmitted all the love she felt for him. He levered himself up on his elbow and reached down to strum her clit with the other hand.

"I'm going to come." Hera bit her lip and closed those amazing eyes. She twisted her hips and gasped.

"Yes. Yes. Oh." His seed erupted from him like a blast of heat, bubbling up and filling her body with his release. The pleasure was so intense with spasm after spasm his body twitched, and shook uncontrollably. Taking a deep breath, he collapsed on top of her. "Hera. Oh my, Hera. I love you more than life."

"And I you, my love," Hera murmured.

He gathered his strength and rolled them to their sides, with him cuddling her close. They lay that way with their bodies still entwined in the roiling aftermath. Zeus tried to gather his bearings.

"Do you miss her yet?"

Hera stiffened and he immediately regretted his words.

"Stupid question I know, but damn it we just got her back." Now he was starting to sound like a whiner, and that just wouldn't do.

Hera giggled, and the reverberation of the sound shot straight to his balls and his cock began to swell again. "Are you laughing at me, woman?" Zeus asked with a mock growl.

"Why yes, yes I am. What are you going to do about it?"

Zeus flipped them over, and with his dick buried balls-deep inside its favorite place, he looked up and grinned. "Ride me, sweetheart." He gripped her hips, lifting her up and down until she took over the motions. Where the woman got the energy he didn't know, and frankly, he didn't care.

# Chapter Eighteen

"Dang it, I hate it when he does that," Malcolm groused.

Selena swayed on her feet, and Malcolm watched as his brother grabbed her shoulders and held her steady. She smiled up at Max with a smile so bright it literally rocked Malcolm's world. He wanted to see her face glow like that every day for the rest of their lives.

Max led Selena to the huge walk-in tub in the center of the bathroom. Max flicked his wrist and the tub filled with steamy water and cherry-blossom-scented bubbles fell over the sides. He closed his eyes and willed his and Selena's clothes away. At times like these, Malcolm loved the ability to will away clothing.

Meeting the amused stare of Max, Malcolm gave him a shrug. "I am not undressing my brother, and don't even think about it," Malcolm said as Max got that gleam in his eye. Malcolm knew that look meant his brother was going to slap him in the back of the head.

"What are you talking about?"

"Don't act all innocent, bro." He turned pleading eyes to Selena. "Lena, make Maxy be nice to me." He gave her his best little-boy look.

"Oh gods but I love you guys," Selena said

Malcolm walked up and grabbed her face in the palm of his hands and kissed her forehead, and then trailed kisses over her eyes and down one cheek to her chin. He reversed the path on the opposite cheek, and then slid his lips over hers in a butterfly wing's caress. Leaning his forehead down, he pressed against hers and looked directly into her silver orbs.

"We love you too, baby. You truly complete us."

"I'm not sure how this works." She encompassed them in a circular gesture with one hand. "But I know we can do it. I mean hello. I'm a goddess and you guys are...What the hell are you guys, anyways?"

Malcolm glanced to Max with a look and spoke directly into their minds, sharing the link with Selena. "*I think Max can explain it better than me. What do you say, bro*?"

"I say, let's get in the tub and ease our weary bodies for this long, tortuous story." Max held his hand out and Selena placed her smaller one in his as he led them into the tub.

Malcolm followed them and sat on the opposite side, sandwiching Selena between them. They all rested their heads on the back of the tub that had been padded, and gazed up at the skylight above. Malcolm watched as Max created a virtual scene, but instead of words he showed Selena in pictures the beginning of how the Ravens were created.

She inhaled and gripped their thighs that flanked her each time a battle scene played out, and when another woman's face came in to view, Selena did a little swirly thing with her finger and fast forwarded the picture. Malcolm smiled at her show of jealousy.

"I will so get you back for that thought, Malcolm King," Selena said.

"A man can only wish for that, goddess."

Malcolm turned his head and instantly, sparks flew between them. Max still stared at the ceiling and with a negligent lift of his arm, wrapped it around Selena, and brought her closer to him. He skimmed his palms up her sides and brushed the underside of her breast closest to him.

"We were so scared we were going to lose you," Malcolm said.

"Me too," Selena whispered.

Malcolm remembered the fear he'd felt when she'd swooped in like an avenging angel. He also remembered they owed her an ass beating. He reached over and pulled her over his thighs, rubbed his palms down her sides, and stopped at the top of her delectable little derriere. He envisioned their hand prints making her ass glow and trailed his hands down, resting them on the firm globes.

"Do not even think about it, Malcolm King, or I swear I'll tie you up and leave you hanging," Selena snarled.

His little darling was threatening him, and his little man down below twitched at the prospect. Fuck, he must be a moron. He let his fingers glide down her crack and pressed forward. Her moan was like music to his ears.

"Are you two done playing yet?" Max asked.

"Hmm?" Malcolm asked. He raised Selena up with a little pressure between her thighs and engulfed her right breast into his mouth.

"Please tell me we aren't stopping?" Selena questioned.

"Oh baby, we are so far from stopping it isn't even on the horizon yet." Malcolm tugged her hair and brought his lips down, sealing their mouths together and lifting his hips, impaling her on his shaft. She gasped and he slapped his own head. "I'm sorry, Lena. Did I hurt you?" He held perfectly still.

"Goddess no, Malcolm, you feel so damn good inside me."

"Are you sure? I just couldn't wait to feel you wrapped around me again. Don't ever scare us like that again." He pumped his hips. "Do you hear me?" Each word was punctuated with a thrust and retreat of his dick inside her.

"And none of that fancy word play like you did. 'I promise to be safe and careful,'" Max said in a parody of Selena's voice.

She slapped water into his brother's face and Malcolm buried his face into her neck, inhaling her scent. He nipped her shoulder and she squealed, even as her pussy squeezed his cock.

"Turn her around, Malcolm. I want that sassy mouth wrapped around my dick."

Malcolm effortlessly lifted and turned Selena to face Max, who stood across the tub with a heavy-lidded gaze that definitely spelled trouble for their girl, or ecstasy. She pointed her perfect ass at him and he couldn't help himself. He gave her a little swat on one cheek, and then the other. She slammed her pussy back down on top of him, and from the copious liquid that eased his entry she'd really enjoyed those love taps.

"I think our girl likes her butt spanked, Max."

"I do not." Selena glared over her shoulder.

"Yes you do. And what did we tell you about lying?"

"Are you two done yet? I feel a little pain right here." Max pointed at his penis. "I think it needs a kiss."

"Oh my, he does look pained. Why, he is so red, and what is this?" She swiped her finger across the weeping end of Max's cock and brought her finger to her mouth.

"Damn but that is fucking hot." Max panted and stepped forward, pressing his dick to her closed mouth, painting her lips with his pre-cum.

Selena hummed and opened her mouth, and took Max to the back of her throat. Max shared the feel of her wet mouth wrapped around him with Malcolm, and Malcolm reciprocated with the feel of her tight heat surrounding his shaft as he pressed forward. She squeezed her inner muscles, letting him know she needed more.

Both men groaned as their Fated held each of them inside her body. Malcolm pushed up and pinched her nipples while Max held her head steady with his hands. They each took care not to hurt her with their larger bodies, shuttling in and out of her at the same time.

Malcolm formed a stream of water in the shape of a finger, letting it massage her tiny bundle of nerves. Her vaginal walls constricted so hard on his dick, it was all he could do not to explode on the spot. He looked up to see Max, his head thrown back and a grimace on his face. He opened his mind, sharing the feel of Selena milking his cock, and shuddered as Max unveiled the ecstasy he felt each time she took him to the back of her throat and swallowed on the head.

"I'm not going to last," Malcolm said.

Max grunted his agreement and Selena laughed into their shared link. Malcolm formed another digit out of water, only this one pressed on her back entrance.

"Easy baby, don't bite me." Max's eyes widened when Malcolm showed him what he was doing to their little darling.

Selena pulled back on a gasp. "What the hell is that?"

Malcolm met her look for look and tried for an innocent expression, but right at that moment, she clamped down on him so hard he feared she'd snap his cock off at the base. He saw her eyes roll to the back of her head, and her mouth opened on a silent scream. He pumped the phallus in and out of her ass in time with his cock.

Every muscle inside Selena squeezed his shaft as he shuttled in and out of her. Her orgasm crashed through and he felt it all the way down to his balls. Pulses of aftershocks rocked her body and she screamed. Spasm after spasm shook her. Selena's voice grew in volume as she came. He continued to fuck her, pulling out and pushing in, slowly prolonging her pleasure until she collapsed in a stupor against his chest.

They let her catch her breath, and Malcolm made the phallus dissipate, causing her to twitch on him again.

"I could almost come just from watching her," Max said.

"That would be a shame when you taste so good." Selena licked her lips, and it was Max's turn to pant. "Come here, big boy." She beckoned Max with a finger.

Malcolm held completely still as his brother stepped forward and closed his eyes, with a look of bliss transforming Max's features. Selena opened wide and took him into the hot cavern of her mouth. Malcolm leaned to the side to see her pull back and lap at the underside of Max's dick.

Malcolm had a little envy until she began milking him with those incredible internal muscles again. She rhythmically squeezed him, taking him to the brink, but neither he nor Max wanted to leave her behind.

Max tweaked her nipples and tapped her clit before trapping it between two fingers. He rubbed it back and forth as he shuttled in and out of her mouth, racing toward his own peak.

They were all so in tune with each other, sharing their pleasures through their link, it was impossible to tell who soared first. Max roared like a lion. Selena vocalized her pleasure with a keening wail. Malcolm grunted. But in the end, they all came at the same time. She took their seeds into her body, licking Max like a favorite treat as he filled her to overflowing.

"I think she killed me." Max pulled his softening cock from Selena's lips.

"Mmm…definitely better than chocolate," she mumbled.

"Please don't share his taste with me love. Ow! What did I say, damn it?" Malcolm rubbed his head. "You're gonna mess with my brain if you keep hitting me."

* * * *

Max rolled his eyes and stepped out of the tub. He reached back inside, lifting Selena off his brother's lap, and carried her into the tropical-style shower with the four amazing waterfall heads. He set the temperature to cool and quickly washed himself, watching Selena through half-closed lids with her head thrown back, letting the water flow over her face. Max saw her open her mouth and fill it with water, and then she spewed it out like a geyser. He laughed at her antics.

"Why do you guys have all this?" she waved her arm. "You could have cleansed us with a thought. Come to think of it, I could've, too."

She amazed him with her quick acceptance of all the revelations she had been shown. "Yes we could, but there is just something about water washing away all the grime of the day."

"Oh sure, and it has nothing to do with a naked Selena," Malcolm said, stepping into the shower behind Selena.

Max marveled at the drops of water that clung to her long eyelashes, and the way her eyes flashed from a stormy gray to a liquid silver. He poured some soap into his hands and tossed the bottle to Malcolm. They both soaped up their hands, while each took their time washing their side of Selena's body.

Max gave her a little push, turning her to face Malcolm, presenting her back to him. He uncapped the shampoo and began lathering her hair. Soap trailed down her back and over her softly rounded behind. Stepping forward, he rubbed his hardening cock up the crack. He massaged the muscles in her shoulders and down her back, pressing on her spine in small circles.

Looking over her head, he met the hungry look of Malcolm, and they both nodded. Max stepped under the spray and Malcolm pulled Selena closer to him, helping her rinse her hair, paying special attention to the bubbles trailing down her front. Max could tell from the tiny puffs of air, she enjoyed Malcolm's ministrations. Rinsing himself quickly, Max opened the door, leaving Selena and Malcolm alone, only to return with a big fluffy towel. He pulled Selena away from a kneeling Malcolm, who gave him a petulant look.

"What?" Max asked him.

"I was enjoying my treat." Malcolm's tongue swiped over his lower lip.

Selena giggled.

"Ow! Dammit, Malcolm, what the hell was that for?" Max asked.

"Doesn't feel too good, now does it? Now will you quit slapping me in the back of the…Ouch! Max, you are a first-class jackhole."

"Thank goodness I'm the brains of the family then, huh?"

"You two stop it. And Max, stop hitting your brother." Selena laughed.

Max tugged on her hand. She stumbled, but Malcolm swooped in and picked her up fireman-style, as he draped her over his shoulder, with a smug look, he passed Max in the process.

Max heard a little tap and squeal. Linking with the two of them, he saw Malcolm slap Selena's ass a moment before she retaliated and smacked his brother's left butt cheek. They both rubbed the little sting with the flats of their hands. Max shook his head at their antics, realizing in that moment there wasn't a snowball's chance in hell they'd ever be able to truly punish her that way.

Reaching around the giggling pair, he flicked the comforter out of the way and lay in the middle of the big bed. "Give her here, Mal."

Selena lay over Max and rubbed her belly over his already engorged flesh. She leaned forward. Her hair formed a curtain, shielding them in their own little cocoon.

"I've read books." She bit her lip.

"Of course you can have anything you want, baby," Max met Malcolm's frown with one of his own.

"No…I mean both of you. Gah!"

Max's head nearly spun in a circle at the image she projected into their minds. Damn, how the hell did they get so lucky with their Fated?

"Selena, you have no reason to be embarrassed to voice your wants. Your wants are our wants. As long as it doesn't endanger your life, we will move mountains to give you anything you desire."

"Less talking and more doing then," Selena said a bit impishly.

"Have you ever tried the reverse cowboy, Lena?" Max asked.

Instead of telling her, Max showed her shocking images that detailed how they wanted her. He felt more of her juices coating his lower belly where she lay.

"I think she likes that idea, Mal."

They took the time to ease her rear passage for their penetration, working a generous amount of lube inside before either man made any move to enter her.

"Scoot down to the edge Max, and I'll help Selena," Malcolm said.

Max held Selena tight and maneuvered them to the end of the bed. He nearly choked on his tongue when Selena grabbed the base of his dick and placed the tip to her opening. She sank down on him, sliding her over his cock. The tight ring of muscle gave way slowly as he and Malcolm both steadied her downward descent. They were all shaking by the time she was fully seated. Malcolm waited until she'd taken Max all the way inside before he helped straighten her legs and drape them over Max's thighs.

Reaching out, Max slowly lowered her until her back was flush against his chest, and then tipped her chin up to capture her lips. Malcolm stepped between their spread thighs and Max felt cool liquid drip onto his balls that had nothing to do with Selena's juices.

Both men were well-endowed and shared a fear of causing her pain. To help ease his entrance, Malcolm poured more slick gel between their bodies. It would've been comical the way he avoided touching Max's dick if Selena hadn't whimpered.

"Are you sure, Lena? We don't have to do this."

"Yes we do. I want it so much I think I might come just from the idea," Selena all but shouted.

"By all means, baby, go ahead and come," Max offered.

"Oh yeah, you should see the way her pussy is fluttering down here," Malcolm said in awe.

"Fuck looking, man, you should feel it."

"Are you ready for more, Selena girl?" Malcolm asked.

Max captured her mouth again, distracting her with little tugs to her nipples. He felt Malcolm as he pressed forward, entering her overly tight sheath. Max felt more liquid pulsing inside, coating Selena to ease Malcolm's entry. Max held completely still as Malcolm tunneled inside. She allowed both of them inside her body, accepting their double penetration. Making their possession complete as they both filled her to capacity.

"Oh yes, I'm gonna come. Oh. Oh." Her voice grew in volume.

Her orgasm bathed them both and in complete accord, Max trapped her hardened nipples between thumb and fingers, rolling them back and forth, and then massaging them with his palms to soothe the ache. Malcolm pulled out to the head of his cock and surged forward. They wanted her to have a vaginal orgasm. It took a lot of patience and skill, but neither man had a problem getting a woman to come that way.

Selena swiveled her hips and Max nearly lost it. She didn't let him gather his control. She squeezed her inner muscles, urging Malcolm and Max into a faster pace.

Malcolm raised her legs and rested them on his shoulders. He ran his hands down her legs preparing to touch her clit. Max knew if he so much as touched her there, she'd go off like a rocket. He communicated his thoughts with Malcolm, blocking Selena from hearing them. She didn't seem to notice as every muscle in her body contracted around them.

Malcolm set up a rhythm of pulling out, and when he pushed in, Max retreated. They surged forward and out in sync with each other, driving her closer to an orgasm to rival all others.

She gasped and tossed her head on Max's shoulder searching for his lips, and he was quick to oblige her. Malcolm yanked her hair, jerking her head back.

Her eyes opened wide and she cried out. He nearly let go, thinking he had gone too far.

"Oh my, don't stop."

He wrapped her hair around his fist and tugged even harder. She laughed, a tinkling sound that had his balls drawing up preparing to release.

She writhed on their dicks, urging them into a faster pace. Max met her look with a fierce gaze and turned her face toward Malcolm so she could see the intense concentration he reflected. Max never broke from the steady pace they set, keeping her suspended between their larger frames.

"Try to push us out, baby. Yes, just like that, bear down on our cocks," Malcolm panted.

They thrust in and out, slowly increasing in speed as her entire body writhed involuntarily, driving them all closer to the peak. Max saw her body begin to glow, encompassing the three of them in a golden bubble.

"Yes. Yes. Oh fuck. Fuck me," Selena chanted.

Max completely agreed with Selena. He loved her so much. Light exploded behind his closed lids and he felt his release bubble up. He felt Malcolm twitch as their cocks rubbed back and forth, increasing her pleasure. His cock hurt so badly from holding off his release, Max feared he may not be able to finish. When his orgasm finally slammed into him, he forgot all about a slow pace and picked up speed. He jarred her body with his thrust, holding her hips so hard he knew she'd have bruises come daylight. It just wasn't in him to give a shit.

She worked so hard to force them into going over the edge.

Release caught them all by surprise, and they couldn't stave it off any longer when Max felt an imaginary touch pressing against his prostate. His seed erupted from him like a tsunami. It crashed as he spurted wave after wave into her flexing pussy. They all gasped, still filling her with their pleasure. Selena shared the overwhelming feeling through their link.

Max could only come and come and come, and from the feel of it, Malcolm did too. He felt their combined juices flowing down between their bodies. Long after they were all spent, her muscles continued to clamp down on the bases of their cocks.

They all seemed to groan in ecstasy, or possibly agony, when the contractions finally stopped. Malcolm was the first to pull out, followed by Max. He picked Selena up, and walked around to the side of the bed, laying her gently in the middle.

"I think she passed out, dude," Malcolm said with his hands on his hips.

With a thought, Max cleaned himself and Selena while Malcolm did the same to himself and the bed. They were too tired to wash up the human way.

Max climbed in on her left side and kissed her parted lips. She didn't even stir.

Malcolm followed suit and snuggled up on her other side. He nuzzled her neck and threw his leg over hers. Max tossed his arm over her chest and closed his eyes.

## Chapter Nineteen

Zeus waited for what seemed an eternity before looking in on his daughter. The last time he looked into the bowl, he'd gotten a picture that was sure to cause him nightmares for years, possibly thousands of decades. He knew when Hera opened her eyes and saw when she noticed him by the porcelain dish, what he planned.

"Darling, do you want me to look first?"

"Do you think they are still going at it? I mean for fuck's sake. What the hell do they think this is, a marathon or something?"

"They are newly mated and they have been separated for weeks. What would you do in their same position?"

"I do not want to compare what I do with you and what they might do with her. If I do, I might have to kill them."

Laughing, his wife climbed from their bed and rested her head on his shoulder. He loved that they were so evenly matched in size, with her just a few inches shorter and much curvier. He didn't like the idea of his tiny daughter and the two overly large men sharing her.

"She is not that tiny in comparison to them, Zeus."

"Ha. Okay. Here it goes." Zeus looked into the clear liquid and zeroed in on his daughter lying between her two men. He couldn't help but think she looked right at home.

Fates really had a funny sense of humor, that was for sure. He waved his hand and a looking bowl very similar to the one he had stood in the center of their room. He wanted his baby girl to be able to contact him anytime she needed. She could also do it with only a thought, but until she got control of all her powers, that would be the easiest and least invasive way.

"You really are a softy at heart."

"What the hell is a Stay Puft Marshmallow, anyways?"

"You caught that, did you?"

* * * *

Hera loved her husband, but sometimes the man was just too arrogant for his own good. Their daughter was definitely the burst of fresh air and energy they needed. Poor Zeus had no clue what went through their girl's mind, which frustrated him to no end. *Bless his heart. You have to love the man for all his faults. He is a great man.*

"Do you think she wants to have a big wedding and all the trimmings the humans so favor?" Zeus asked.

Hera watched him shudder and, turning her back, she hid her mirth behind a slight cough. If their baby wanted a big white wedding with a horse-drawn carriage, she knew Zeus would make it happen.

"Oh honey, you will look so fabulous in one of those tux things with the bowtie and coat with tails."

"Bullshit. I won't do it. She will have to have a toga-themed wedding, or maybe a nice Greek wedding with the Grecian style of dress. Yes, I can do that."

"What the hell is the difference between the two?" Hera asked with one hand on her naked hip and the other on the post at the head of the massive bed they shared.

She saw his eyes flare and follow her movements like a lion stalking its prey. She loved it when he went all animal-like on her.

"You are trying to distract me with your dirty thoughts and your sexy body. But I am telling you right now, I will not, and I repeat, will not dress up like a monkey in a suit."

Hera released the pole and trailed her hand down her neck, between her breasts, and stopped right above her mound. She extended her middle finger and dipped between her lips, rubbing around her clitoris in small circles. She closed her eyes in bliss, dipping her finger down lower to her vagina and pushing the tip inside.

Zeus jerked her hand out of the way and captured her finger between his lips, sucking her cream inside his mouth.

*Heh, I win!*

* * * *

Cronus tossed another idiot out of his path, watching as the body slithered down the black walls and landed in a heap of bones and blood.

"You can't keep doing that to my beings, Crone." Hades shook his head.

"Don't fuck with me, boy. I have my powers back," Cronus snarled.

"You are not at full strength as you may think, boyo. And don't think to come into my house and rule me."

Cronus took an involuntary step back before he noticed his mistake. *Show the devil you're scared and you will suffer for all eternity.* For beings like them that was indeed a long, very long time.

"I meant no disrespect. I appreciate you allowing me to come here." The words tasted like acid, but sometimes he had to do things he'd never do, unless in extreme situations.

"You don't eat crow well, my friend."

Cronus blinked as Hades snapped his fingers, astonished to find himself back inside his compound. Hades was obviously a lot stronger than he'd given him credit for. Cronus made a mental note to send someone into Hades's realm. Knowing your enemy inside and out could mean the difference between winning and losing. And Cronus did not like to lose. The Ravens may have won the battle, but he would win the war. The smell of sulfur was thick, and that was when he realized he wasn't on Earth, but back in hell.

Closing his eyes, he found what he was looking for in the form of a betrayer with red hair and snapping green eyes. He'd heard her companions call her Jaklyn and vowed to find the bitch and make her pay for helping Selena escape him. He'd gotten out of worse places, he could do it again.

* * * *

Jaklyn looked around at the empty home and wished she would've thought to grab the goddess when she'd transported back to the lair of the dead one. That was what they called Cronus. When she looked into his soul, there was only death and suffering for everyone around him.

Cronus had a black inner core that scared the holy living hell out of all his followers, but not Jaklyn. She'd seen the worst of men and women and survived. Her aunt and grandma had taught her how to see inside things and learn the weaknesses of people to use against them. Those lessons were passed down from generation to generation.

She and her band of warriors all had special abilities. They'd formed a group when they were little more than children, protecting their families from the demons who preyed upon them.

She had no clue they would enter into a world far beyond what she'd ever known.

"Okay. So now we have met a goddess and her protectors. Now what?" Link Adams, her best friend, asked.

"Now we prepare. Because this fight just went to the next level," Jaklyn said.

"Yes!" Link pumped his fist and bumped knuckles with his cousin. "We so totally rule Halo, man."

"You two are such dorks." Jaklyn laughed.

"But you wuv us anyways, right?" Abe Adams said.

"Let's get out of here, guys." Jaklyn turned and headed out the door.

"Do we gotta? I mean, dude, check out the digs for real," Abe whined.

Jaklyn spun on her heels to look at the two goofballs she considered her older, much less mature brothers. "Do you hear yourselves? Do you really want to be caught here by those two overgrown men, or, how about their way larger friends, hmm?" Jaklyn asked.

"I think their way larger friends would be quite okay with you being here, considering one of the two overgrown men zapped you here."

Jaklyn spun back around and nearly toppled over at the too-quick motion. The speaker stepped from the shadows and steadied her with an arm around her waist, bringing her into intimate contact with his harder-than-hard body. She tilted her head back and looked up into green eyes set in a face that could surely grace magazine covers.

He chuckled, a low, deep sound that had her toes curling in her combat boots.

"You think I'm handsome?"

"Stay out of my thoughts," Jaklyn snapped, and slapped a hand over her mouth.

"My name is Grayson. You need to learn to shield your thoughts." He made it sound like an accusation.

She bristled at his tone. Link and Abe moved to stand behind her, and she was shocked to see the man in front of her flare his nostrils, inhaling their scents.

"You are not mated to these two fools, are you?" He didn't give her time to answer. "No, you're not, thankfully. I would hate to have to kill them."

"What the heck are you talking about?" Jaklyn asked, truly confused.

He closed his eyes, shielding his thoughts from her probing gaze. "I need to go. I have spoken with Malcolm King, and he would like you to stay here. There are safeguards in place to help protect you until we can get back."

"I—we don't need protection," Jaklyn countered.

"Yes you do. Now don't argue with me." Grayson tapped her nose.

Blinking, Jaklyn tried to dispel the aura of power the man wielded like a sword. She was spellbound as he moved without warning, capturing her lips in a full-bodied kiss. He anchored her body to his with his steel-band-like arms, hugging her close. She went up on tiptoes, giving him better access.

He released her just as quick and took a step back, and then another until he blended into the shadows. She knew he dematerialized the same way the goddess had done earlier.

"Wow I think he just claimed you, Jaky," Link said.

"Shut up you two," Jaklyn yelled.

"No shit, Sherlock." Abe punched his cousin in the arm.

"Let's get out of here, before he returns."

Jaklyn was cut off mid-thought when she heard Grayson inside her head, as clear as if he stood in front of her. "*Baby, if you so much as try to leave I will know, and I will not be happy. Now be a good girl and get some sleep. There are several rooms to choose from, just make sure it is not in the same one as the idiots you call friends.*"

"Hey, my friends are not…" She slapped her hand over her mouth again. "Ow. Damn it, that fucking hurt." She licked the inside of her mouth, tasting the familiar taste of copper, letting her know she split her lip open.

When an unseen tongue swiped inside her mouth, soothing the little hurt, she jerked and before she knew it, the sting completely disappeared.

"*You taste divine, Jaklyn,*" Grayson rumbled.

Jaklyn looked around, checking to see if he'd returned. Link and Abe stared at her as if she'd grown two heads, and maybe she had. "I think I'm losing my ever-lovin' mind," she mumbled.

"I think we should chill here for a while. Ya know, catch our bearings and regroup," Link said, looking more like the soldier he was instead of the laid-back man he presented to the world.

She would trust her life to these two men and the others who made up their group. "Where is everybody else? Did they not get transported here like us?"

"I'm going to do some recon. You two check your phones and text the others." Abe barked out the orders. Jaklyn and Link quickly complied.

# Epilogue

*Six weeks later...*

"I am not wearing that…that, oh whatever the hell you call it. And you can't make me," Zeus said defiantly.

"Now all you need to do is stomp your foot and throw yourself to the ground to complete your temper tantrum," Hera joked.

Selena covered her mouth to stifle the giggle that threatened to bubble up. It was a losing battle, and one she gave up when her father looked at her with puppy-dog eyes and his lower lip puckered out.

"Oh my gawd, you big baby, it's not that bad." Selena laughed out loud, she couldn't help it. Her dad looked so adorable. Of course she'd keep that little bit to herself.

"Yes. Yes it is. Look at me. I look like an idiot, and that job is saved for your two idiots, not me," Zeus said. He pointed at the door where Max and Malcolm were getting ready.

"But, daddy, you know how much I want this. I always dreamed of having my father walk me down the aisle."

"You play dirty, little girl. That isn't fair. Not fair at all." The love that shone in her dad's eyes made his words sound like terms of endearment. After so many years of wondering who she was, where she came from, she now had the answers. Of course she wasn't fooling herself. She knew there was still a lot to learn about her newfound family, but it was something to look forward to.

* * * *

Selena turned and picked up her small bouquet, admiring the way her two rings shone, even without any light. When her men had gotten down on bended knee the morning after their joining with a platinum band ringed in diamonds in the palm of their hands, Selena had fallen a little more in love with them. They'd spoke in unison, like they did with many things, and asked her to share the rest of eternity with them, and it was all she could do not to scream yes, yes, yes she'd marry them.

Now, her life would be perfect if her best friend, Tamara, wasn't attempting to stay as far away from her as possible. She'd threatened bodily injury if Tamara weren't here today to be her maid of honor.

A commotion in the hall had her looking up in time to see Tamara rush past a stunned Rafe, before she slammed the large door in his face. The shock on the Raven's face was priceless in Selena's estimation.

Breath sounding labored, Tamara smirked at the bellow they heard from the other side of the door. Selena rushed over and wrapped her in an embrace she knew the other woman couldn't break. Now that all her loved ones were here, she was ready to get married.

"Thank you for coming, Tam. I was beginning to get worried."

"Oh yeah, right! Like *I could not* come, when you sent that big-ass oaf to get me." Tamara snarled.

"Did Rafe hurt you? If he did, I'll cut off his balls and feed them to him one at a time." Selena stepped back with her hands still holding Tamara's arms, to look up into her best friend's eyes. The only thing she could decipher in her gaze was longing. Opening her mouth, she wasn't sure what to ask, or how to explain all that had occurred since she'd last seen Tamara.

"Gods, but I love my bloodthirsty woman," Max interrupted, as he strolled into the room.

"Look here, now, it's my manly bits she's threatening. Be happy if it was yours, not mine." Rafe growled, coming into the room with a glare in Tamara's direction.

"Hey. Why doesn't he have shoes on? How come I have to wear shoes if he doesn't?" Zeus and Hera joined the others, filling Selena's room. The once quiet room was filling up with more and more people, making Selena happier than she thought possible.

"Why are you wearing shoes to a beach wedding anyway?" Malcolm asked, coming in behind Max. Both men had on similar outfits of loose white slacks with a silk button-down, top left untucked, with a beautiful corsage made up of purple and pink flowers, bedazzled with crystals, pinned to it. She was one lucky girl.

"I thought you said you wanted a church wedding." Zeus looked to his wife. "You said she wanted me to walk her down the aisle." He stabbed Selena with an accusing look.

"I did, Dad, but there just wasn't enough time to get it all arranged." The look of horror and disgust on her father's face threatened to double her over in laughter. You'd think she asked him to walk on hot coals while chewing broken glass.

"That's because she's done nothing but travel to all her clubs and check in on them. Spending days at each one, and then coming back to her club in Kansas City and doing the same there," Max said, folding his arms across his chest with a disapproving look at her.

Selena stared back, waiting for him to squirm. Malcolm, bless him, walked in and draped his arm across her shoulders, adding his glare to Max and then Zeus. She reached up, rubbing his chest over his heart, melting as he covered her hand with his larger one.

"Okay, I give," Malcolm said in a stage whisper. "What the hell are we glaring at?"

It was too much. The giggles she'd tried so hard to suppress finally erupted, and once she started to laugh it was impossible to stop.

"I think she works too much."

"She wants me to wear a monkey suit."

Zeus and Max spoke at the same time, completely ignoring Selena.

"Stop it, both of you," Hera admonished. "You can take off the tie and jacket and the shoes." She pointed at Zeus, and then turned to stare at Max. "You leave my baby alone. She never travels without one of you with her, and I know she shares her feelings with you, even if you are not with her." She finished with a regal hand pointing in Max's direction.

"Okay, people. I have kidnapped the priest, and hogtied the guests, so let's roll." Vin grinned, rubbing his hands together as he walked through the open doorway. Vin stopped and stared at Tamara.

Selena widened her eyes. "Please tell me he's joking, right?" she wheezed out between fits of laughter.

Max strolled over to her and grabbed her hands. "He's kidding, sweetheart. Now you go and put on your dress. I don't like all these yahoos seeing you in a robe."

Her father coughed something that sounded suspiciously like "look who's talking" to her, but covered it with a flick of his wrist. Within the blink of an eye he had stripped down to slacks and a shirt. Would she ever get used to the fact she was the daughter of a god?

"Damn, but that feels much better." Zeus grabbed his wife's hand, leading Hera out of the room, but not before Hera winked at Selena over her shoulder.

"Are you scared your darling girl is going to make you put that back on, you big baby?" Malcolm called out. "Ouch. What was that for?" He glared at the laughing pair walking out of the room, rubbing the back of his head.

"That's for sassing me, boy." The laugh that accompanied the comment reverberated throughout the room.

"Hey, I didn't do it this time." Max raised his hands in surrender.

"No, but you thought about it," Selena groused.

"I think about lots of things, baby." A blush stole over Selena at the pictures Max projected into her head.

The man was just too much for her equilibrium. With a growl Selena dematerialized into her own suite and gazed at the gorgeous gown laid out on the bed. The beautiful tiara her mother had given her sat inside a velvet box, beckoning to be worn. Hearing that all the goddesses received something similar when they joined with their Fated, she finally felt accepted. Not that her siblings didn't make her feel welcome. But they all treated her like spun glass, like they were afraid she'd break or something. Just because she was close to a foot shorter than her brothers and sisters didn't mean she was weak.

"Of course it doesn't mean you are weak, sister mine." Asteria, Selena's sister, materialized beside her.

Since she was found all of Zeus and Hera's children, had made it a habit to literally pop in whenever they felt like it. Selena loved all her siblings, but she felt a real connection to the goddess of the stars. Asteria appeared closer in looks to Selena, and was only about five inches taller. Her hair was more golden blonde instead of white blonde like Selena's, and she had crystal-blue eyes with a just a hint of silver.

"I'm sorry. I should've shielded my thoughts." It was hard to remember other beings existed, let alone that she was one too.

"You have nothing to be sorry for, goddess of the moon. We do not think you are weak or fragile. We are just grateful to have you back." Asteria sniffed.

"I love you, sister mine." And she really loved the formal way they all spoke.

"As I love you, Selena. Now, let's get you ready." Asteria clapped her hands while a beautiful grin graced her face.

* * * *

"Gods, but she is beautiful." Max marveled as their bride started down the rose-petal aisle that led her to them on the arm of her parents.

"Yes, and she is all ours, bro." Malcolm agreed.

They could see the effort it took Zeus to place his feet in the sand, but Max could see it cost him dearly to let the grainy ground touch his bare feet. He saw his future father-in-law lean down and whisper something to Selena. She giggled and shook her head.

"I bet he just offered to take her out of here," Max said.

"She obviously didn't take him up on it. Damn, look at that scowl on his face. You'd think this was a shotgun wedding or something the way he's glaring at us." Max stared at Selena, barely hearing what Malcolm was saying.

"What do you mean? Nobody has a shotgun," Malcolm fairly shouted. "Ouch, damn it." He touched the back of his head where Max smacked him.

At the outburst, Selena stumbled in her approach, pinning Max with a look that promised retribution. He shrugged his shoulders until her mouth tilted up at the corner. Damn but he really did love his bloodthirsty woman.

"Who gives this woman to these, um, men?" the priest asked.

"Who the hell do you think, boy? Ow! What was that for?" Zeus rubbed the back of his head.

"I learned that from Max. Now answer the man," Hera whispered.

"Her mother and I do," Zeus answered, if a bit reluctantly.

"Good boy. I will give you a special treat when we get home."

The chairs that had been set up on the beach were filled with Selena's siblings and several other gods and goddesses. At Zeus's roar, the whole group seemed to dissolve into raucous laughter, earning them a look that promised payback from the big man himself.

"Ack. Truly mom, couldn't you have said that with your inside voice?" Asteria asked aloud, causing the laughter that had just died down, to start all over again.

* * * *

Malcolm smirked at the look on Selena's father's face after he got a whack in the back of the head. He had taken Selena's right hand in both of his while Max held her left. They had all the Ravens on one side of the aisle while Selena's best friend Tamara stood up front holding the bouquets.

Zeus finally took his seat in front with his wife, after issuing what Malcolm was sure a silent warning to the others to hush if the glare he shot them was anything to go by.

Humans weren't invited to the momentous event out of necessity. One just never knew when Zeus would send a bolt of lightning into one of his kids. Or hell, even a flying pigeon that looked like it might take a crap on his head might get zapped.

Malcolm shut the mental door on Zeus and concentrated on the words of the ceremony. The priest brought all their hands together and said a prayer. Malcolm said the right words at the right time, tightening the invisible bond between them, and then it was Selena's turn as she repeated them, followed by Max, with so much conviction no one could doubt the sincerity of their vows.

Malcolm's heart knocked his ribs so hard he worried the sound could be heard by everyone. The look on Max's face was one that he was sure mirrored what was written all over his own. They had finally found the *one* person who completed them, and they were scared shitless it would all disappear.

"*I'm not going anywhere without the two of you,*" Selena murmured in her soft southern drawl through their shared link. It was getting harder to shield his thoughts, but Malcolm really didn't want to.

They didn't plan a reception, thank the lord. Malcolm couldn't wait to whisk Selena away to their little hideaway her father had given them as a wedding present.

Finally, the longwinded man wrapped up the ceremony. He was escorted back to the airstrip, where hopefully Rafe or Vin would remember to wipe his memory and send him home with a large donation to his church.

Vin hadn't lied when he told Selena that he didn't kidnap the man. Rafe did, but he'd promised to make it up to the priest. If Rafe made a promise, he kept it, even if it took him a human lifetime to do it.

Malcolm waited for all the well-wishers to hug and kiss Selena and shake his and Max's hands. He laughed at the sight of Zeus lifting his feet and wiggling his toes to rid them of sand.

"All right, people." Max raised a glass.

Malcolm was astonished to see everyone had flutes in their hands.

"Thank you all for coming. Please find your way home." Max threw back his head and swallowed the golden liquid in one swallow.

Selena laughed, took a sip, then handed her glass to Max. He downed it and waggled his eyebrows at Malcolm. Taking the hint, he drank his champagne in a single gulp. "Party's over," Malcolm crowed.

* * * *

"Dude, did you see the look on Zeus's face?" Malcolm asked.

"Nope, I was too busy looking at our girl. I think Selena has something she needs to tell us." Max stalked closer to where Selena stood.

"Oh. Um…I love you guys."

"Nope, that's not it. But we love you too. Try again, sweetheart," Max teased, crowding her.

"Will someone let me in on the big secret? I'm ready to get on with the bow-chica-bowwow," Malcolm said.

A man only had so much patience and his had been stretched thin. Like a predator stalking its prey Max prowled closer, invading her space, giving her no room to maneuver.

"All right already…Geez, can't a girl have a secret?"

Max watched Selena take a deep breath and smile, showing a brilliant flash of teeth. "I'm pregnant."

"What?" Malcolm clutched his chest, making Max want to smack him.

"Are you sure?" The air seemed to freeze in Max's lungs while he waited for confirmation.

"I am very sure, and I can even tell you when it happened."

Selena went on to describe in minute detail the moments she was sure it happened, the morning after she'd been back in their arms after they fought Cronus they'd made love again, one right after the other.

By the time she'd finished, they were all naked, and Max had a hard-on to rival a light pole. He noticed Malcolm wasn't in any better condition. He didn't realize he still held Selena's hand until she gave it a little shake.

"Damn we're good," Malcolm said.

Max didn't even bother to slap his brother this time. Malcolm was spot on. They were more than good. They were great.

"Yes. We are more than great." Selena repeated his thoughts. She tugged them toward the four-poster bed and proceeded to show them all how great they were, using her hands and her body to take them all to heights they'd only been to with her.

# THE END

# ABOUT THE AUTHOR

I'm a full-time wife and mother who has loved to read and write since childhood. At the age of thirty-two, I survived cancer and decided I could do anything. Four years later, after meeting many wonderful writers, several of whom I can call friends, I decided to write a book. Now four years later I've attained my first goal, becoming a published author.

I love to write and have all kinds of stories in my head waiting to be written. The best part about my new journey is that if I don't like it, I can re-write it, unlike real life, so I always make sure there's a happy ending.

I'm creating new worlds, and I hope you all enjoy them with me. I can guarantee you'll always have a hero or two you'll love, and a heroine you'll want to be.

***For all titles by Elle Boon, please visit***
www.bookstrand.com/elle-boon

**Siren Publishing, Inc.**
**www.SirenPublishing.com**

CPSIA information can be obtained
at www.ICGtesting.com
Printed in the USA
BVOW06s1632250417
482158BV00016BA/414/P

9 781627 418294